S0-ABD-723

DISCARDED

LOWELL PUBLIC LIBRARY

LOWELL PUBLIC LIBRARY

SEARCH
FOR THE
DRAGON

SEARCH
FOR THE
DRAGON

Jack Lange

DISCARDED

LOWELL PUBLIC LIBRARY
1505 E. COMMERCIAL AVE.
LOWELL, IN 46356

BookPartners
Wilsonville, Oregon

3 3113 01818 9615

Library of Congress Cataloging-in-Publication Data

Lange, Jack, 1925–
    Search for the dragon / Jack Lange. -- 1st ed.
        p.   cm.
    ISBN 1-58151-026-8 (pbk. : alk. paper)
    I. Title.
    PS3562.A48494S42   1999
813'.54--dc21   99-35367
                                                                          CIP

Copyright © 1999 by Jack Lange
All rights reserved
Printed in U.S.A.
ISBN 1-58151-026-8

Cover design by Richard Ferguson
Text design by Sheryl Mehary

This book may not be reproduced in whole or in part, by
electronic or any other means which exist or may yet be
developed, without permission of:

BookPartners, Inc.
P. O. Box 922
Wilsonville, Oregon 97071

For Jocko,
whose seafaring skills
made it all possible,
and
Robin Redfoot,
Gwen, Lorrie, Dick, Gil,
and a host of others who
gave lots of support

The events in this story happened during one month in 1977. By then, the U.S. government had spent more than a decade in vain attempts to stem the rising tide of recreational drug use in the nation. Despite all efforts, the decade following saw the highest levels of drug abuse in recent history.

Intelligent observers attributed the failure of the "war on drugs" to a profound miscalculation by the authorities. As early as 1970, novelist and social critic Gore Vidal wrote in the New York Times (26 September) that legalization and honest marketing of drugs, at low prices, would make it "possible to stop drug addiction in the United States within a very short time." Without the huge profits to be made from illegal drug sales, the suppliers—from organized crime bosses down to playground pushers and addicts themselves—would not have their present incentive to recruit new users.

Vidal went on to say, however, that nothing so sensible was likely to occur: "The American people are as devoted to the idea of sin and its punishment as they are to making money—and fighting drugs is nearly as big a business as pushing them. Since the idea of sin and money is irresistible (particularly to the professional politician), the situation will only grow worse."

The prophecy has been more than fulfilled. The crime syndicates whose early activities are hinted at in this story have proliferated and reached everywhere in America, and people who were enticed into drug use and supply by dreams of easy money fill its prisons. The dynamics of these fictional characters' adventure reflect that reality.

Prologue

Running without lights, the wounded vessel lumbered through the black night like a stricken sea creature hiding from predators and the hand of death. Her belly, weighted with water, held her low in the stiff seas against all the will of her design to rise and fly with the wind in her sails. Huge waves rolled her with callous regularity, adding indignity to her death throes.

Her engine still ran the bilge pump, but the propeller and shaft assembly were lifeless beneath her battered undersides. No match in any case for the sea's insidious invasion, which would've taken her under hours ago but for the steady bailing of the three men, the woman and the boy aboard. It was a battle that waxed and waned, with an outcome at least as uncertain as the fate that ruled them so capriciously.

Benjie, stopping to catch his breath, looked through the open hatch at the starless sky and Dynamite's silhouette at the wheel. Despite his misery and fatigue, he smiled. But for a chance encounter with Weeto in a Lauderdale marina and the string of bizarre events that followed, he and Dynamite might still be high and dry. Beached, of course, with dead-end jobs that seemed for the moment a preferable stew to the one they were in now.

If he was looking for scapegoats, his old buddy Josh was closest to hand and the most likely candidate. But he knew where his shadowboxing was taking him--home to his own heart and conscience. Had he merely drifted into his choices, allowing Josh and Dynamite to throw him off course and ride the easy current? Or was it a flaw in his nature, as fated as the forces Dynamite always claimed to believe in?

The empty bucket in his hand was a stark and shuddering reminder not only of how it might end but what it said about all his efforts. How was it possible for a single month to undo twenty-two years of a life's course line?

Chapter One

Dynamite stirred at the sound of Benjie's rising. Unable to see him in the February darkness of seven in the morning, she wondered if she imagined it. Lately she was waking at crazy hours after only a few hours of sleep. Benjie too. She could say it was due to the crazy hours they worked but knew that didn't begin to cover it. Turning in her bunk, her hand caught the bare flesh of his thigh as he was rising. At its widest, the V-shaped aisle between bunks was barely the length of her arm. She knew he'd be stooped slightly to keep from bumping the ceiling beams. He always remembered. Lately somehow it made him look vulnerable and apologetic.

"How come you're awake?" he whispered, as if there were others aboard.

He had made a habit of slipping out of bed early each day to do his stocktaking and agonize over their plight. But lately she was thinking it was a way of avoiding her in the early morning hours.

"I heard the same bomb go off," she whispered back loudly, grinning in the half darkness as she reached for him. Her hand grazed his dangling penis. She felt his body shift away and knew he had other things on his mind.

"Sorry, didn't mean to disturb you. You need your sleep," he said quietly.

"What're we whispering for?" she asked aloud, her irritation showing. She hadn't intended anything but an affectionate pat. Another clue to the thick fog their relationship was drifting into.

"Why so early?" she added, trying to conceal her annoyance.

"Early start. I'm going to Lauderdale," he muttered. She sensed him retreating from her and felt a momentary rush of forgiveness. Then he spoiled it as his tone suddenly changed. "I told you yesterday, remember?"

With his constant reminders, how could she forget? The Humbers were due back in a few days. They'd have to move out and into an apartment if they didn't find another boat to caretake. Benjie, who'd been haunting the local docks and marinas for weeks, checking bulletin boards and newspaper ads, thought they'd fare better in Lauderdale. That would mean changing jobs again, and she wasn't sure she could find anything that paid as well as the one she had now. Rent saved by caretaking somebody's boat could be lost twice over if they ended with lower-paying jobs. But Benjie had this hair up his ass.

"I must've forgot," she snapped. "Rots of ruck."

His stony silence as he slipped into the passageway told her he was on a downer again, beyond her reach. Fact was, they were stuck in dreary jobs and scavenging like crazy squirrels storing nuts for a catastrophic winter. Not to ward off calamity, but to restore what they had lost, to recover a style swept away in a storm.

Their descent had begun with the loss of the *Candy* to that fluky storm. Hurricane Faye should have blown itself out down in the Gulf States. Instead it looped north with a new burst of energy to lash across New Jersey, taking their boat and all they owned. Too late they raced back from Minnesota where they'd been visiting her family. But Faye got there first, leaving a wake of wreckage and a litter of broken boats. Dozens of vessels anchored like *Candy* out in the bay had simply disappeared, dragged out to sea, splintered and swept away, or buried beneath the storm's new sandbars.

Their odyssey together had started as a fantasy of Benjie's on the other side of the continent, in San Francisco where they first met. They sailed the thirty-foot sloop—engineless from the time they dumped it overboard along the Baja coast—down half the length of North America's west coast and, after a transit of the Panama Canal, halfway up its other side. Only a first leg, an appetizer to the intended lazy circumnavigation of the world. But with the boat's disappearance, the memory of the journey was beginning to thin and shred. It would be years before they saved enough for another boat.

Dynamite resisted an impulse to join him in the main cabin, where she could hear him pumping water for his morning coffee. In his present frame of mind she knew he wouldn't appreciate her company. Just as well. His bad moods were becoming tedious. Unable to shake him out of his dark moods, she had drifted into the habit of simply avoiding them.

She punched the pillow and rolled over on her belly, angrily wondering if they'd ever been in love. They'd been consorting sexually for nearly two years and she still wasn't sure. Was that the reason she always resisted his talk of marriage?

Her nipples, grazing the rumpled sheets, went hard with a reminder of desire and neglect, igniting new anger. She was perfectly aware of her impact on men, and wore the bruises of their pinches and propositions from her nightly work in the cocktail lounge. Men stared and whistled at her too often for Dynamite to miss the value they attached to her body. Lately, they were mistaking her for a celebrity, some new girl on television, Farrah-something-or-other. She'd never seen the actress, but when some of her middle-aged droolers asked if she was related, Dynamite wasn't above pitching the cousin ploy to up her tips.

That was another thing. She guessed that her earning twice as much as Benjie rankled him. After losing *Candy* they hiked south to Palm Beach for the weather and the boating scene, and she was first to land a job. The pay was under minimum but the tips were something else, fifty to a hundred bucks on nights when the joint was jammed and swinging. Benjie, unable to find anything but low-scale work at the boat yards, scraping and painting hull bottoms, took a job as fry cook on the night shift at the same hotel where Dynamite worked. The pay was only a fraction over minimum, but at least they had similar schedules and weren't just strangers passing in the night.

Damn, she hated mental ruminations. They only went in vicious circles like mad dogs chasing their tails. It was one of the reasons she was so easily persuaded to drop out of school when Benjie came along with his boat and his fantasy of circumnavigating the world. Her love affair with water surprised her more than him. For a farm girl who'd never been in anything bigger than a rowboat and never seen an ocean until she went west to go to school at Berkeley, the chance encounter on the Sausalito docks had all the elements of a meeting between fire and water. Nothing could possibly come of it. She took it for a joke at first.

When the toast-colored man in sneakers and cutoffs slipped down the mast of the wretched-looking little boat she stopped to look at and offered to take her on as first mate, she laughed. Even after she made it clear she didn't know the ass end of a boat from the front nor a binnacle from a barnacle, he persisted. By then the current was flowing and it seemed as natural for him to invite her below for wine and a smoke as it was for her to accept, without giving false impressions about crewing or screwing anything else.

Following him down the ladder, she was surprised by a freshly varnished interior, a sharp contrast to the shabby condition topside. Rays of afternoon sun beamed through two round portholes, illuminating the little cabin like klieg lights. A little corner galley next to the hatch was separated from the dining alcove by a carved post and counter. Two kerosene lamps, gimbaled on the bulkhead over the table, gleamed golden copper from recent polishing. Books lined shelves above the settee and a tiny black-iron heating stove occupied a niche of porcelain tile. Everything looked miniaturized, like a carefully scaled dollhouse. The rich glow of varnish and copper reminded her of Grandmother Inger's small polished house in the village. She loved it.

When he said he'd soon have the topside as bright and shining, she didn't doubt it. He had an old-fashioned touch, a care for detail and perfection, which appealed to her prairie sense of order.

He also surprised her with his talk of going around the world in the little boat—alone if need be. She might have felt it a put-on but for his understated delivery and the resolve in his gray-blue eyes. Between sips of dago red and marijuana tokes, he even wheedled out of her the story behind her nickname, something she didn't often talk about.

Raised with two husky brothers, what they didn't teach her about self-defense she taught herself in coping with the oversexed farmhands who drifted in for work and thought they could help themselves to the farmer's daughter. One such lout, when she was still a skinny twelve-year-old, cornered her in the toolshed with obvious pointed intent until she calmly struck a match to a stick of dynamite from the shelf behind her. She chased him beyond the barns and halfway across the back pasture before she finally threw it away, seconds before it exploded. Her assailant was never seen again and was soon forgotten, but the story and the name stuck. Inger became Dynamite, which suited her better than the foreign-sounding name meant to preserve her grandmother's memory.

Dynamite dreamed she woke from her reverie and found Benjie gone. Bounding up, she forgot to duck and bumped her head on a ceiling beam. Star-dazed, rubbing her head, she cried aloud with an anger going beyond the focused pain. She was mad at the beam, the boat and her own stupidity. She was mad about dozing off. But mostly she was angry at Benjie for sneaking off without a word.

When she finally did awaken, there was no bump on her head but Benjie was gone. Remembering she was nearly as tall as he, she stooped to miss the low beams. But a pain throbbed in her head all the same. Even the morning, dawning through the porthole, was a somber gray, a pall dragging on her spirits like a protracted decision. She knew she wasn't one to put up with boring routines for long.

Benjie lucked out with the first car coming along Flagler Drive and got a ride all the way to Lauderdale. The driver wasn't headed that far but, when it came out that Benjie had been to sea in a small boat, something lost and envious stirred in the middle-aged salesman's heart. He took him all the way, right down to the water-front where the big marinas were clustered in a forest of tall masts and high-rise hotels. Bahia Mar, Pier 66, Jack Tar. For one who disavowed belief in superstition, he had to admit to some amazing coincidences. Others would have called it luck. Dynamite declared it his destiny.

Once in awhile it came inversely, in devastating events such as the storm that took *Candy* or the brutal slaying of his father when he was fourteen. But for the most part chance smiled benignly on him, a fact he could hardly ignore. He lucked out in storms at sea which might easily have done him in. Fortuitous encounters occurred in unlikely places, such as the run-in with the Humbers (whom he only met briefly in Panama) just as they put in from the Caribbean and needed caretakers for their boat while they went to California for extended visits with children and grandchildren.

Dynamite, of course. She dropped into his life like a godsend, a veritable blast on the hazy horizon of his expectations just when he was on the verge of risking it alone. Green eyes and straw-blond hair, skin blessed with an uncharacteristic Nordic ability to adapt to sunshine. She tanned like an ad. But Dynamite was much more. She possessed both intellect and sensuality. Her good looks and body curves brought the kind of flattery and attention that might have turned any other girl into an empty-headed sex tease. Aware of the first, she displayed it ostentatiously. The second she tended to ignore.

Anxiety was the price he paid for the lavish gift, a constant fear he might lose her, and lately the strain of their jobs ashore raised that specter like a waving flag. His vulgar job, catering to pampered tourists, depressed him beyond the demeaning quality of the work itself. He'd come to despise the smell of burgers, fries and sputtering grease. The thought of Dyna being ogled and pinched every night in the lounge repelled him in another way. She deserved better than that.

Lately, frustration compelled him to reconsider alternatives he thought he'd put behind him. Going back to college and completing medical school, for instance. It would take three or four years even if he didn't specialize. How many more years to build a practice and accumulate enough money for the kind of boat he wanted? Not all doctors got rich overnight; his father was proof of that. Besides, how long would Dynamite sit still for that kind of schedule, trading today's reality for some far-off speculative future?

He could feel things coming to a head like the soggy day knotting for rain. Living on the boat these past months, even tied to a dock, had somehow camouflaged reality. But the Humber's impending return reinforced the depressing notion that he would never have his own boat again.

Too many things irritated him lately, and he wasn't often successful in hiding it from Dyna. He tended to avoid her when he got in such moods—it only increased the tension between them. Back on the boat, he hadn't intended leaving with a rift between them. He sneaked back into the forward cabin, seeking a kiss of reconciliation. But she was asleep, her face a scowling mask of concentration framed in a sunburst of radiant hair. He had left her undisturbed, telling himself she needed the rest. Or was that an excuse, another evasion?

The overcast sky looked as dark and sullen as his thoughts and as unwilling to make up its mind.

Chapter Two

An hour later, as Benjie stopped to admire a handsome sloop tied to an outer pier, a familiar face popped out of the hatch. Recognition flashed in the man's eyes, then he turned and abruptly ducked below. For a second Benjie couldn't recall the name. It was foreign and a nickname—the "crazy Spic" some called him, the best cut-rate diesel mechanic in Marin County. He had torqued the injectors on the old Perkins and gave it a final patch job before the *Candy* sailed out of San Francisco Bay, making a gift of his services by refusing to take a dime.

"Weeto?" Benjie called out. "That you, Weeto?"

The man's frowning face reappeared, his index finger pressed to his lips. Weeto climbed on deck, snapped the padlock on the hatch and stepped on the pier with his satchel of tools.

"Yeah, I know you—the crazy raghead with that big stick of dynamite," he mumbled, grabbing Benjie's elbow and propelling him down the dock. "Sausalito, two years ago. I remember her name—but I got to tell you I don' remember yours."

Benjie glanced back at the white sloop placidly nudging her big white fenders against the pier. The scripted name on her bow swirled in golden Gothic, a writhing imitation of the sinuous mythical beast. *Dragon*.

"Benjie," he said, then smiled apologetically. "I couldn't think of yours either at first."

"So watcha doin' here? Don't tell me you awready been around the world in that little rag-rigged teacup." Weeto's eyes constantly darted about warily as they strode along the pier. When they reached the central dock, his pace and grip slackened. He shot Benjie a look of friendly interest.

"I thought about you a few times. I wondered whatever happened to you two crazy kids. Who quit first—you or the boat?"

"The boat." Benjie sighed. "Nobody's fault. Lost her to a storm."

"Too bad." Weeto's eyes locked on a dockworker walking toward them. When the man veered off to a side pier, Weeto looked back at Benjie. "What about the girl friend? She quit too?"

"No, we're still together. Caretaking a boat in West Palm Beach at the moment."

"Still not married?"

"Her call."

Weeto nodded and patted Benjie on the shoulder. "I shoulda been so smart with women."

Benjie grinned back. He noticed Weeto's thick, dark hair was receding. Gray along the temples was beginning to marble the black. He only had a few years on Benjie, but worry or work was already aging him. That and his New York accent—tough, weary, and skeptical—combined to make him seem a generation older. He looked stout as seasoned timber otherwise, his stocky frame hard and weathered as bent oak.

"Come on, I'll buy you a beer." Unlocking the trunk of an old, dented white Chevy, Weeto tossed the tool satchel among a litter of tools and spare parts sufficient to outfit a machine shop. Benjie saw the car carried a Louisiana plate.

"No, my treat. I still owe you a big one for that favor in Sausalito, or have you forgotten?" Climbing in the passenger side, he decided he wouldn't mention the engine conked out and had to be thrown overboard. No fault of his in any case, it was a wonder it went as long as it did.

"What, that three hours I spent setting the injectors?" He waved it off and started the engine. "Kid's play, I gave it to God. I thought He might do me a favor with my ex-wife if I did one for others, like it says in the Bible."

"That all settled?" Benjie asked awkwardly.

"Don't I wish!" Weeto hissed.

"She got custody and won't honor your visitation rights," Benjie guessed.

"You don' know the half of it, friend." Weeto's sour glance was perhaps only meant to be funny. With New Yorkers Benjie was never sure where cynicism left off and humor began. He stared at the road ahead, the seconds ticking away. A thick black cloud was coming from the west to meet them. Two blocks down the road, a waterfall was pouring from the sky. The day had finally made up its mind.

"So tell me," Weeto said abruptly. "Where'd you and Dynamite go in that rag-rig before you lost it?"

For the next twenty minutes, while they made their way to a small upriver marina, Benjie summarized their ill-fated cruise, ending with the ironic loss of *Candy* not to a storm at sea, but one that caught her trapped in a snug anchorage.

"Tough luck," Weeto offered as the car coasted to a stop in the parking lot of a marina for do-it-yourselfers. The rain had vanished as swiftly as it appeared, the fierce sun was raising steam clouds from the wet pavement.

"So watcha gonna do now?" Weeto asked when they were out of the car.

"We're saving for a new boat."

"Jeez, that's gonna take some time, eh?" Weeto speculated, leading him down a gravel path.

"A few years. We're both working—" He halted as Weeto abruptly veered off. Stepping onto the grass, the Puerto Rican whistled at two Latino guys working on a hull. When they looked up, he fired a volley of Spanish at them. The two men nodded back, then returned to their work. Grinning, Weeto turned back to Benjie and directed him to a snack and beer bar. It was little more than an open shed with insect screens for walls, its charm springing from the accidental decor of sea debris and shoreside discards. Cable drums, kegs and barrels served for tables and chairs, abalone shells for ashtrays. Nets and glass balls decorated posts and rafters. A hangout for local boaters, though at the moment they had the place to themselves. Weeto led Benjie to a table where they could look out over the hauling ways to some of the boats docked beyond.

"Nice," Benjie commented. "You come here a lot?"

"I live here. On a boat. Behind that shed there." He pointed, then signaled the approaching waitress with two fingers. "Not one of your stick-and-rag rigs, jus' an ol' fishing boat. Belongs to a frien' of mine who only goes out to impress new girlfriends. He lets me live aboard and I keep his old engines running."

"Hey, good deal." Benjie explained his caretaking arrangement with the Humbers, inadvertently reminding himself of the urgency of his own situation.

"You still set on long-distance stuff?" Weeto asked suddenly. "Goin' round the world? Dynamite's not scared out of it yet?"

"She loves distance sailing."

Weeto lifted one of the mugs of beer the waitress put on the table. "Excuse me for sayin' it, but a sexy-looking number like Dynamite—I don' figure it. But what do I know? I been figuring women wrong all my life."

Benjie raised his glass. "*Salud, amigo.* May you find in time the one you can."

"*Salud.* I don' ask no favors. Only to get my bitch ex-wife off my back."

Benjie stared back at him blankly. The Puerto Rican's dark eyes narrowed and he leaned closer. "Look friend, when I first seen you by the boat I acted like I didn't know you, right? It's because I thought you was somebody else, a private dick hired to find me."

"Why?"

"It's my ex—she gives me so much trouble, using her rich daddy's money to put cops and private eyes on my tail." He gulped a mouthful of beer, as if it was needed to get the words out. "Well, it's because I took the boy. He's with me now, been with me almost two years."

Mistaking the surprised expression on Benjie's face for disapproval, he rushed to defend himself. "Look, Chico don' mean nothin' to her, she could care less! She's only doin' it to hurt me.

She's sick in the head, you know? An unfit mother!"

Benjie shrugged. "So she got custody."

"What else? The judge and lawyers, they din' give a damn what I tol' them. How she slept all day and partied and whored all night. She let that baby cry his head off, with his pants all wet and full of shit. Half the time she forgot to feed him, or she was too drunk to care!" Weeto clenched his fists.

"That lousy judge! A blind man could see through her lies. Not jus' what I tol' them, friends and neighbors testified too—"

"So you just grabbed the kid and ran?" Benjie repressed the thought there was another side to the story.

Weeto nodded. "First down to L.A. but in two months they're closing in. I sold my car and bought an old one under another name and split. First to Portland, then Seattle." Anger provoked by the painful memories weakened his grasp of English. He blurted out his narrow escapes, which included one in snowbound Chicago. "Thirty degrees below zero! Can you believe it, man? So much snow an' cold I couldn't leave the apartment to go to work. But not so bad it put the bloodhounds off the track. Plainclothes or private cops, I dunno, but I hear them askin' my name to the desk clerk. I jump back in the elevator to get Chico on the third floor. First I jam the elevator doors with my shoe, then I get Chico and we grab everything we can wear and go down the fire escape. I left my car in the garage. We caught the El to the bus depot and took the first bus south, to New Orleans. I changed names again and bought that fancy white Chevy you jus' rode in, and we came down here. Last March, almos' a year ago."

"Maybe you're through running," Benjie offered, trying to sound optimistic. "Maybe they stopped chasing you."

"Ha! I learned one thing about Anglo law—even if it's blind to justice it's got a very long arm. Even if her rich daddy stops hiring his own army, she's still got the cops to chase me down. Even if she din care no more, the cops will. I tol' them to shove the system, I thumbed my nose at the guy in black robes. You think they gonna let me get away with that?"

The waitress brought fresh beers. Benjie waited until she was out of range again.

"Amigo, if you know that, why do you keep running? If you really think they're bound to catch you—"

"I din say that!" Weeto interjected. "I said they gonna go on hunting. I din say they gonna catch me!"

There was logic in his determination but it was the logic of the fugitive. Benjie wondered if he understood the reach of the forces stacked against him. Every police unit across the country, state and local, the FBI, Social Security, the IRS and employers' records—they were all ways of tracking even with aliases and fake ID. He stopped short of telling Weeto to turn himself in and beg the court for leniency.

"You give those guys too much credit," Weeto pointed out. "For them it's just a job, and sometimes they don' move so fast." He slammed his fist onto the tabletop. "For me it's everything!"

Benjie knew they were debating in circles. Seeing the torn look on his friend's face, he took the easy way out. "Weeto, I'm sorry. I mean that. You must really feel for the little guy. How old's he now?"

The mechanic's eyes brightened like sky washed by a storm. With the easy quickness of tropical weather, the face shifted from the gray of storm clouds to a blazing grin of sunshine. "Hey, you wanna see his picture?"

He started fumbling with his wallet, then glanced at his watch and smiled. "Better still. He goes to pre-school, like kindergarten. Whenever I got time, I pick him up at noon so we can eat together."

A few steps outside the bar, they were whistled over by the same two Latinos Weeto had spoken to earlier. Cubans, he would later explain. Benjie couldn't help but notice the wariness in their voices, even though they spoke in Spanish. Nor had he missed the subtle glances and gestures they exchanged when one of the other yard workers approached too closely.

Chapter Three

Chico's school was actually a private home close to the marina, brightly painted and with a well-equipped playground set up in the front yard. Weeto pointed it out as they passed by, continuing to the corner where he made a U-turn before returning to park along the fence enclosing the property. Before he got to the gate, a shriek rose above the chatter of the other children as a small boy raced to greet him.

"Poppi, Poppi!" he squealed, scrambling to climb the gate if Weeto hadn't opened it first. He leaped into his father's arms, jack-knifing his legs while jabbing words and punches. He squirmed free seconds later and ran down the sidewalk toward the car. Reaching it ahead of Weeto, he opened the door and jumped in.

Undaunted by the stranger beside him, the boy slammed the door, rolled up the window and snapped down the lock button on the sill. Kneeling on the seat, his hands wildly spinning the wheel, he vocalized the engine sounds of his getaway.

Opening the door, Weeto grabbed Chico and tickled him under the arms. He went into paroxysms of squeals and squirmed like an eel fighting to escape.

"Eh, what kind of manners you got?" Weeto scolded. "Say hello to my friend Benjie."

Slapping him on the rump, Weeto pushed him to the middle
and climbed in. Benjie saw that Chico, like most children, was
prettier than parents had a right to expect. This one had something
special beyond the gift of his mixed Anglo-Latin heritage. Beneath
golden skin, his spirit shimmered with promise, dark eyes flashed
excitement. His movements were all darts and explosions.

"Come on, show Benjie how good you talk Spanish," said
Weeto. He fired a salvo of Spanish at the boy as he slowed to turn
into a Burger King parking lot.

"Me llamo Jorge Alvarez," the boy recited mechanically, his
interest elsewhere.

"That's his new name, which he keeps forgetting," Weeto
explained to Benjie. He turned back to Chico. *"Y donde vamos?"*

"A *Burgher Keeng*!" he screamed. Benjie decided the name
sounded even more ludicrous in Spanish than it did in English.

Father and son ordered burgers, fries and cola drinks. Benjie
settled for an apple turnover and a carton of milk. If there was any
question whether the kid was sufficiently fed and cared for, it was
answered by the way he picked at his food and used a French fry as
a dipper for the ketchup, which he ate more of than anything else.
Food didn't interest him so much as the paraphernalia it came in.
Drinking straw skins were ammunition for his blowgun. Air piped
through a straw caused bubbling eruptions in the brown lake of his
cola. Paper napkins were quickly fashioned into sailboats and
airplanes, one of which soared over the heads of startled diners
before his father put a stop to it.

But his exuberant play didn't diminish his interest in the
men's conversation. Nor engaging in it. He slipped back and forth
from English to Spanish with a facility Benjie could only envy. He
didn't miss a thing.

"A sailboat, *que bueno*!" he raved when he heard where
Benjie lived. *"Eh, Poppi, un velero, un velero!"*

"He's not like his poppi," Weeto explained, winking. "He's
crazy about sailboats and can't understand why we live on a
stinkpot. He heard somebody call it a stinkpot last week and now
he thinks all powerboats are stinkpots."

"Stinkpots, stinkpots," Chico mimicked.

Between prattle, pranks and language lessons, some messages slipped through. Benjie managed to convey his concern about finding a boat to caretake. Weeto knew of none at the moment. But since his work took him to marinas all over south Florida, he'd keep his eye out. "You kidding yourself, man. To do charter you gonna need something forty feet or more and with a good diesel. You can't touch nothing like that under forty thousand, not even old used stuff. You think you gonna save that kinda money in a few years? Not by workin' and payin' taxes. Unless you got a rich uncle or you gonna rob a bank, you never gonna see that kinda bread, friend."

A wave of depression swept over Benjie as strong as he'd experienced looking out at the empty Jersey horizon where *Candy* had vanished. Was he kidding himself? Had wishful thinking made him as blind to his own circumstances as he had felt Weeto was to his? Neither could admit being tied to impossible dreams, each waiting for some miracle to happen. Only the high-spirited kid, dipping his finger in ketchup to make blood smears on his forehead and keeling over to prove he was mortally wounded, was in touch with reality. At least he knew when a bullet or an arrow had stopped him dead.

Benjie's sinking spirits must have been more visible than he could have imagined. The boy, rising from his dead trance on the seat, looked at him sympathetically. "Eh Benjie, I'm not dead, not really!"

The laughter that followed revived both Benjie and Weeto's flagging spirits.

"Quien sabe?" Weeto asked. "Who knows, you might win a jackpot. I might get lucky and find out my ex-wife died. We're all pawns in the hands of God." He grabbed the boy roughly, wiped away the ketchup smears and pulled him to his feet. "Let's go, monkey!"

In the car the same play between father and son continued. A rare relationship, unabashedly physical and volatile. Benjie could only compare it with his own childhood and wish the bond with his father had been less stiff and formalized. His father had been a good and kind man but for whatever reasons—his own rearing, the press of work and philanthropic duties—he'd never been a playful man.

Chico sounded a warning as they coasted past the school. *"Mire, Poppi! Hombres!"* Two men in suits, their backs to the street, were talking to the lady who ran the school. Weeto grunted an expletive and gunned the car forward.

"What...?" Benjie turned in confusion, grabbing the dashboard. "They could be fire inspectors or—"

"Could be, but they ain't," Weeto snapped. "I recognize one, the same big guy I saw in Chicago!"

Eyes grimly fixed on the mirror, he floored the gas pedal and they shot down the road. At the first corner he braked abruptly and turned right. As they swerved in a squeal of tires, Benjie glanced back and saw the two men running across the street towards their car.

Benjie broke into a cold sweat at the thought of cops or FBI agents chasing him. He'd never defied constituted authority in his life, not in any real sense. Scenes over the years from television and movies of high-speed chases ending in bullets and crashes and smashed, bleeding bodies, made his heartbeat stitch ominous warnings. Ketchup smears on the forehead might have been a grim symbol of what the afternoon had in store for them.

He hadn't reckoned on Weeto's quick reflexes and preplanning. Considerable thought had obviously gone into contingencies. At the next block he hung a left into a clearly marked dead-end street. It was bisected at its terminus by a private gravel road crossing the drainage ditch which otherwise separated the school road from the rest of the tract like a moat around a castle. Once back on the school road he headed east before picking up a state road and reversing direction to speed west until they were well out of the city. Turning onto a dirt road lined by tall casuarinas, he rolled down it for a quarter mile before coasting to a stop.

"We change the license plates here," he announced. He pushed Chico back into his seat when he started to slide out after him. "No, monkey, you stay inside!"

Taking a Florida plate out of the trunk, Weeto quickly mounted it in place of the Louisiana plate on the rear bumper. Then he spit on it and dusted it with dirt. Not satisfied, he kicked it a few times.

"New plate on an old clunker—whatta you think?" Weeto asked, squinting at Benjie.

"Looks fine," Benjie said. "But what about registration papers—"

"Yeah, yeah, I know," Weeto snapped irately. "I din mean it to get me cross country, jus' across town. To gimme time to think!" Disgusted, he stamped his foot and began pacing in circles at the back of the car. One clenched fist punched the palm of the other hand, as if to force an idea by pounding it out. "Where to now, eh? Where to go from here?"

Benjie felt useless. He could only think of possible destinations, and this desperado needed plans and strategies.

Weeto angrily kicked a tire, then brought his fist down hard on the fender.

Chico crawled into the back seat and pressed his face against the rear window, his big eyes liquid with concern.

"Que pasa, Poppi?" he shouted.

"Nothing, *nada*," Weeto reassured him. Relieved, the boy reverted to his antics, making faces and pounding on the glass.

"Eh, Poppi, mire! Un velero!" A napkin from lunch folded into a dunce cap on his head had been transformed into a sailboat, which he now began skimming across the imaginary seas of the window.

"Crazy monkey," Weeto grumbled. Suddenly, he jerked his head skyward again, and split the air with the Spanish version of a banshee cry. *"Aaiiy, aaiiy!"*

He grabbed Benjie's shoulder and began shaking him. "Amigo, I got it! You need a boat to go sailin' round the world, but you got no money. And me, I got to get outta this country, fast! There's a boat waiting for us, a big velero that can take us anywhere in the world!"

"What, you mean steal it?"

"Not exactly, friend. They gonna sink it anyway, to collect the insurance. Why not take it out of the country, change the name and never bring it back? Those two Cubans I talked to, they're—whatcha call it—scuttlers. The boat you saw me on, the *Dragon*, that's the one they gonna sink. I went there to check the engine and make sure everything's working to get them outta the harbor."

"Jeeeesus," Benjie breathed. Like all boaters, he'd heard about Sunday sailors anxious to get out from under vessels they no longer wanted. Some, stuck with long waits or drastic price cuts, looked for easier ways. An accommodating marine surveyor, yacht broker or down-and-out sea captain might be induced by a suitable fee to arrange burial of the boat in deep waters. There were a dozen variations to the stories. He'd heard them on the West Coast too, occasionally catching newspaper articles about scuttling rings getting caught and busted. But this was the first time he'd ever come face to face with anyone actually involved in the racket. And obviously Weeto's was a well-organized gang, not just dock bums hired on the spur of the moment to convert someone's seagoing albatross into an insurance payoff.

"Jesus, Weeto," he sighed again. "That's what you're into?"

"Hey man, we're not hurting anybody. Nobody's breaking legs or dumping some poor shit overboard in concrete. It's only insurance money an' if the rich don' mind stealin' it first, why should I feel bad? They take ninety percent of the money. All we get is maybe ten percent and that's gotta be split five, six ways."

"I was thinking of the risk," said Benjie, unsure what he was thinking.

"Look man, I'm givin' you the chance to get your boat." Weeto kicked at the hard marl of the roadbed, emphasizing his point. "Right now, not five or ten years from now. You get a good look at that mother? A sixty-footer, probably half a million to build. In your whole life you never gonna be able to buy a boat like that. I'm givin' it free to you…on a platter. All I want is a ride to South America for me and Chico."

Benjie knew he couldn't say no. That beautiful boat, a splendid Rhodes design and as unthinkably out of his reach as the *Queen Mary*, was going to be sunk anyhow. How much better if she survived to give service and pleasure to those who would appreciate her, instead of ending as debris on the ocean bottom?

He questioned Weeto about the ship's provisions and equipment and how to camouflage her identity, but the mechanic had an answer for everything. She was equipped and outfitted for distance cruising. Fake papers were no problem, Weeto had a packet of registrations stuffed in the trunk of the car. With a few alterations one could surely be made to fit the boat.

"And the food lockers are full," Weeto continued excitedly. "She's loaded. We can sail that mother all the way to South America without stopping for nothing! The reserve tank is full and the main tank at least half, prob'ly three hundred gallons of diesel aboard. And she's got a sweet Mercedes to putt-putt you all the way down if the wind plays tricks. Man, I tell you, she's made to order."

"What about the Cubans?" Benjie asked. "Will they let you take off in it just like that?"

"Why not? They getting paid anyway. I'll esplain I got this Anglo to take the boat off our hands and save us the trouble of sinkin' it. Maybe give them a thousand dollars and say you're paying to take it off our hands. You know, make them an offer they can't refuse. You willing to go half on the money?"

"No," said Benjie. "If everything goes okay, I'll pay the full thousand. You're gonna need a stake when we get to Colombia."

"You set your mind on Colombia? Why not Venezuela? Prob'ly I can find my kind of work there better."

"Good thing you invited a rag sailor along, amigo," Benjie laughed. "Colombia's a broad reach all the way down. Venezuela's a beat into the wind and bucking the current all the way. Besides," he added, winking, "I've been to Colombia. We were there on *Candy*. I know just where and how to sneak us in."

"Eh Poppi, I got to pee-pee!" Chico abruptly called from the car. While father helped son by the side of the road, Benjie's thoughts steadfastly clung to the luxury of being master of a boat again. It didn't occur to him to calculate how he was going to support the care and maintenance of such a vessel—nor what Dynamite's reaction might be.

On the way back to town they stopped for gas and Weeto called his Cuban friends from the pay phone. Going back to his boat was out of the question; he surmised the cops had it staked out by now. The Cubans knew where he kept the key. They would board when it looked safe to do so, and get the nearly four thousand dollars he had hidden in the lining of his shaving kit.

"You explained the deal to them?"

"Enough. Jus' that somebody's lookin' for me and I gotta get out of the country. We're meeting at six o'clock when they get off work."

"You decided when you want to leave?"

"Why not tonight, if it looks okay?" He glanced at Benjie as if reading his mind. "I know, you've got your girlfriend problem. Chico and me, we'll go to an afternoon movie while you take the car and get Dynamite and your things. Try to be back by seven o'clock. And don' come loaded with baggage. We don' wanna wake up the marina when we go to the boat."

"Don't worry, everything we own fits in two backpacks."

"Good, we don' wanna sound like a bunch of noisy *turistas*."

"Turistas, turistas," Chico mimicked. *"Donde vamos, Poppi?"*

Benjie couldn't follow Weeto's burst of machine-gun Spanish—except the word for sailboat.

"I jus' tol' him," said Weeto winking at Benjie, "if he was good and minded me, we'd take him for a ride in your sailboat tonight. Don' forget to play your part, skipper. It's your boat."

Weeto and son got out at a downtown theater and Benjie slid behind the wheel. Weeto started to walk away, then turned back and stuck his head in the window. He squeezed Benjie's hand on the wheel. "Good luck with the girl friend, amigo. Don' lemme down, eh?"

His eyes told Benjie that he was Weeto's last hope. He nodded solemnly.

On the drive to West Palm Beach, Benjie sorted through the bizarre events and emotions of the past few hours and knew he had made the right decision. He didn't really know what the penalties were for complicity in a child-kidnapping case, especially one that took the child out of the country, but he really didn't care. In a showdown, if it came to that, he knew he wouldn't say or do anything to threaten that wild, warm father-son relationship.

Reminded of the break in his relationship with his own father nine years earlier, he still felt the pain. Bloody scenes of the television newscast unrolled in his mind. The rumpled suit on the pavement, the hole in the sole of his shoe flagging his thrift and indifference to material things. A pathologist whose added forensic skills were among the best in the Bay area, it seemed ironic that his volunteer work with the free clinics should end as an unsolved case on the police blotter. Knifed and kicked to death in a hospital parking lot, apparently by assailants infuriated that he only carried five dollars in his wallet, his case had dwindled to little more than a fading statistic on the burgeoning list of unsolved crimes. Oddly, despite his recollection of minute details, he could not visualize his father's face.

He turned back to his luck of the moment, which reprieved him from his grief and the morning's worry and made him light-headed with excitement. He speculated about Dynamite's reaction, and in a startled moment realized he might have to make a choice between a wooden mistress and a living mate. Many men had, and the wife wasn't always first choice.

He could feel amused, because he was certain he'd never be put to the test. In most ways Dynamite was more open than he to chancy dares and risky ventures. Sometimes eager to jump into situations that scared him, she was often oblivious not just to what he considered ethics but even to ordinary caution: illegal money exchanges, shady characters, food bought from pushcart vendors, shopping alone in the parts of strange cities notorious for robberies and muggings.

Balancing this understanding of her propensities, or maybe just needing to suppress his own distaste, he felt he had to deceive her about some of the details. For starters, she didn't have to know they were accomplices in a child-snatching. If it came out later, safely out to sea or in Colombia, it couldn't make her change her mind. Not knowing might even protect her from prosecution if they got apprehended.

He didn't intend telling her anything about Weeto's connection with a boat-scuttling gang, either. He reasoned it was to spare Weeto embarrassment, but a blip trailing on the end of that thought indicated it was just as much to spare himself.

LOWELL PUBLIC LIBRARY

Chapter Four

In his nervous state, Benjie put it to her badly. Too late he realized it sounded as if they'd be crew on some other skipper's stolen boat. She simply said, "No."

Backpedaling, he hastily explained that the boat was to be theirs, describing the sixty feet of splendor scheduled for a watery grave if they didn't take it.

Dyna studied his face and shrugged. "Maybe." When he said it was to be a one-stop, possibly a nonstop sail to South America, she nodded. The smile she'd been suppressing under her pout broke out. From her perch on the cabin top where she was sunning herself, she grabbed his hand and pulled herself up. "See? Didn't I say you were born under a lucky star?"

"Don't gloat, it hasn't happened yet."

"Hey, I feel it in my bones," she countered, squeezing his hand and hugging him. "A bad morning always brings luck in the afternoon."

She was always inventing after-the-fact aphorisms. No matter that often they contradicted each other, it was a sign of her best mood. Benjie was rising into a mellow mood too, with her sun-warmed skin assaulting his senses, but he knew time was short.

They had to quickly get packed and checked out to meet the deadline with Weeto.

Just when everything seemed set and they were strapping the backpacks to leave, a change of plans arrived in the form of an old friend. A voice hailed them from the dock.

"I forgot," said Dynamite, glancing out a porthole. "Some guy was here earlier looking for you. I'd have invited him aboard, but I wasn't dressed."

It was Josh, a surfing buddy and his only close friend in high school, whom he hadn't seen in years. Joshua Vanderbilt Slocum was his full improbable name, the gift of a Navy-captain father with a droll sense of humor or an inflated ego. Josh, the wild Indian of their school days, scourge of teachers and systems, bane to grim-minded students and their demanding parents alike. Challenger, rebel, defying the petty and conventional, putting down all that seemed false and pompous, the great balloon-breaker. Wild hairdos and outrageous clothes were only the tip of the iceberg. Beneath was a mountain of pranks and practical jokes sufficient in number and ingenuity to jar a school system and topple a school board. As he nearly did once, before someone finked on him and he had to answer to the juvenile authorities.

"Josh!" Benjie shouted, bounding from the hatch to the dock, torn between joy at this apparition from the past and dismay at its timing. "Whatcha doin' here?"

"Looking for you." The suave reply was in measured contrast to his appearance. The two friends locked arms in greeting.

"You've been out of circulation," Benjie said. "Where have you been hiding?"

"Recently or generally?" Josh grinned. "Generally taking in the world. Recently India and Afghanistan."

"Afghanistan!" Benjie smirked and nodded. "Figures. Studying yoga or doing hashish?"

"Both," he replied smugly.

His long hair, black and kinky as Persian lamb, was pleated in dreadlocks. Just as thick and curly, a beard blanketed him from cheek to chest like a student if not a guru of eastern mysticism. But instead of saffron robes and sandals, he was wearing worn-out sneakers, cutoff jeans and a sack-like Mexican poncho. A big leather bag hung on a strap from his shoulder and a green surplus-store bedroll tied with sisal rope lay on the dock next to his skinny legs and sockless ankles.

Any other time Benjie would have been overjoyed to see this legend from his past, this brightest of wits and best of all friends. Not that Josh necessarily saw him the same way. Just as Benjie was the loner, Josh was the leader and was much too busy defending and fighting to parcel himself out in big chunks to anyone. His friends and enemies numbered in the hundreds. But there was unspoken understanding between them. It was as if Josh held him in higher esteem than he held himself. And vice versa.

Even so, Benjie found himself silently cursing his arrival. Time was running out. And from the looks of the bedroll at his feet, he hadn't just come for an hour's chat.

"I can come back another time," said Josh, as if sensing his friend's anxiety. "I didn't come with an engraved invitation, did I?"

Benjie shifted awkwardly. "Oh Josh, you know I'm glad to see you. It's just bad timing. I'd ask you aboard, only—we're just on our way out. I mean we're leaving for good and not coming back. It's not our boat, you know. We've only been caretaking it. It's...well, it's all very complicated."

The patience and understanding Josh had learned in India reflected in his steady gaze. He reached for his bedroll.

"Jesus, don't walk off!" Embarrassed, Benjie grabbed his elbow and walked him to the outer end of the pier.

"Look, it's so crazy you're gonna think I flipped my lid. We're on our way out to—" He searched for the right words, "—to steal a boat."

"Not so crazy," Josh responded matter-of-factly. "I once stole one in Newport. Borrowed it, more accurately, to get to the Balboa side. I didn't have the change for the ferryboat."

"No jokes, Josh. I'm talking about a sixty-footer. Not just something to get to the other side of the bay!"

"I see what you mean. That is a big mother. Maybe you could use some help. I happen to be out of school, out of work and between amusements at the moment. Free to dare and do."

"It's not a pleasure cruise, Josh, and I'm not in charge. It's to get somebody out of the country. We're leaving tonight for South America."

"Ah, prime choice! First on my list. Haven't seen nearly enough of that continent. So big, you know."

"Josh, you can't just—you need passports and visas." His voice trailed off, seeing defeat in Josh's amiable expression.

"Not to worry, friend. Two things I'm never without—my toothbrush and my passport." India's mysticism hadn't tamed the free spirit within him. "As long as it's South America, let's pick a country like Colombia. We could deal some dope and make the trip profitable as well as entertaining. We can fly up to the Andes and bargain directly with the Indians for our coca leaves. Why deal with the middle if we can go straight to the source?"

His high-pitched voice, impudent as it was imprudent, carried like a megaphone over placid waters. Benjie shuddered and glanced quickly about.

"Don't even joke about it around here! It's not exactly redneck country, but coke scares the whiskers off these old retired folks."

"Really? With Coca Cola just over the line in Atlanta? Don't they know how the 'real thing' began and why it was first served in a drugstore? The Quechuas in South America chew the coca leaves all their lives, yet dispense with the habit when they come down to live in the city."

"Drop it, Josh. Dope's the last thing I wanna deal. It's no part of our plans. We're not even coming back here, at least never in that boat."

Josh flashed an exaggerated grin. "Good, I'm tired of it too! Nothing but concrete and freeways and big, big jails. I've only been back a month and already I'm anxious to get back to the savages."

"Josh, it's not my boat—"

"I know. Belongs to somebody else. You just told me—you're stealing it."

"I mean, it's another guy's setup. I got invited along only a few hours ago."

"Somebody you've known long?"

"We knew him in San Francisco, he worked on our engine once. Ran into him again by accident today."

"Sounds like a brief and rather tenuous relationship," Josh remarked. "Can you trust him?"

"I'd bet my life on him!" Benjie snapped back. He'd placed his trust on nothing but a gut feeling, against all the evidence of Weeto's nefarious activities. "He's a hard-luck guy but an honest Joe—"

"Who steals boats just for kicks?" Josh interrupted, smirking.

"You're needling me, Josh. He's an honest injun. Circumstances forced him into a corner."

"So he's stealing a boat, with your help, to make what isn't a pleasure cruise to South America. What business then, if not pleasure? And why you? Why not invite his friends along?"

"Because he needs somebody who can navigate and handle sails. We deliver him to South America and drop him ashore and…and Dynamite and I get the boat."

A low whistle escaped between Josh's teeth. "Sounds like he's doing it the hard way. Why not fly down? Unless he's on the run from some people with big-big connections. Is the Mafia after him?"

As much as Benjie thought he could trust Josh, he knew that one wrong word in the right ear would bring ruin down on them all. "Enough already. Better if you don't know more. Just know he's got legitimate reasons for getting out of the country. And right now a boat's handier than a plane for his exit, okay?"

"*Mais oui, d'accord.* By the way, does Dynamite know the full score?"

"Enough." He clipped the word, resenting the cross-examination. He didn't see Dynamite coming up behind him.

"Okay, you guys, I'm inviting myself to the party. What's the pow-wow all about?" Hands on her hips, she glared suspiciously at them. Josh's eyes swept over her with obvious approval.

"Benjie's been giving me all the reasons I shouldn't go along on the cruise. I'm ready, willing, able and eager but he doesn't want me. My old school chum! I almost get the feeling it's something personal, like bad breath or BO."

"Maybe he feels you need more protecting than me," Dynamite laughed, sniping at Benjie. "It could be dangerous, you know."

"Danger's not often my enemy. Boredom is." Grinning, Josh's small black eyes, shiny as obsidian, shifted between them. "Is it a case of odd man out—two's company, three's a crowd? Maybe my Rasta hairdo isn't to his liking?"

He winked at Dynamite and, with a grand flourish, whipped the hairpiece from his head to reveal a knobby scalp recently shaved. Benjie roared with laughter and shook his head in mock disbelief.

Josh held the wig out at arm's length. "Alas, poor Yorick," he recited solemnly. "I knew him well. Well enough, in fact, that he was once a living part of me." He patted and smoothed the disheveled strands. "Malheureusement, fashion fades like time and life. Hair power like flower power has gone out with the tides of surfeit. When I took my vows at the ashram in Katmandu, they shaved it all off. Nobody said anything about not saving it for a later time or another karma. Who can say what old fads may come sweeping back on the next tide?"

"Is the beard for real, or is that a prop waiting for the next act?" Dynamite goaded, instinctively taking to the skinny comedian who combined a sackcloth appearance with the sharp tongue of a raconteur.

"If the skipper has Navy rules aboard, it shall certainly come off. I'm tractable as a recruit. But at the moment it's still attached." He tugged his beard and winced. "I promise more fun and frolic aboard if I'm allowed to join the cruise. Benjie may have forgotten my credits as a jester. I speak only of the legitimate ones on stage." Flourishing the wig in front of him, he bowed from the waist to Dynamite's applause.

"Well, why not!" she asked Benjie. "Who's the skipper, after all? Isn't it up to you to decide what crew we need for a safe passage?"

"And a pleasurable one!" Josh chimed in. "I can cook, sew, swab decks, stand watches, handle firearms, speak Hindi and Pashto, recite the Upanishads and the Bhagavad-Gita. I can roll a tight joint and a neat bedroll, perform card tricks—"

"Enough, Jester-Lester!" Dynamite patted Josh's head. "I've never had a chance to play pampered passenger before. Your price is right."

Benjie threw an arm around his friend's shoulder. "Come on, old buddy, our ship's waiting. If the Coast Guard intercepts us, you can always claim you were shanghaied."

"What's my excuse?" Dynamite interjected.

"Put the blame on Ben, Jen," Josh sang. "Say he's a slaver and I'll swear to it. He lured you with false promises, really intending you as gringa bait for a Colombian capo's white powder! Who could doubt your eminent qualifications?"

Even though he was joking, Benjie felt distaste. Not only the unsavory connections but the air of complicity were touching Dynamite, and her laughter implied she accepted them. The doubts he'd just put a damper on flared again.

He was still nervous about the car. After dropping the boat keys in a sealed envelope for the Humbers at the dockmaster's office, he redusted the license plates with a handful of dirt.

Josh raised an eyebrow. "Traveling hot all the way, are we?"

"It's not what you think. It's not stolen. It's just that some of the wrong people are looking for it."

"Uh-huh," Josh grunted. "The cops or the Mafia?"

"Don't ask so many questions, Josh. Like they say, 'what you don't know can't hurt you.'"

"And a lack of curiosity can sometimes kill you!" Josh retorted. "But for the non and now, I'm sealed to silence. Promise, Captain. My solemn word."

He pressed a finger to his lips in bug-eyed solemnity and Benjie wondered if he was ever serious about anything.

Chapter Five

It was already dark when they reached Lauderdale. Benjie found the theater and drove slowly by the flickering marquee. There was no sign of Weeto and his son in the lobby. Circling the block, he parked on a side street across from the movie house. He glanced at the glaring McDonald's arch to his left and his stomach growled. At the same time he caught sight of a paper airplane soaring along the ceiling behind the big glass panes.

"If you need to set up a secret meeting, why pick a park bench or a dark alley?" he commented to the others. "Might as well eat while you're waiting for business. Latin practicality."

"What's with the kid?" Dynamite asked, frowning. "Is he going too?"

"He thinks it's our boat and we're going off on a pleasure cruise," Benjie admitted. "So play your part. And don't hassle Weeto with a lot of questions."

Dynamite wasn't to be sidetracked so easily. "Are there others you haven't mentioned? A wet nurse or a nanny? Who changes his diapers?"

"He's almost six, for Godssake! You'll be lucky he doesn't try to change yours."

"Wow, a Latin rake aboard," Dynamite droned flatly. "I can hardly wait."

A few minutes later, Weeto and his son glided into view, a yawlish mainmast trailing a jigging after-spar, the boy skipping double-time in an effort to match his father's stride. Weeto carried a huge shopping bag.

Benjie flicked the headlights and the two headed for the car. As he got out to meet them, Chico broke free and dashed past him for the car.

Expecting that Josh would be a problem, Benjie was surprised by Weeto's ready acceptance. He assured the Puerto Rican that neither Josh nor Dynamite knew anything about his personal problems or of the scuttling ring. "How'd it go with the Cubans?"

"No problem," Weeto said quietly. "It's gonna be cold out there tonight and they jus' as soon not get all wet. I din give them no money, so you don' owe me nothing. They're getting five hundred apiece anyway without having to work for it."

"All set for tonight, then. What time do we leave?"

"I thought you were the skipper. What time is right for a sailing trip to the Bahamas?"

Benjie grinned. "Around midnight. That gives you crossing time for daylight arrival. No point in running onto reefs in darkness."

"Good. I need a few hours to hide some things and ditch my car. Maybe you can take Chico and catch a movie with your friends. I'll meet you back here. Eleven o'clock, okay?"

By the time they got to the car, Chico was already acquainted with the strangers inside. Dynamite thrust her head out the window.

"My God, Benjie, you were right! He's...i-n-c-r-e-d-i-b-l-e!"

"*Adorable*," Josh lilted in French from his corner in the back.

"Careful, he's learning how to spell now," Weeto said proudly, peering inside. "Nice to see you again, Dynamite. Bet you don' remember me from so far back."

"The guy in greasy coveralls who spent a day inside our engine. How could I forget?"

"That's me, the grease monkey!" He laughed and extended a hand to Josh who had emerged from the back door like a jack-in-the-box. His thin frame exaggerated his six-foot-three height. "Hey, who needs a mast with you along?" Weeto teased. "We can jus' hook the sails to you, right?"

Josh laughed and they shook hands, but Benjie sensed ripples beneath the calm surface as they gave the car back to Weeto and headed for the theater.

After four consecutive hours of movies, they shuffled red-eyed into the theater's lobby at five minutes to eleven. Benjie shifted the sleeping bundle on his shoulder. Chico had fallen asleep hours earlier, apparently more comfortable in Benjie's arms than in Dyna's. Benjie speculated about the boy's aversion to women. Perhaps there was only one side to Weeto's story.

"Here, let me hold him awhile," Dynamite coaxed. "He won't know the difference."

Chico protested sleepily for a moment, then settled into her arms. Benjie saw she enjoyed the feel of the child. That maternal side of her surprised him. Babies were the farthest thing from his mind and, he had thought, from hers.

As they stepped outside a taxi pulled up and Weeto waved from the front passenger seat. Waking at the sound of his father's voice, Chico squirmed from Dynamite's grasp and ran to him. The others gathered their gear and piled in back.

Directing the taxi to the hotel in front of the marina, Weeto led them toward the lobby. At the last moment, he turned left and strode along the shuttered shop arcade, past a cocktail lounge. The laughter and singing of the patrons inside covered the sound of their footsteps as they went through an unlocked gate directly onto the docks. Once inside, Weeto lifted a dumpster lid to retrieve his tool satchel and a half-filled gunnysack, which rattled metallically as he handed it to Benjie. More tools, he thought as he hoisted the sack over his shoulder.

Benjie noted the night was overcast. No moon or stars. Cold, too. Temperature in the low fifties, he guessed, even in the protection of buildings. Exposed to the wind out at sea they could expect a further drop in temperature and perhaps conditions.

Calculating wind, currents and time of crossing, he walked to the end of the long pier in silence, ignoring Josh and Dynamite's animated talk and Chico's incessant jabbering. The cold was a blessing in one sense. As far as Benjie could see there were no parties in progress aboard the adjacent boats and nobody was topside.

Not until he stepped aboard their vessel, her fenders musically squeaking against the dock, did the tension began to fade. Making no effort to conceal their movements, they turned on the cabin and running lights, started the engine to warm it up, checked fuel and water and went about the many chores of getting a boat ready for sea.

Glancing through the chart drawers, Benjie beamed at what he found. Gnomonic charts for ocean crossings as well as coastal and harbor charts were all neatly stored in numbered sequence. They had the crisp feel of freshly minted money. Tables of computed azimuths lined the shelves above the chart table, along with the nautical almanac and a thick new Bowditch. The polished sextant, an expensive German model, gleamed in the cushioned green felt of its case. Within minutes they were ready and hauling in dock lines as they eased away from the pier.

There was only one bridge to pass through, just beyond the Customs pier where incoming yachts returning from foreign waters were required to put in for inspection. The bridge clanged its warning bells in instant response to the *Dragon's* three horn blasts, and seconds later they motored into the commercial basin. Picking up the buoy lights, they turned left and followed them down the channel and out the inlet. Not until they reached the outer buoy did Benjie allow himself to look back, fearing he would jinx them if he checked too soon. He chuckled to himself, wondering if Dynamite's superstitious habits were rubbing off on him.

Behind them, nothing. Only an illuminated harbor glaring with the intensity of a floodlit stadium.

He had Dynamite take over the wheel while he readied the sails for hoisting. Winds were eighteen knots, but coming from the north they could easily increase before morning. Unfamiliar with the boat's performance, he raised only the jib and a reefed main. Best to motor-sail until morning's light, and not so fast as to arrive on the other side in darkness. The rocks, islets and reefs of the Bahamas had been taking vessels since the time of Columbus and still occasionally claimed overenthusiastic crews who failed to act with caution.

The wind direction was in their favor—but its intensity was not. Blowing against the Gulf Stream, it changed normal three- to five-foot waves into eight- to twelve-foot slammers. Striking broadside, they created a rolling motion in the vessel and regularly washed aboard, dousing the helmsman and everyone else on deck. Chico, refreshed from his nap at the movies, refused to stay below. Dynamite found six complete outfits of foul-weather gear, but nothing in a child's size. But a bulky life vest and an adult jacket with the sleeves rolled back served nicely. She was his self-appointed guardian, keeping him off the decks and in the cockpit with a safety harness either tied to a cleat or in her hand. Chico finally gave out around three in the morning and she went to sleep with him in the forward cabin.

Josh, on the wheel then, had been unusually quiet thus far, initially more frightened than anyone guessed. His anxiety had nothing to do with the theft or fears of apprehension. The sea was what scared him. Although raised on an ocean coast where he had surfed its shores as a youngster, he'd never been to sea in a sailboat before. While he'd been in powerboats and sailing dinghies on lakes and protected bays, he had never been out where the raw mind of the sea held sway. The stormy night, with waves thumping and boarding with impunity, made it fearfully ominous. Human life seemed dispensable in the indifferent black environment of the rolling waves.

It took several hours for Josh to find his sea legs and quiet his fears. He could see from the obvious calm, even relish, in Benjie and Dynamite that they were in less than severe—possibly only moderately bracing—sea conditions. Being a fast learner, by the time the drizzle came and went he had acquired the confidence most novice sailors possess—an overconfidence bordering on fool-hardiness.

"Nothing to it," he shouted, steering with one finger. "How fast can she go when you really open up?"

"Sixty feet overall, maybe fifty feet at the waterline," Benjie calculated aloud. "Twelve knots hull speed, but likely seven or eight average."

"Whatta you think her tonnage is?"

"She's wood, she's heavy. Around thirty, I'd say."

"That much, huh?" Josh whistled between his teeth. "We got a floating gold mine under our feet. Thirty tons of grass—know what it's worth? Only a few million is all!"

"You're confusing displacement with cargo tonnage," Benjie laughed. "There's a big difference."

"So even half that, only a third, you're still talking millions!"

His exuberance resulted in inattention and the boat began to fall off course. The sails began luffing wildly, threatening to shift to the other side until Benjie reached over and corrected the wheel. Weeto shook his head. "And a million years in jail when they catch you, turkey!"

"He's only jiving," Benjie interceded.

"The hell I am!" Josh retorted.

"I don' like that talk, even when it's jus' horsing around," Weeto grumbled, getting to his feet. He nodded at Benjie, then headed for the hatch. "I'm going down awhile. Call me when you want me to stand my watch."

Josh had the good sense to stay silent until Weeto was below. "What's with him? That's the second time he's stiffed me." When Benjie offered no quick consolation, he added, "He wants us to think he's a bloody tough *hombre!*"

"It's your brand of humor," Benjie explained. "Not everybody knows when you're fooling around."

"He sees me as competition!" Josh snorted. "Like that gay expression, 'Today's trade, tomorrow's competition.' The Mob hates us bloody amateurs more than the cops or professional rivals."

"Mob? Weeto?" Benjie laughed.

"So who's he bloody running away from then?"

Benjie shook his head. "It's bloody well none of your business!"

"You bloody well better believe I'll be making it my business before he steps ashore in Colombia," Josh grunted, and adjusted the wheel. "How'm I doing anyway, Skip? Okay for a first-time helmsman?"

"Your first time, really?"

"Yeah. I've never been to South America before, either," he added sheepishly. "That was all bullshit."

"So, where were you then the past three years?"

"India and Afghanistan—before the Russians came in. Before that, Greece and Turkey. Mexico and Guatemala before that." Josh placed his hand over his heart. "Scout's honor."

In the binnacle light Benjie saw the wild look he remembered from the past, signaling a secret beyond the absurd reality everyone accepted and practiced. Josh—a mongrel mixture of Greek, Armenian, Italian and Irish, and raised as a Roman Catholic, was often accused of being a Jew, while blond Benjie, the half-Jew, was more often taken for a German or a Swede. Benjie's "Jewishness" was no more than something imposed by his name, Weinberg. True, his father had come from a Jewish background, but he hadn't been to temple since he was a boy in Brooklyn. Benjie had never been inside a synagogue in his life. His religious training came from his mother's churches, Anglican and Presbyterian, depending on her preference in ministers. His father, though a confirmed agnostic, believed religious training had a sound social effect so long as children were subjected to occasional skeptical critiques at home. As a dedicated amateur philosopher as well as a pathologist, he was as qualified at dissecting ideas as cadavers, and until his untimely death, Benjie continued the churchgoing for the discussions it generated at home. After that, it all seemed pointless.

At five o'clock he spotted the Bimini radio tower light, only a few degrees off the heading, an indication he'd calculated the push of the current about right. He told Josh to forget about the compass and steer for the light. Dynamite came up from the cabin, rubbing her eyes, volunteering relief at the wheel. But Josh was still enjoying his new toy. A chronic insomniac, he was more alert at night than during the day.

Dynamite threw an arm around Benjie and nodded at the cabin. "If we ever decide to have one, let's make it a kid like him. His kind I can enjoy. He wears you out, but it's worth it."

"He's still sleeping?" Benjie asked.

"Like he's on downers. No surprise he wore himself out—did you ever see so much energy?"

"Not since Josh was trying to close down Jefferson High School," Benjie replied.

"I heard you had a habit of playing with dynamite when you were a kid," Josh interjected.

"Only in self-defense and against a real slob," she explained, her tone and her expression tinged with disgust. She stared off in silence, then added suddenly, "How about some coffee, guys? Provided there's some aboard and propane in the stove tank. Anybody remember to check that?"

She kissed Benjie lightly on the cheek, then went down to the galley. She returned a few minutes later to hand up steaming mugs of coffee and then relieved Josh at the wheel. She was all smiles.

"So there was propane," Benjie teased.

"There's everything, stores galore! Enough to last a year! It would have been criminal sending it all to the bottom."

"Not to mention the lady herself," Benjie added, feeling good about the sleek vessel which carried them safely through the stormy hours of darkness. "She's a beauty, isn't she?"

"She's gorgeous!" Dynamite raved. "I can't believe the luxury below, it'll spoil me! What creep would want to sink her? Did Weeto say who she belongs to?"

"To us now," Benjie joked. "I don't think he knows. I'd rather not know either. Yeah, the secrets are slipping out," he turned to Josh. "They were gonna sink her for the insurance. Our taking her doesn't seem so criminal now, does it?"

"So why the scruples over the morality of hauling pot?" Josh shot back. From a pocket of his poncho under the rain slicker, he fished out a tin box of homemade joints.

"Not one of the top lines but I've had worse," he said, lighting up with an old Zippo. He took a drag and passed it to Benjie.

"Neat, we're in smokes again!" Dynamite yelped from the wheel.

"First in months. Where from?" Benjie asked after he puffed and passed it to Dynamite.

"God knows these days!" Josh lamented. "I picked up this stash in New Orleans on my way through. A dealer friend of a friend of mine. I would have brought more but I travel light and didn't wanna get busted in one of those cracker towns."

"Mmmm, nice," Dynamite sighed.

"Wait'll we get to Colombia," Josh cooed back, rolling his eyes. "Like the coffee, Colombia's got the best. Mountain grown, as they say."

"You and Mrs. Olson! She'll get you for that," Dynamite giggled. "Is it really so much better?"

Josh raised an eyebrow. "You never had Santa Marta Gold when you were in Colombia? You're in for a treat. God's own acres of heavenly treats! Smooth as velvet and cheaper than tobacco."

"You just told me you were never in South America," Benjie said, his smile fading.

"Right, man, but it doesn't mean I don't have friends there."

"You have friends there?" Dynamite said enthusiastically. "Maybe they can be a little help to some friends of yours."

"In whatever quantity we might want!" he said pointedly.

"She only means a personal stash," Benjie told Josh. "Not the boatload of stuff."

Josh grinned mischievously. "Let the lady speak for herself."

"Oh, that's crazy!" Dynamite sounded properly shocked. "Hauling it up in this? In a boat that's hotter than a Fourth-of-July firecracker?"

"It won't be so hot once we change names and papers and give it a paint job. Benjie's counting on that or he wouldn't have gone for it in the first place."

"In foreign waters, sure. And our deal was never to return her to U.S. waters. I gave my word."

"Tell me, how you think you could pull it off?" Dynamite interrupted, anxious to explore the new option Josh was proposing. "I mean, even supposing you somehow found the cash to make a buy and got it up here, how do you make connections for a sale?"

"Merest details," Josh tut-tutted, dismissing her question with a wave of his hand. "You won't even have to enter U.S. waters if your deal with the pirates is that important to you, Benjie. We lay off in the Bahamas and arrange for fast powerboats to ferry it across."

"Yeah, but who? How do you make your contacts?" Dyna wanted details.

"The least difficult part, take my word." Josh was smooth with confidence. "A few phone calls and I'd have all the buyers we need. My New Orleans friend has connections in Key West and Miami. A few jingles and some negotiating on price..."

"You're serious, aren't you?" She acted shocked but Josh detected something else.

Benjie stretched and yawned. "He's pulling your leg, Dyna. Can't you tell when he's joshing?"

His pun was lost on her. She had been sucked into those dark recesses where schemes get hatched. Twirling numbers and tumblers, she was busy opening and checking closets and cellars she never dared to peek in before. The lure of easy big money was drawing her into a labyrinth of intrigue that promised only profit and pleasure. No downside.

Josh grinned at Benjie and shrugged. But he knew that Dynamite was sniffing the bait. A little patience was all that was needed in her case. Benjie would take much more convincing.

Chapter Six

At daylight the island was in sight, no more than a mile off. Benjie had Dynamite fall off and head south. A string of uninhabited keys and islets ran from Bimini along the edge of Great Bahama Bank. He wanted enough light to read the waters before they went on the bank in search of an anchorage. As he headed below to consult the charts, he ran into Weeto, who lurched out of the forward cabin at the same time.

"Hey, why din you wake me up? It's morning awready." His sleepy face came alive when he glanced out a porthole. "There's land there! Why are we heading off?"

"Killing time. I'm waiting for more light before we go on the bank and anchor."

"You got a place in mind?"

Benjie pointed to the chart. "Any of these will do. The winds are shifting to the east, we're lee of the keys. All we do is pick an opening, go in close to one of the islets and drop the hook."

"How long we gonna stay?"

"Just long enough to change the name and numbers. Too close to home to dawdle here."

"I'm with you on that. Which way from here?"

"Not much choice. We can't go though the Bahamas without clearing in, and what we need now is distance." Benjie lifted the local chart and pointed his pencil to the overall chart beneath. "We'll continue south, down through the Old Bahama Channel, hugging the bank where the current's not as strong."

Weeto's eyes followed the pencil on the chart. "*Aaaiy*, so close to Cuba?"

"Can't help it. But don't worry, there's a law of the sea, the 'right of innocent passage'. Even if we stray into Cuban territorial waters, we're not in violation."

"Yeah, but does Castro know that?"

Benjie's laugh didn't fully dissipate his own concerns. "Don't worry, *amigo*, we'll keep close watch down through here in the narrow part. Then we'll head off this way for Great Inagua."

"We gonna put in there?"

"No, that's still English-speaking. If we have to go in anywhere, we'll put into Haiti. That's French and we can always play dumb foreigner if they get too picky with our boat papers. Which reminds me, did you bring them?"

"A whole box full. And the paint and stencils." Weeto dug in the shopping bag he'd acquired the night before and came up with a shoebox. He dropped it onto the chart table. "Take your pick, frien'!"

"Your friends weren't pikers," Benjie clucked in wide-eyed surprise at the stack of documents. "Did anybody know you were saving them?"

Weeto clapped him on the shoulder. "Ain't you glad I did, though?"

Studying the papers, Benjie saw most were Florida registrations. But a few were out-of-staters. Two were federally documented vessels on the rolls of the U.S. Coast Guard: one in St. Thomas, the other San Diego. All found graves in the Florida Straits.

The San Diego papers contained the Coast Guard renewal stamp from last September; it was still a valid license. Moreover, the vessel was described as a Kettenburg sloop of fifty-eight feet, as close a match as he could hope to find. *Dragon*'s brass letters on the transom could be switched to read *Gorda*, a favorite word in

Spanish meaning "fat female." The lettering and numbers on the bow needed only to be painted over. The documentation papers needed a bit of alteration, changing the vessel's name and the owner's. The bottle of ink eradicator from Weeto's shopping bag would do it nicely. Everything was coming up cherries.

The day, too, looked much more promising. The previous night's messy cloud-and-rain pattern appeared to have passed through. The sun was out and it looked like they were in for a spell of good weather. The Miami radio confirmed Benjie's own observations, forecasting clearing weather with winds shifting to the east. He found an opening on the bank with enough charted depth and piloted from the bow as Dynamite steered the *Dragon* into the lee of a small rocky islet. The rattling of the anchor chain roused the only remaining sleeper aboard. Chico came running topside in his underwear.

Before Dynamite could stop him he bolted up from the cabin and out of the cockpit, heading for the bow where Weeto and Benjie were paying out anchor line. Josh, on deck midship alongside the cabin to relay signals of the anchormen to the helm, had his back to the cockpit. When Dynamite called out to him, he turned and grazed the boy streaking past him. Swept off his feet, Chico went clean under the lifeline and vanished over the side. Josh dove in after him.

With the engine running in reverse to dig in the anchor, there was added danger. Dynamite threw it in neutral before abandoning the wheel and running to where Chico went over. The others ran back from the bow. Josh already had a hand on him but, as they saw, it was hardly necessary. Showing only a fleeting surprise as he surfaced, he coughed, then broke into a grin and began squealing.

"Eh, Poppi, mire! Soy un pescado!" He sucked in a mouthful of water and spouted it at them, thrashing in the shallow crystal water, The cove echoed with his giggles.

"Never mind bein' a fish! You awright?" Weeto called down. Another shrill squeal and another jet of water from Chico's mouth provided the answer.

"He can swim all right, then?" Dynamite's question was more confirmation of her relief.

"Like he says, a *pescado*. He loves the water." He called down again, sternly this time. "No time to play, monkey. We got work to do." He jerked his thumb backwards. "Out you go!"

Chico protested, then dutifully climbed the boarding ladder Dynamite hung over the side. The water temperature may have been in the seventies, but the chilly northern breeze was enough to chatter his teeth. Leaving the others to finish the anchoring chore, Dyna took him below to dry him off and heat some milk on the stove.

As he watched with strained politeness from the table where he sat bundled, his conversation was sullen and in Spanish. As Dynamite explained the engine propeller and its dangers—blades churning like knives—he stared back blankly. Surprised at his turn-around from the night before, she confronted him. "I know you speak English. Why not with me? Or is it because your dad's not here?"

"No," he answered in clipped ambiguity.

Dynamite smiled down at him. "That's at least understandable in either language. But which question does it answer? Why not English so we can both understand?"

"Ingles es feo."

"English is what? What does *feo* mean?"

"Feo means ugly." His face showed what he meant.

"Ugly?" Dynamite pondered, as amused as she was confused. "How so?"

"You make funny sounds in English—the, there, this. Like your tongue is twisted and you can't talk so good. *Muy feo!*"

She stifled the urge to laugh aloud. Repeating to herself a few of the 'th' words like father, mother, brother, she decided he had a point. They were odd sounds, as comical as she sometimes accused the Castilian tongue of sounding.

"You mean like a speech impediment, a lisp?" When she got no response, she asked another way. "Do you know what a lisp is?"

"Por supuesto!" he replied at once.

"There you go again! Why can't we talk in English?"

"Porque no puede hablar Español?" he retorted. She understood and started to laugh.

Coming down the ladder, Weeto heard the last of this and began loudly scolding the boy. "What you got for manners, Chico? That's no way to talk to a lady! I'm ashamed of you!" He smiled apologetically at Dynamite. "He was askin' why you don' speak Spanish."

"That much I understood." She put her finger into the milk to test the temperature. "The answer is, I'm lazy. We were nearly two years in Latin countries. I could have learned Spanish, I guess, but I didn't take the time to master it."

"Que lástima," the boy sighed with a condescending air.

"It means, 'What a pity,'" Weeto translated, then frowned at Chico. "That's terrible, monkey! That's like an insult. You owe the lady an apology."

"No, he's right," she intervened. "All that time among Latinos and I can hardly put two words together."

"My fault," he countered. "I'm always tellin' him what a beautiful language Spanish is. I don' want him growing up not knowing it."

"Good for you, you're right!" There was more to this macho grease monkey than the gruff exterior he displayed around his son. Opening a cupboard she found a sealed box of cookies. She put some on a plate and placed them in front of Chico along with his glass of milk. Her movements, she noted, were as carefully scrutinized by the father as by the son. Perhaps his distance around her was grounded in something other than disinterest.

When Weeto bit into one of the cookies, she offered him a glass of milk to go with it.

"Or a *café-con-leche*," she added, showing off a bit of her Spanish. "I just have to spoon in some instant—"

"No, no, thanks." He put a hand up, already headed for the stairs. "I got to help Benjie topside."

"I'll get some breakfast together," she called after him as he bounded up the steps. Only slightly shorter than Benjie's, his squared body suggested bulk, even fat at first glance. But beneath his baggy clothes one caught the outline of solid muscle, the primal strength of the manual worker.

Turning, she saw carbon-copy features in the face of the boy across the table. Chico sat in silence. Same sheen in the curly black hair, same dark brown eyes and long lashes, and the same way of tilting his head to one side, as if viewing the world suspiciously. But he'd be taller than his father and finer-boned, not so husky. The dimple-dented chin must have been inherited from the other side.

Calling them to breakfast, they were hardly seated when interrupted by the sound of an approaching helicopter. Fearful glances flew around the table before they all rushed up on deck. A chopper was coming straight for them from over the open straits, from Florida way. All froze, fearing the worst. Benjie's face went pale.

Less than a hundred feet astern of them, it banked sharply and turned. Emblazoned on the side was the bright orange and white lettering of the U.S. Coast Guard. They watched breathlessly as it completed its turn and continued south, following the line of the bank on some routine exercise or patrol.

"Too soon for them to be looking," Weeto whispered to Benjie as the others headed back down. "They won't know it's missin' until Friday. We got three days before they come snooping."

Benjie could think of other possibilities. "Unless the dockmaster or one of the boaters sees it's gone and calls somebody on it."

"Fat chance! They don't know whose boat is supposed to be at the dock or on a trip somewhere—and they don't care."

Benjie, aware of the odds Weeto had been successfully battling for years, wasn't willing to subscribe to his optimism. That little lucky streak he felt earlier in the morning was fading like a bettor's pass. The chopper had come close enough to read the name; maybe they routinely noted it in their log.

When they returned to the breakfast table, Chico mimicked chopper's engines and pointed his syrup-dripping fork in Dynamite's face. *"Eh-lee-cope-tair. Digale!"*

"He's askin you to say it too," Weeto translated. "Your first Spanish lesson."

"Just a continuation. We covered the canned goods and breakfast preparations this morning—why stop now?" She winked at the others. *"Digale!"*

"No, no, no, no, no," Chico scolded. Not the command word—he wanted helicopter in Spanish.

"Eh-lee-cope-tair," she obliged.

"Bueno," said her pint-sized teacher. "That means good."

Dynamite kept a straight face. "Thanks teach," she said. Chico frowned at her. "I mean, *gracias, maestro.*"

"*De nada.*" He bowed solemnly. "That means, it's nothing."

"*De nada,*" she repeated dutifully.

The lesson lasted only as long as the meal. When the men went topside to finish the work on the hull, Chico bounded after them. He wanted sandpaper and a paintbrush too. Weeto rigged a fishing pole and line for him, and threatened to throw him overboard if he didn't stay put. He snapped the boy's harness to a cleat in the cockpit. The threat, Dynamite decided, would have little effect on Chico given his interest in the variety of sea life visible in the glassy waters. She ducked below to do the dishes and clean up the galley.

While Benjie worked on the transom from a rubber Avon in the water, the other two were on the bow, sanding and painting over the areas where the name was scripted on the sides. They worked hurriedly, ears and eyes alert not only for the sound of choppers but for any sign of sails that could be sneaking up on them on silent winds. As they worked, Weeto thanked Josh for diving in after Chico when he fell overboard.

"*De nada,*" Josh quipped, then grinned. "That means for nothing."

They even managed to share a laugh in the aftermath.

Dynamite, overhearing their conversation through the open ports, began to understand what lay beneath Weeto's rough exterior. What other storms had he weathered in raising the boy alone or in the mob-related activities now forcing him to flee the country? The question spun not only a web of sympathy but a thread of interest on a level her instincts told her went beyond her perception of him as a dedicated father and lodged in her loins.

In little more than an hour the painting was finished and the brass letters on the transom rearranged to spell *Gorda*. Hauling anchor, they motored off the bank and raised sails. In her full suit, she was a towering skyscraper of immaculate white, dwarfing her human crew on deck as she filled with power and knifed along the bank for Cuba. Then as she stiffened to her element and went scudding, a few aboard who'd never experienced the thrill of a giant wind machine gaped in awe at the splendor of its silent propulsion.

Dynamite, at the wheel, felt the morning irritations fall away as the sails filled, the hull vibrating beneath her feet as they picked up speed. A line of Shakespeare suddenly popped into her head: "We have laughed to see the sails conceive and grow big-bellied with the wanton wind."

The image made her laugh and she glanced at the boy, who was jigging his pole over the side. She had no wish to grow big-bellied for even such a prize. Not yet. Josh's talk of pot and the millions to be made in a single haul had the power to invade her thoughts and alter all their destinies. Sunlight sparkled across the water's surface like a carpet of diamonds and stirred her Viking love of water like an acid high. Josh's schemes lent themselves to a sense of adventure, like the gulls cawing and swooping away to unknown destinies. The sudden interest in riches—new to her—conjured images of avarice in herself she wouldn't have imagined. But it's not simply greed, she told herself. It was more the thrill of daring it, the challenge of winning the prize.

Glancing at Benjie, who was putting final touches to the sail trim, she saw a new image emerging. Even though he was skippering the boat, she felt more in possession of it than he did. He brought to everything, even what he owned, a sense of tentativeness like a renter or borrower who knows the article will have to be returned. A stewardship pervaded whatever came into his care, whereas she acted on impulse, devouring and discarding at will. He acted as if his actions mattered. She knew they were largely fated, like the lodestones and prayers that carried some of her ancestors to safe shores and plunder—and others to Arctic deaths or drownings at sea.

Benjie scanned the horizon, looking for signs of weather or approaching unfriendlies. Edginess was still perched on his shoulder, persistent as a bobby bird at sea. He felt only temporarily lucky, never permanently charmed like Dynamite and Josh. It was as though his subconscious knew in advance that his dream would end in disaster, and he felt deprived even of its momentary pleasure.

He disliked his habit of caution. It robbed him of a spontaneity and joy he thought he saw in others like Dynamite and Josh. He loved his blond gift at the wheel but ached at the thought he could lose her. Nothing yet threatened their relationship except the ritualized habits of work and saving, and an uncertain future. A reminder, if he needed any, that nothing is forever, least of all love.

He sensed that Josh was a powerful draw on Dynamite. Not physical or sexual—more like the kinship of iron and magnetism, close cousins meeting for deviltry rather than mating. He told himself he'd relax once they were safely through the straits and out of reach of the Coast Guard. But his cautious side warned of other concerns besides arrest—some, doubtless, that he couldn't yet imagine.

Chapter Seven

One of those unimagined snags was about to surface in Miami. It had been triggered weeks before, when the widow of the *Dragon*'s last skipper acceded to the suggestion of her late husband's law partner that she seek a speedy disposition of the white elephant in the water.

For reasons unknown, her husband had registered the vessel solely in her name. It wasn't part of his estate, which would take months to go through probate. She learned he had recently remortgaged their home, as well as the vacation house in St. Thomas, and bought the two Cadillacs in the garage on time, not for cash. She couldn't even dispose of his car without going through the process and letting the tax authorities and legal mercenaries take their bites. Contemplating the disarray of her finances, the widow made the one decision that made sense.

Not that she didn't understand the need for laws and lawyers. Law had been Karlie's professional lifeblood. How else, he once laughingly asked, could a Polish kid from an immigrant steelworker family make it to the top of the slag heap without being an All-American linebacker or a screaming rock star?

Whenever he heard the old cliché about a lawyer and his briefcase out-stealing any ten men armed with guns, Karlie always grinned. He never openly knocked the fraternity, but she could tell he had about as much respect for the profession as a hard-hat for bureaucrats and pencil pushers. If you didn't come home with dirt on your hands, you hadn't been working.

But where was his dirt? She could guess but preferred not to. There was protection in that. What she didn't know she couldn't be accountable for, nor have to carry on her conscience to confession. Karlie had died on a business trip to Switzerland. She would have been with him, but for a flu attack a day before the flight. Then, when authorities called, she had to go anyway, dragging herself out of her sickbed, doped up with Dristan and Valium, to claim the body and arrange shipment home. Thank God for Harold, Karlie's junior partner, who dropped everything to go with her and help with the details.

There wasn't any problem with Swiss authorities. They all spoke intelligible English and there was no mystery about the death. He died in his hotel room of an acute myocardial infarction. Forms had to be signed, however, questions answered, red tape satisfied on both sides of the Atlantic. In her sick, dazed state she wasn't up to it. Never good at dealing with the authorities, she always had boyfriends or husbands—Karl was her third—shield her from such tedium. Harold took charge and handled everything, reminding Helen again she functioned best on the arm of a man.

This was dramatically underscored when Harold showed her the pathetic state of her finances. She couldn't believe it at first. Karlie had always been secretive about money matters, but he made a few things perfectly clear to her. There were cash deposits of several hundred thousand each at two banks in Nassau and at least one in Grand Cayman. She even remembered the names of the banks because she accompanied him there a few times. But nowhere in his desks or vaults at home or in the office, nor in the safe deposit box in the bank, could she and Harold find passbooks or other proof of assets. Contacts with the offshore banks confirmed the accounts, but they'd been closed months earlier. Where had all the money gone?

Karlie wasn't a gambler, though many of his high-flying friends and clients were, and he often went on trips with them to the casinos in Nassau and San Juan. When Harold, as executor, put it all together she was left with less than a hundred thousand in cash and paper negotiables and the real estate was all highly mortgaged. And more was tied up in the yacht Karlie had recently purchased than in all the other assets combined.

"Suppose the money wasn't his in those offshore accounts," Harold speculated. "What if he was only caretaking it for others?"

Helen had already asked about files on his clients and his secretary, Mary Jo, had told her there weren't any—Karl kept it all in his head. Helen knew from experience his remarkable power of recall. He could read the stock market quotes in the morning and remember them with amazing accuracy when a client called him at home that night. He knew the most recent exchange rates on foreign currencies like the mark, pound, franc, and peso and quoted them like racetrack betting odds.

When Harold suggested an insurance payoff on the boat as a means of solving her immediate financial problems, she needed very little coaxing. She already knew from the yacht broker that a boat the size of the *Dragon* might take months or years to sell even at a greatly reduced price. Meantime without regular care and maintenance, it could start deteriorating fast. Slip fees were extremely high and insurance cost an arm and a leg. In fact, it was the arrival of the adjusted premium billing the day before that prompted Harold to drive her to Lauderdale to check the boat for valuables. It also provided the perfect opportunity to bring up the subject again.

"Be sure to pay it," he cautioned, explaining that hippies and others frequently stole boats for the dope trade. The following Tuesday, after receiving the last of the replies from the island banks confirming the closed accounts, he brought the matter up even more forcefully.

"I've done some checking for you," he said, handing her a creased note with a figure inside. "That's what it'll cost you to have someone take it out to sea and scuttle it. Even less than the broker's commission if and when he finds a buyer. You understand what you have to do, Helen?"

She nodded consent but avoided his gaze while he gave her detailed instructions. The boat itself meant nothing; boats made her seasick. She didn't mind the ones before, small sportfishing boats to take clients and friends for a day of fishing in Biscayne Bay. But his sudden whim for an ocean-going yacht and his talk of sailing it to their home on St. Thomas, and perhaps across the Atlantic or around the world, greatly upset her. But she had little say in financial decisions and there seemed to be plenty of money. If he wanted to buy himself an expensive toy, she could hardly protest.

She did as Harold instructed and drove to Lauderdale at midday on Friday. After an hour aboard and a desultory inspection of lockers for any valuables they might have overlooked, she left the brown paper bag of money in the galley. Then she locked the hatch and slipped the key under the seat cushion in the cockpit. The shopping bag that had carried the brown bag of cash now contained a few jugs of Beefeater and Tanqueray gin. Harold had warned her not to strip the boat, that would look suspicious. But a few bottles of booze couldn't hurt, and she needed a few martinis to help forget the day's sordid business.

Three days later when she returned to Lauderdale and found the boat gone, her reaction was one of genuine surprise. She first searched the piers, thinking the dock boys might have moved it. Appropriately outraged, she reported it to the dockmaster, who then sent his assistants scampering in futile searches around the marina. By the time the police and Coast Guard were notified she felt bona fide indignation, her face suffusing with the same anger experienced by any law-abiding citizen victimized by crime. Some of the anger carried over into her phone call to the insurance agent, who was reduced to calming her down and reassuring her of a speedy disposition of the matter.

However, her injured innocence was given less than forty-eight hours to jell. On Thursday morning two of Karlie's clients rang her doorbell with anything but condolence or friendship in mind. She instantly recognized one as the man featured in the state televised crime hearings, the same baldheaded man who had embraced Karlie in Nassau.

Rude questions were asked, in hostile tones, about places where Karlie might have stored cash and valuables. Cruder actions followed. They began ransacking the house. Her initial protest, made as she was volunteering the key to Karlie's desk, brought such a resounding slap to her face that she nearly fainted. Terror took over.

After wrecking the desk they had her open the wall safe. They examined the interior and contents with the scrutiny of detectives looking for hair strands. They smashed drawers and stuck knives in picture frames and the backs of upholstered furniture. Carpets were rolled back where they weren't nailed down. Walls were rapped for empty sounds that could reveal hiding places. All the while Frank, whose name she remembered from the crime hearings, interspersed his questions and orders with penetrating glances at her. His shaved head and jutting chin reminded her of Nazi generals from old war movies. So did his manner of barking commands at his aging sidekick, who spoke only in mumbled assents or nods and took his lead from the other like a shadow. At Frank's direction he even crawled into the low attic covering the sprawling one-story house and searched it with a flashlight.

When she finally summoned the courage to ask what, specifically, they were looking for, she was stunned by the response.

Paper! Not money as she'd supposed, but sheets of paper! Lists of names and numbers!

"Whose names? Numbers for what?" she asked.

"He never told you? You haven't a clue?" She averted her eyes to escape Frank's penetrating gaze. "All those trips to Europe and the islands and he always took you along for cover. You never knew? Never guessed?"

She shook her head. Frank put a finger to her chin to raise her gaze. Fearing he was going to strike her again, she spoke in quick, desperate tones. "He never told me. I never asked and he never said. I still don't know. God's truth, I swear it!"

A moment's security emerged in the midst of her ordeal. Her ignorance of Karlie's financial affairs provided a margin of safety. She couldn't be punished for what she didn't know, could she?

"It never occurred to you why he visited banks on his trips to Switzerland and the islands?"

"Client business is all he ever said," Helen replied weakly. Any fool could have guessed it had something to do with laundering money and hiding it in safe places. But now she was beginning to see another connection.

In a rush she explained the mystery of the disappearing funds and closed accounts in Karlie's estate. She detailed Harold's exhaustive and futile searches with the island banks and wondered aloud if Karlie might have transferred the monies from the closed accounts to a new Swiss account. But which bank, and in what city? Weren't the numbers secret, known only to the banker and the account holder?

Suddenly, she understood.

While killing time on the *Dragon* the week before, she came across some curious scribbling in a plastic tube on the shelf above the chart table. She was drawn to it by the elegant gold lettering emblazoning it. German Gothic, she thought it was called. All swirls and curlicues, graceful but so decorative she could seldom identify words or letters even in English.

Rolled up inside were several sheets of heavy embossed paper with a series of numbers in scrawled ink running down the page. Recognizing Karlie's hand, she didn't bother removing them, certain they were corrections or calculations having to do with celestial navigation. A few weeks before he'd bought an expensive German sextant and spent much of his spare time taking practice shots and working out the equations or whatever they were called. Reminded of him and the mess he'd left her in, she flung the tube angrily back onto the shelf. It bounced and rolled down an opening behind the paneling. She scarcely gave it another thought.

Relating all this to Frank and his shadow brought a sudden new flicker of interest, since they didn't know about the *Dragon* nor the fact it was kept berthed in Lauderdale rather than Miami. Her rapport with them vanished the moment they began asking for details and she had to confess the vessel was missing.

"Missing?" the shaved head asked, moving closer.

"Stolen," she bleated, heart aflutter with another half-truth. "They think hippies. Probably for—you know, smuggling dope."

Silence reverberated like a threat. When she dared to look up, Frank's stare was still riveted on her but his look had softened and his voice had the timbre of new tactics.

"Helen, dear Helen," he coaxed, "hasn't it occurred to you that your missing money or its equivalent is probably hidden somewhere on that boat, too?"

"We searched it, Harold and I—"

"A boat has a thousand hiding places."

"But we—" she began, then trailed off in the certainty she'd missed the point again.

"Too late, too late," she keened, rocking and wringing her hands. "They've sunk it already, it's gone."

"Sunk it? They?" Frank's words hung in the air.

"Do you see what we must do, Helen? We've got to find that boat, no matter where they've sunk it, even if it's a thousand feet down. And you'll help us, won't you, with every little detail about the boat and who you hired to scuttle it?"

Of course she'd tell them everything. Everything. Only then did she realize she shielded herself from all the sordid details and had little useful information to give. "Harold made all the arrangements," she said.

It took two phone calls to establish a lead and put them on track. The first was to Harold's office where, not so surprisingly, two of Frank's henchmen were conducting a separate interrogation. With information Harold supplied, another call went to a man called Paco. Helen was surprised they let her sit there and listen to the conversation.

"Listen, Paco, a lady friend of mine had her boat turn up missing," he sang cavalierly, this man who could bark like a general and jingle lawyers in his pocket like loose change. "Yeah, disappeared from a Lauderdale marina earlier this week. I thought you might run me around the area in your powerboat. Check first to see if some hippies might have borrowed it and parked it elsewhere. The lady left some valuable jewelry aboard and she's offering a reward for its recovery. Who knows, you might get lucky and collect it!"

Setting a place to meet in two hours, he dropped the phone and grinned at his older partner. "A fishing expedition, Harry. With some Cubans. Brush up your Spanish."

Convinced by now her missing assets were somehow tied to the boat and reassured by Frank's manner that the matter of locating and raising a scuttled vessel was no great task, she needed to stake out her claim. She found her excuse when he asked for pictures of the boat, which she eagerly supplied. She even offered to share in the cost of the recovery operation. "You can deduct my share of the expenses and whatever you think is a fair share in the reward."

Frank stared in astonishment a moment, then his face turned playful under the shiny dome of his bald head.

"Helen, Helen, don't you know about laws of salvage at sea?" He clucked his tongue and shook his head sadly. "Don't you know it's strictly finders-keepers, losers-weepers out there?"

Weeto's two Cuban friends, also employees of Paco, on whose boat Weeto and Chico had been living, had already admitted their part in Weeto's plan before Frank and Harry came questioning them. Although they denied any knowledge of where the boat was headed and what others might be aboard, Frank was, for a moment, skeptical of their explanation and it looked as if they might be subjected to persuasion by force. But sheepishly volunteering the information about the two strangers who came looking for Weeto the morning after he left restored their credibility, and the questions took a different twist.

The strangers had claimed to be private investigators, looking for Weeto to bring him good news. Naturally suspicious, the Cubans' first instincts were that they were cops or immigration, *la Migra*.

A possible fortune was waiting for the boy if they found him in time—so the man said. He produced identification to prove he wasn't official, only a private tracer from a company in Texas. Taking the strangers at face value, the Cubans admitted they thought Weeto and Chico had gone off in a boat. They claimed they didn't know the name of the vessel and, since in truth they'd never seen it, they couldn't provide a description. Of course, they had no idea where it was headed.

At first relieved to hear the *Dragon* was still afloat, Frank become suddenly agitated at mention of the two investigators. He and his partner seemed worried the strangers weren't what they pretended to be. Paco, translating, made them repeat what the

Texan said about a possible fortune waiting for the boy. Frank had Paco take them over the conversation again and again to study the words used and physical descriptions of the men.

To their surprise, the Cubans were rewarded with crisp hundred-dollar bills and promised more if later they came up with additional information. Warned never to mention their interrogation and to forget they ever met Frank and Harry, they were told to be as silent about the encounter with the Texans but to report anything new they might learn about the missing boat or the people on it.

Paco supplied Frank with a picture of Weeto and his son which had been left behind on the boat with their belongings. As they were about to leave, Paco asked Frank what he was going to do next.

"Find the *Dragon!*" Frank grinned, sunlight reflecting on his gold-capped teeth and bald head. "We're gonna put on the goddamndest boat hunt you ever saw. From Boston to Brazil, Panama to the Azores. If she's afloat we'll find her. Bet on it!"

Chapter Eight

*D*ragon, newly christened *Gorda,* slipped out of Lauderdale under cover of darkness, and a week later she glided into Colombian waters in broad daylight. Fair winds and smooth sailing wore away even Benjie's worry. The only scare occurred in the channel off Camaguey, when they drifted close enough to Cuba to see shore lights. Dousing their own, they drifted until dawn, then powered out to avoid any encounters with Cuban gunboats. Timing their entry, they slipped through the Boca Chica opening to Cartagena harbor in late afternoon and motored up the twisting channel to the anchorage fronting the Club de Pesca as the sun was setting. Arriving at dusk, they could put off clearing Customs until morning.

After midnight, when the yacht club restaurant was closed and most of the townspeople asleep, the rubber Avon was quietly lowered over the side. Benjie powered his two passengers across the bay to the rotting docks where local trading schooners unloaded their cargoes of fish, produce and charcoal. Behind loomed the open-stalled marketplace, sprawling for blocks along the waterfront in the shadow of the old walled city, dark and deserted now. He had no understanding with Weeto beyond an offer to help if it was ever needed. The boat would be there at least a few weeks, maybe a month, so he could complete some topside changes to further disguise the vessel before moving on.

Weeto's plans were far more uncertain. Knowing nothing about the city or the country, he'd have to feel his way around, take a room in town to first size things up and find new identification and travel papers in case he had to leave. He thought Venezuela, with its oil riches and fleets of tankers coming and going, might be more rewarding in his work as a diesel mechanic.

Typically brusque in departing, he took the bags Benjie handed him, murmured a laconic farewell, and walked away. Recognizing the departure as something final, Chico mimicked his father with a "good luck, *amigo*," and the same quick handshake.

"*Buen suerte,* Chico," Benjie whispered back, pausing a moment to look after them before he bent to his task. He yanked the starter cord and the silence shattered around him, making him feel exposed and destitute. He'd miss them both.

Harbor entry went like clockwork next morning. Local customs laws dictated working through a ship's agent, and an hour after Benjie dinked ashore to notify the dockmaster of their arrival, an agent appeared on the docks with a Customs official. Taken to the vessel anchored offshore, they made a cursory inspection below, their attention focused more on Dynamite in her green bikini than any of the provisions or supplies.

After checking boat papers and passports and finding nothing amiss, the officer made out a crew list for the three of them and issued shore passes valid for a month. The gentlemen politely stalled and poked around until they were offered a bottle of Scotch each, then found pressing reasons to get back ashore to other duties. Josh, quietly observing the show from his seat under the cockpit awning, called to Dynamite as Benjie ferried the officials back to shore.

"Methinks I saw two lean and hungry men, who would sell their etceteras for almost anything!" He grinned broadly. "You gave a great performance, Sarah!"

"Under the circumstances, I thought a little distraction was called for." She sawed the beach towel across her fanny, then delicately tossed it aside. "You can always count on the Latin male to hold up his end of the performance. Machismo demands it. Macho-men, whether they feel it or not."

"Shrewd observation. And a modest one," he added, surprised again at her lack of vanity. "Or do you claim personal experience with the Latin male?"

"Ho-ho-ho," she crooned mockingly. "I don't have to go around the world to know it's round. You noticed too, I wasn't the main attraction. A bottle of Scotch sells for a week's wages down here."

"I noticed—if you're going to insist!" Josh's smirk betrayed a multiplicity of insinuations. His shaved head was sprouting a five o'clock shadow. Pure punk or recently released prisoner.

"Nothing feels right to those guys unless they come off with a little *mordida*," she continued. "It's like a point of pride with them. No self-esteem unless they make off with a bite."

"Interesting," Josh mused, tilting his head back. "Makes the whole country look promising, if you get my drift."

"No. Explain."

Josh laughed. "I was thinking of our New York friend and his precocious kid. In a country like this it shouldn't be difficult to get fake ID and work permits."

"Stop bullshitting, Josh. You were thinking how easy it might be to arrange a shipment of pot by bribing the right officials."

"Oh, it occurred to you too!" Josh pounced eagerly. "But what would Benjie think if he heard us discussing such evil specula-tions?"

It pleased him that she was beginning to advance her own suggestions. From time to time during the trip, he jokingly reminded them of their floating opportunity, the open mine under their feet waiting to be filled with Santa Marta gold. He was careful not to push and, having seen Weeto's violent reaction to the sugges-tion, avoided any mention of it when he was around. Knowing as well that Benjie would bolt at the first sense of pressure, he left it as a joke when Benjie treated it that way, leaving Dynamite to wonder if he was just kidding.

They went ashore like jubilant sailors on shore leave. Back on land, Josh's wit found its feet again and Dynamite, as if released from a nagging toothache, was ready to let the past take care of itself. Even Benjie, willing at last to accept the good fortune snatched by criminal means, seemed ready for a new start. At his suggestion, they recklessly lunched at the expensive yacht club under a banyan tree in a corner of the old Spanish fort built to protect a king's treasure from marauding pirates and enemy states. They had wine with the broiled lobster and a dessert wine with the flan. Afterwards, instead of waiting for the three-cent bus they used the year before, Benjie hailed a twenty-five-cent taxi into town. Dynamite raised an eyebrow at his extravagance.

The outer forts and old walls of the inner city were as elegantly sanctified by time as Benjie remembered them. Inside, the cobbled streets were as noisy and thronged with pedestrian shoppers as his imagination always pictured. Warmed by the mild winter sun and glowing inside from the wine, they set about exploring the city on foot.

The same restoration projects were still in progress, not visibly advanced from the year before. The cathedral was still encased in rickety scaffolding. Glimpses of flowered courts and cloisters behind facades of stone and grillwork romanticized the security and slower tempo of an earlier time. But history, he knew, had put a stamp of violence and bloodshed on the fabled city where the continent's treasure was once gathered and stored for shipment to Spain.

Dynamite too was caught up in the mood of the city, surprised it imprinted itself so vividly on her memory. Like rock music and strobe lights, the street sounds and sights assaulted her senses. Hawkers of goods called out to them, others jostled them for attention, money changers whispered bargains as they passed. Soft-shelled iguana eggs, said to promote male potency, were strung like ping-pong balls in necklaces hanging from the rafters of pushcarts. Men bought them in multiples and swallowed them on the spot like oysters. The baleful producers of these aphrodisiacs dozed in the well of the carts, tethered by twine.

Vendors hawked American Kents and Marlboros from stacked boxes on the sidewalk, smuggled contraband that sold for less than half the Florida price. Josh reminded them that smuggling was an old and sometimes honorable profession.

"At times it's the only way to outwit tyrants and confiscatory taxes, not to mention impositions by religious demagogues. One could argue," he added with conviction, "it's mankind's most persistent expression of free trade in a world where special interests always seek protection from competition through legal restraints."

Dynamite only half listened, knowing the lecture was meant for Benjie. Her blond voluptuousness attracted stares and whistles from young males, but it didn't bother her. She let it caress her as part of the light-and-shadow show of the afternoon sun while they browsed the narrow, crooked streets and arcades. Perhaps because she'd been there before and, memory flooding her with images generated a powerful sense of déja vu, she felt not only the pull of the town's obvious tourist appeal, but a narcotic sense of belonging.

Attracted by an emerald display in the window, she stepped through the door of a jewelry store and had the utter certainty of having crossed the same threshold a thousand times before. Not when they were there in *Candy* a year earlier, but in some far-off time in another life. The scent of incense struck her with instant familiarity.

As if awakening to a false dream about herself, she was struck by the beauty of the stones and metal resting on their cushions of velvet behind the locked glass cases. Green was her favorite color and she was in a forest of green-winking fires. One in particular, isolated in a case of its own, an emerald the size and shape of a small bird's egg, hung from a gold pendant like a dollop of green lava, surrogate in some weird way for the iguana eggs the men sucked and swallowed. She stared transfixed. A nearly irresistible urge assailed her to smash the glass and take it. She wanted to seize it in her hand, feel its cold fire on her cheek and in her mouth—she wanted to swallow it.

In a daze she turned away, shaking her head at the middle-aged jeweler who came padding up to her in house slippers. Returning to the men outside, she hardly knew what to make of the strange experience inside. She chalked it up to the wine and sun, the kaleidoscopic sights and sounds of a quaint city, and the sudden release of tension after days at sea under threat of discovery and apprehension.

They stopped at a juice bar and took a table on the open end, overlooking the clock tower and main gate fronting the plaza inside the walls. Ordering tall cool glasses of *chino*, a local concoction of sweetened orange juice, Josh reminded them they had no pesos. An eavesdropper behind them leaned closer and whispered, "Eh, mee-stair, you want to change Amedican moh-nee?"

The young man at the next table was more a kid—fourteen or fifteen but already adult in his savvy. "Only twenny-four, maybe twenny-five pesos they give at the bank. I give you twenny-seven for one doe-lar. How many doe-lars you want to change?"

"No," Benjie said, shaking his head.

"Is good deal, frien'. You can't do more better no place." Streetwise eyes, brown and lively, darted in all directions. Benjie turned nervously away.

"Thirty pesos!" Josh piped up and turned in his chair to face the kid. He opened the flap of the big leather bag he carried on his shoulder, as if intending to pull out his money.

The boy's hand waved a warning. "No, no, no, *señor,* not here!"

"Don't get involved, man," Benjie warned Josh. "It's strictly illegal."

"I got to fix it with my frien' first, to get the pesos," the boy told Josh. "He won't give thirty, maybe twenny-eight the most. How many doe-lars you want to change?"

"Two hundred, maybe three."

"It's probably a scam," Benjie cautioned him. "They've got more tricks than a hat magician."

The kid turned to him. "No scam, man. You see by the wall where it says *Salida?* The man there, the one with the hat, that's my frien'. We get the pesos, enough to change three hundred U.S. We give you twenny-eight."

"Thirty," Josh insisted.

"Twenny-nine."

"Thirty." Josh began buckling his leather bag.

"Okay, mee-stair, thirty." Flashing a wide grin, he added, "You pretty big Amedican crook, eh?"

"And bring the money here, not by the wall."

"No, no, no, is no good! Too many peoples, too many police mans. Is too dangerous." His nervous glances said it all. "Otherwise, maybe we all go to jail!"

Josh, who nodded agreement, again ignored Benjie's warning glance. The urchin darted off towards his friend.

Benjie was disgusted. "Do you know what you're letting yourself in for?"

"A little." Josh scratched the itch from his morning head-shave and smirked at Dynamite. "You mean, like they might have a friend posing as a cop, hiding around the corner? While we're making the exchange he pops out of the stonework and while they run off with the money, I dash the other way to save my skin? Or in the excitement they shuffle bundles and I end up with a wad of paper instead of the six thousand pesos I'm due? Or...? I could spend the rest of the day reciting the scams I've heard or read about or seen employed in my travels. Not to worry, friends. I've been a practitioner of the magician's arts since I was old enough to manipulate a deck of cards. India only honed my skills. Remember that our word 'fakir' comes from that ancient part of the world."

"When it comes to fakery, these guys aren't exactly pikers," Benjie muttered. "I've heard tales to curl your hairpiece. They can lift a watch from your wrist so smoothly you don't know it's gone till you see them running."

"Pickpockets! The lowest form of thievery and easiest to guard against!" Josh scoffed. "*Señor,* want me to change some doe-lars for you? Five percent more than the going bank rate, fella!"

"No thanks," Benjie replied testily, looking away.

"Why not, for heaven's sake?" Dynamite asked in sudden annoyance. Benjie glared back.

"Because I don't like taking chances. Ten percent doesn't outweigh my vision of a Colombian jail."

"Look who's talking about taking chances," Josh mocked. "As if we left Florida with the blessing of the fuzz!"

"Just remember one thing," Benjie snapped, doubly annoyed at being reminded of the risks he had just taken. "If you get into trouble with the local fuzz, leave us and the boat out of it, okay?"

"*Mais oui, d'accord!* Friends are to help, not hurt. I'll play wetback like your friend, Weeto. I was a stowaway on a freighter."

"Don't worry, Josh," Dynamite assured him, patting his hand. "I'll come visit you in the local lockup."

"Alone or with this ex-friend of mine, who seems to want to turn his back on me if I get into a legal fix?" Josh asked.

Benjie nodded in the direction of the gate. "Your friends are back at their post. Don't forget to check who's on the other side of the wall before you start counting your money out to those dudes."

"So, he is concerned about his friends," Josh sneered. He gave Dynamite a wink and strode off across the plaza without looking back.

Dynamite lowered her voice, leaning closer. "He's planning a little con of his own, if I know him." Two men had moved in on the table next to them.

"Jesus, he's not going to do something stupid, is he?" Benjie wondered aloud. "This isn't California where the cops play kneesie with bad boys. They break bones here!"

"Oh Benjie, don't you think he knows that?"

Her words added insult to his growing irritation. Two men at the next table were staring at him and whispering. Instantly his heart sank, certain they were plainclothes cops or agents of the DAS, Colombia's equivalent of the CIA, FBI and DEA rolled into one. After the money exchange they'd arrest them all, or at least threaten to unless bribes were paid. Maybe not cops or DAS agents at all, only members of a gang with fake credentials to put the squeeze on visiting foreigners after sucking them into illegal transactions.

Having heard dozens of stories of the chicanery and double-dealing of the Colombian underworld, he was ready to believe the worst. Down there, traffickers made drug deals, then collected informer's fees by notifying the authorities. Stories alleged that Colombian officials were often themselves the principal traffickers in this two-way dealing, like having their cake and eating it too. What else could you expect of a country where contraband American cigarettes were sold openly on the streets, the vendors never disturbed by the police so long as they took out a license? What was to be thought when banks had a special window, *la ventana siniestra,* where illegal dollars could be converted with no questions asked?

A second glance at the pair at the table dispelled his concern. Unlikely types for cops or underworld thugs, Benjie thought. One had distinctly feminine airs. In his teens or early twenties, darkly handsome in a wan, thin way, he flaunted his sexual interest unabashedly. His companion was fortyish and urbanely attired with polished nails and carefully styled gray hair—stiffly bouffant, as if teased by blowers and cemented in place with lacquer spray. His eyes were no less searching but more discreet. A rich old "auntie" and her young faggot friend enjoying the scenery. A blond American was fair game even if he was with a *gringa*!

Dynamite, noticing them also, recognized the older man as the jeweler who padded over in house slippers to assist her with the bird's egg emerald. She too caught the meaning of their gaze and leaned teasing across the table.

"How does it feel being peeled in public?"

Benjie grinned but couldn't stop his face from reddening. "As long as they don't touch, who can complain? Anyway, better than handcuffs. I thought at first they were DAS agents."

"They would have devoured you by now if it weren't for me. Aren't you glad you've got me for chaperon?" Straightening, she smiled pointedly at the men and winked. They responded as unreservedly, breaking into broad grins as if acknowledging a secret they all shared.

"Jesus, Dyna!" Benjie whispered, aghast. "What're you trying to do, encourage them?"

"Would it scare you if I did?" She raised the ante purposely. "Who knows, they might be interesting...."

"With faggots yet! What's got into you?"

"Oh Benjie, in this wicked city where everything goes, how can you be so narrow-minded? Smuggling and piracy, five hundred years of looting and plunder. Rape, pillage and slavery, torture by the Holy Inquisition. After all that can sex be anything more than an innocent pastime no matter what form it takes?"

"Well, I'm not against sex, as you surely must know," he backpedaled, wondering why he felt so defensive.

"But you don't approve of some of its forms."

"Do you?" he retorted.

"Life's too short not to be open to new experiences," she cooed seductively.

"Like Josh, you mean! Willing to dare and do, devil take the hindmost! Did that, that—" he sputtered, searching for the words, "—that juvenile bit of folderol impress you?"

"Shit, Benjie, it's not what I meant at all!" Her anger flared for only a moment. Recognizing her part in escalating the argument, sensing its causes went deeper than the moment, she relented at once with a wink and a grin. "I was just amused, seeing you on the receiving end of those amorous glances. I wondered if they could do anything to you that I haven't done."

Leering, her green eyes glinted against the champagne sunlight of her hair. She flicked the tip of her tongue between generous lips that never needed painting and whispered, "Now I've got you blushing!"

Josh appeared in the wall gate and leisurely crossed the plaza, stopping once to check something inside his shoulder bag.

"Just like you warned, Benjie," he grinned sheepishly as he came to the table and slumped his long frame into a chair. "A plain-clothes cop in a niche of the wall. As the money changed hands, he came out of the woodwork blowing his whistle. They yelled and we all ran. Lucky for me, he chased after them."

"The set-up, you mean," Benjie asked cautiously. "What about the money?"

"Five hundred pesos." He paused, his face glum. "How much is that, twenty dollars American? The rest is paper."

He held the pesos and paper up for them to see.

"I told you those guys were up to something. How much did you give them?" Benjie asked with concern.

"Well, I intended changing two hundred and that's what I counted out to them...." He stopped to draw out his moment, his face still frozen in dejection. "Actually they got ten pieces of play money."

"You fooled them with play money?" Benjie asked incredulously. Dynamite pressed her fingertips to her lips to stifle the laughter.

"No, they saw the real stuff when I counted it out, just as I saw the pesos they were dishing out. Since I was pretty sure they had a switch in mind, I was ready with mine."

He pulled a plain white business envelope out of his bag. "I always carry a few of these, never know when I might have to write home. Besides they serve another purpose. Notice the bottom edge is slit. Inside is a smaller envelope, intact. It holds the play money. The envelope is never out of sight, only the bottom edge. Logical since it may have to be ducked if some wrong people happen by, yes? At the critical moment a bit of prestidigitation causes the good money to fall into my bag before I hand them the envelope that's never been out of sight. It's especially useful when the fake cop jumps out of the wall and everybody starts yelling."

Unable to contain himself any longer, he began rumbling with laughter. "Amateurs, rank amateurs! Imagine the egg on their faces right now!"

"The shit, you mean!" Dynamite began to laugh. "A three-way split of monopoly money! Out five hundred pesos, but worse—outscammed by a *gringo*!"

Prodded by the image of swindled swindlers counting the fake money in disbelief, she struggled to control herself. "Who…who, I wanna know…gets blamed for it? The fake cop, the setup kid…or…the sleight-of-hand man?"

"It really amuses you, does it?" Josh was surprised and pleased, infected by her hysteria. It had risen to the point of tears, attracting the attention of nearby patrons and the waitresses behind the counter.

"Oh God…Jesus! Josh, you devil, you! The kick of the week! Imagine what those guys are saying…right now."

"Yeah," Benjie stated sardonically. "They're probably pow-wowing now on how to have your head on a platter. Don't think it's over. These locals play for serious. Twenty bucks may be a joke to you but to those guys it's a week's pay."

"Stop playing sorehead," Josh advised him. "I have no intention of keeping their money. I know they'll come looking and I intend to be right here when they do. Okay? That little switcheroo was just to let them know they're not dealing with a rube. I'm doing it for us all. We're fresh out, you know. We could use a new stash."

"Oh, wow, yes!" said Dynamite, wiping tears from her eyes and cheeks. "And you think they can set us up?"

"Or lead us to the ones who can." He turned to Benjie. "Any objections?"

Sensing he needed to score some points of his own, Benjie could only mumble morosely, "Just let us know our share."

"Then I suggest you two amble along. My friends, two of them anyway, are headed this way looking like the sheriff and his deputy at high noon." He grinned, grunting, "No point having unarmed men and defenseless women around if there's going to be a shoot-out on the plaza. You do your shopping and I'll meet you back at the boat. Hopefully the candyman will get back in time to bring us all dessert."

"You're the tops, lollipops!" Dynamite sang, rising and planting a kiss on top of his shaved head.

"Why do you only say and do that when Benjie's around?" Josh joked, leering.

Dynamite winked and Benjie seethed. Following her into the dappled sunlight and up the cobbled street, he felt nothing but disdain for his old friend. Josh had pulled the rug out from under again, making him look like a fool, dismissing him like a schoolboy, treating them both like charges needing his protection and largesse, as if he were the proverbial magic uncle conjuring tricks and goodies for the children.

Who needed his lousy stash anyway? Pot was nice, and for a high among friends in an intimate setting, it crowned the scene. Sure he enjoyed it, but it was hardly even a steady habit, considering how often it wasn't available or priced beyond his means. Doing without was no sweat, so why all the fuss and delirium? Why make out he was bringing home the treat of the month? Candyman, indeed!

He was almost angrier at Dynamite. She played up to his act like a straight man. He couldn't believe her fake enthusiasm. When did they ever go out of their way for the stuff, take stupid chances or splurge when money was needed for important things? Suddenly she's acting like Josh was the gallant knight charging off to slay the dragon and bring her back the golden fleece.

Ruefully, he sensed he was mixing his myths and metaphors, as if the widening rift in their friendship was breaking up his ability to think straight, too.

Chapter Nine

Josh didn't make it back that night. Both Benjie and Dynamite were concerned that something might have happened to him, but calling the police was out of the question. If he was merely delayed in making his marijuana purchase, bringing him to the attention of the local fuzz would endanger him more and put them all under suspicion. If he was already busted, there would be nothing they could do until morning.

The next day Benjie practically had to restrain Dyna to keep her from rushing into town to check with authorities. "He probably lined himself up with a foxy Latina for the night," he suggested. "He's not a kid and we're not his guardians. He might even resent us poking our noses into his business."

Still Dynamite was worried and her fretting interfered with Benjie's arrangements for some necessary boat work. He wanted a figurehead carved for the bowsprit and some changes in the taffrail. That and a new paint job. Giving the entire hull a fresh coat of paint would disguise the vessel beyond easy recognition. He could worry about interior changes later.

When Josh arrived around noon, hailing them from the dock, it was only to hand over a brown bag of marijuana and pick up some of his personal things.

"So you spent the night getting laid," Benjie chided as he was ferrying him out to the boat. "Didn't you think we might be worried?"

"Sorry, but when opportunity knocks you don't walk away. Yeah, I got laid," he shouted over the outboard noise, "about humpteen times!"

Dynamite cooed over the brown bag's contents as if it was spun gold. Her prior concern disappeared once Josh climbed aboard. She didn't even ask where he'd been. Not until he mentioned leaving again, that he'd returned only to bring them their grass and pick up his things, did she display any sign of curiosity.

"Oh? What's up, or is that a secret?" she asked after hearing he was on his way to Barranquilla and Santa Marta.

"Adventure," he said, his face beaming with enthusiasm. "And yes, a secret—even from me! Call it an expedition into sensory perceptions. India was all mind over matter. This country's all mindless matter, physical sensation—sight, sound, smell, taste, touch. Pure animal vitality devoid of scruples or social strictures. Take what you can while you may, tomorrow is only a promise. Such is the modus vivendi I sense here—wicked, delightfully pagan!"

His tongue made a licking journey around his lips, his eyes glinted lasciviously. "Worth exploring in depth. I'm told it's even wickeder where I'm going!"

Dynamite plied him with questions but he parried with generalities, saying only that friends from the night before were taking him to visit friends in the other towns. "I'll be gone a few days, if you must have a timetable. How else can one get to know the natives without living among them?"

"He didn't even ask us to go along," Dynamite huffed when Benjie returned from taking him ashore.

"I noticed." He tried teasing, "Maybe it's only for swinging singles."

"Shit, what're we—squares or something?"

"We couldn't go anyway," he reasoned. "I have to line up carpenters, and tomorrow I want us to start the painting."

"That's not the point. He could have asked at least."

Josh didn't turn up again for four days. Busy painting the hull and directing the work of the shipwright, Benjie enjoyed his absence. Dynamite's ire at being left behind simmered, but she shed it the moment Josh returned, welcoming him back like the prodigal son.

Benjie's peace of mind evaporated the moment Josh climbed aboard and revealed the point of his trip. He went to the port cities to scout the terrain of the contrabandistas and make liaison with the underground connections to set them up for a big purchase.

"A big purchase of what?" Dynamite asked. Too naively, Benjie thought, unless she was a step ahead and merely probing him for more information. For the moment Josh chose to ignore her question.

"What a country, the devil's very own! Anything goes and everything has a price. Smuggled goods from all over the world sold openly over the counter! If it's not in stock, place an order and they'll get it for you!" He breathed deeply, as if the air had a fragrance only he could detect. "Delicious!"

"Delicious for whom?" Benjie baited. "The predator or the prey?"

"They're all predators, that's what makes it so wickedly challenging. No innocents, everybody fair game. Even the street children are wise old hustlers at eight or nine. *Increible!*" he sighed in Spanish.

"From flesh to diamonds, everybody's got a deal. I could have bought raw emeralds by the pound. Which reminds me..." He removed a tissue packet from his shoulder bag and handed it to Dynamite. "I saw you eyeing the green baubles in the jewelry store the other day. It cost me nothing—a gift from a local admirer of the blond *Americana* with the strong laugh and winning smile."

Dynamite opened it. A small polished emerald twinkled like a tiny square green eye in her palm.

"Admirer? Josh, what're you talking about?" she asked absently, transfixed by the gem.

"The day of the money exchange," he reminded her. "The men at the next table. They said you smiled and winked at them."

"The two faggots!" Benjie exclaimed.

"Tut, tut," Josh chided. "Mustn't call gift-givers nasty names."

"You're joshing," Dynamite drawled, seeing it as another put-on. "You mean the old jeweler and his pretty young friend? And we thought it was Benjie they were ogling!"

"Oh they were, they were! Their admiration for you was of another—shall we say, Platonic order? But don't imagine they're so one-gaited they can't appreciate a pretty woman's smile, especially when it conveys an understanding of their appetites and a willingness to live and let live."

"But why bother sending a gift? And to me?"

"Using you for an intermediary?" Benjie sniped.

"Good question, and not what you might think. It's not bribing the wife to get at the husband, if you know what I mean." His eyes rested on Benjie, enjoying his confusion and embarrassment. "Actually, it turns out Sergio is a wholesaler in precious stones. If I'm to believe him, he's from a family that's been in the gem business since before the time of Columbus. Here in Colombia they were only a step behind the first explorer, Jimenez de Quesada, so they had first crack at the mineral wealth of the New World. You can guess what that meant—a hand in the operations of the famous mines of the interior. Nominally owned and operated for the Spanish crown, you can just imagine what was siphoned off!"

"He's fabulously wealthy, you mean," said Dynamite.

"Not exactly, not anymore. I gather there's more aristocracy than wealth left in the family, otherwise Sergio wouldn't be engaged in the grubby business of money-making."

"And we made all those snide remarks!" Dynamite rolled her eyes. "Don't tell me, he understands and speaks perfect English."

Josh grunted amusement. "Yes, enough to understand he was the object of your fun. But obviously he wasn't offended. He found you both, as he put it, 'refreshingly North American.' He was also greatly amused at my little charade with the cops-and-robbers gang. Turns out they were as rank and amateurish as I suspected, just a band of teenagers with no connection to anything. If Sergio hadn't intervened, I might've wasted a lot of time finding out for myself. As it is, he steered me to his own sources."

Benjie stared at him in disbelief. "You mean somebody you never met before—a foreigner and a gay at that—invites you to his townhouse, puts you in touch with his pusher and provides a call girl all in that first night?"

"Not a call girl." Josh looked wounded. "She came free, gratis, *cortesía del patrón.*"

Benjie shook his head. "In this land of thieves and predators, as you call it, how were you able to find the one altruistic person in the country? Your luck amazes me!"

"Not luck, advanced planning," Josh purred. "Señor Sergio Jimenez-Valdes thinks I'm aristocracy too. Oh, not of such ancient lineage as his family. The Vanderbilts, I think, can only claim a paltry hundred years or so. But the name has a certain ring, in a class with the DuPonts, Rothschilds and Rockefellers, which makes up for what it may lack in lineage, don't you think?"

He grinned with wicked pleasure. "My middle name, as Benjie may remember, happens to be Vanderbilt. Something my Navy father hung on me. In any case, there it is in my passport: Joshua Vanderbilt Slocum. Latins, as you know, use double names, the mother's as well as the father's. They often think our middle names reflect paternity on the father's side as it does in theirs. It helped to leave my passport in a conspicuous place where it could be checked for authenticity. In it I carry a bank passport showing a six-figure balance in my checking account."

"He bought that?" Benjie asked.

"Why not? A maverick, hippie offshoot perhaps, but these days America's wealthy families also produce their share of kooky offspring, yes?" He gave his beard a smoothing stroke, purring like a contented cat. "The fact I was a penny-pincher, preferring the extra five percent of a risky street exchange to the legal bank rate, helped cinch my credentials. Only the rich or the desperately poor are that anxious about their money."

He nodded at Dynamite. "When I said I had friends with a very large yacht looking for merchandise they might take back to the States for profit, I didn't have to enumerate what I had in mind. Emeralds and other gems which he could personally arrange in just about any quality or quantity one might want.

Heroin, cocaine and marijuana. Naturally he'd supply the connections. Friends who—"

"You're not involving us in your schemes, I hope," Benjie
interrupted, frowning.

Dynamite scowled at Benjie. "Hear him out. Where's the
harm in that?"

Josh ignored their bickering. "It's a nation of entrepreneurs
even when it comes to contraband goods. You'd expect a single
mob or syndicate to be in control. Not so. Just dozens of competing
groups and individuals, ready to dicker and deal. So buying's no
problem. It's the risk of getting it past all those in-between
people—security guards on the docks, the DAS, the cops and
Customs agents—they send the price skyrocketing so that—"

"This is crazy talk," Benjie broke in.

"Let him finish," Dynamite sniped at him from across the table.

"They send the price soaring," Josh continued, "unless you
find a way of bypassing the docks entirely. There's more work
loading up at sea, but it offers the advantage of cover and cost. You
put me onto the idea, Benjie—"

Josh pulled a road map from his bag and spread it out on the
table. "You mentioned the fiord area north of Santa Marta, where
there's good protected anchorage for small boats. You said if we got
blown off course and made landfall here instead of Cartagena,
you'd put into the fjords rather than risk the hassle and thievery of
Santa Marta."

Benjie nodded. He'd heard stories about the notorious port—
stories of thieves who boarded vessels in the dead of night and
stripped them clean. Money lifted from pockets and rings slipped
from fingers of people as they slept. Some reported anchors filched
from under them, waking to find themselves drifting out to sea or
washed ashore.

"Ask any boater, it's a *malo* port," Benjie confirmed with an
involuntary shudder.

"In every way," Josh agreed. "I spent the better part of my
time getting chummy with the American drifters and boaters there.
Some desperate gringos are hanging out around there, looking for
the piece of change to launch them into their own gig. Two at least

could be induced for a small fee to bring a load out to a vessel waiting offshore."

"So if anybody squeals, they'd be squealing on the wrong boat!" Dynamite remarked, obviously impressed and excited.

"Exactly! The old switcheroo, befuddle them with a bit of razzle-dazzle. The suspect boat will never arrive in the U.S. waters and the Coast Guard will wonder how it slipped through the net."

"This isn't a football game, Josh!" Benjie exploded. "We don't simply walk off the field if we lose and try again next week. Losing means jail, prison terms. We're talking boat confiscation and God knows what all once they figure out the *Gorda* is really the *Dragon*."

"True, my friend, and I quite understand your concern," Josh responded soberly. "You've got Dyna-baby, you've got each other and a way of life that suits you both. With a little work chartering and some careful budgeting, you can squeak by without having to resort to slob jobs on the side. You've got everything to lose and only money to gain, and money just isn't that important to you. Why should you stick your necks out?"

Josh shrugged indifferently. "There are other boats and skippers just waiting for the right scams. Or I might go it alone, on a plane out of here or a slow freighter. Emeralds could be profitable and you don't have to cart them out by the bale."

"Which explains the emerald," Dynamite observed. "You made him think we were into smuggling emeralds."

"Contemplating it, anyway," Josh replied evenly. "He wouldn't have made a gift of the stone to the beautiful and understanding *norteamericana* if he thought otherwise. I think it was meant as a sample in case I wanted to check it against his appraisal value."

"It's an incredible shade," she sighed, holding the stone up to examine it again in the light.

"A match for your very own eyes." Josh bowed gallantly. "It certainly is your color."

"And she's certainly not keeping it!" Benjie bristled.

"Ho, and why ever not?" Dyna objected. "Of course I'm keeping it! 'Neither an Indian giver nor taker be, which is why I pocket what's given to me.'"

"He gave it to Josh!" Benjie shouted angrily.

"He meant her to have it," Josh corrected. "He was quite specific. And you needn't fear any strings attached."

Benjie sprang from the table and began frantically pacing between the ladder and the bulkhead. "This thing is so bizarre, so crazy," he growled. "I can't believe it! First you involve us in that money exchange where we might all have landed in the pokey. Then you pick up with a pair of gays—perfect strangers—and go looking for contraband deals. You accept gifts, no doubt you led them to believe you had all the money in the world and it was just a matter of deciding what candy you wanted to buy. Didn't it occur to you, you might be wasting their time? Or that they might break your legs if they ever found out?"

He stopped and glared at Josh. "Didn't you ever ask yourself where the money was for a big buy? A boatload of pot—what would it cost? Fifty? A hundred thousand? More? Unless you really have Vanderbilt connections, where was the bread to come from?"

"Benjie, you're the world's worst worrier," said Josh, grinning and shaking his head. "And for all the wrong reasons. Out there on the high seas where you have a hundred legitimate reasons for worry, you never do. But get you ashore and involved in the normal commerce of men and you're all nerves. Not that it matters, since you've made it clear you don't want in, no matter what the profit. I could probably swing a deal for ten thousand dollars. Maybe less."

"That's all?" Dynamite asked anxiously.

Even Benjie was jolted. He always felt ultimately protected from Josh's schemes by the huge amounts of capital he thought were necessary. Josh had just demolished his strongest defense.

"Like a down payment on a conditional sales contract," Josh explained with a shrug. "The balance is paid when the goods arrive at the other end. Buying on terms we'd have to pay more, but who cares when we're talking big profits? And don't forget the benefits of buying on credit—"

"Yeah," Dynamite breathed, comprehension dawning on her face. "Like an insurance policy. 'No payoff for squealers, only silence collects!'"

"Exactly," Josh stated.

"They'd let you sail off with only a token payment?" Benjie queried suspiciously. "No collateral—just your word for the balance?"

"No, not hardly," Josh admitted. "Unfortunately the ilk we're dealing with isn't a club where a gentleman's word is his bond. They'll insist on tangible collateral."

Benjie glanced sideways at Dynamite. "What's the catch?"

Josh laughed, then turned his attention to Dyna. "Is there any wine aboard? I've got a thirst and I think we could all use a smoke."

Chapter Ten

Dynamite broke out a gallon of Gallo red, last of the wine stock. "Enjoy it, *amigos*," she said as they savored it. "There's no more after this. And if you've priced wine down here, you know we won't be buying it often. All imports are from Chile and Spain and heavily taxed."

Josh sighed. "Life can certainly crimp one's pleasure when the cash flow's insufficient."

He plucked the tin box out of his bag and lit one of the joints. They were machine-rolled, as elegantly compacted as cigarettes. Benjie took one from the box he offered, eyeing and sniffing it appreciatively.

"How much, machined like that?"

"I didn't ask," Josh admitted. "These were a gift. A bit of bait, so to speak. Almost worth a little extra, yes?"

"Beats my rolling all to hell," Dynamite droned.

"Not bad," said Benjie after his first draw.

"Santa Marta Gold," Josh crowed. "Just a sample of the quality they supply."

"Quality guaranteed?" Benjie wondered aloud.

Josh smiled knowingly. "By the ton."

"What about cost?" Dynamite interjected, obviously anxious to get back to business. "How much will it cost overall—a hundred thousand, two hundred—?"

"Nothing so high as that," Josh assured her. "If we—"

"Back off just a minute!" Benjie blurted out. "We haven't discussed the down payment yet. Where's that ten thousand coming from?"

"Shit, Benjie, we've got that much between the two of us," Dyna offered. "With what's left of your inheritance and what we saved working in Florida—"

"And just like that, you wanna toss the whole bundle on a wild bet, huh?" he snapped, angry she was so quick to reveal private matters. He suspected she'd already laid it out for Josh.

"Bet your boobs I would," she replied hotly. "If the odds look stacked in our favor, who wouldn't? A ten-thousand-dollar chip riding on a million or so is about the best odds I can think of. But I'd like to hear first how he thinks he can swing the collateral."

"The most obvious asset is the boat itself," said Josh, then paused to sip his wine. "As you explained, Benjie, a documented vessel is proof of clear title. You can't file it with the Coast Guard unless you can show it's free of any loans, liens or claims. So anyone assigned the documentation papers would have a hold on the boat, right?"

"Wrong," Benjie countered. "Only U.S. citizens can document with the Coast Guard. A Colombian would have no legal hold on a vessel unless it stayed in Colombian waters where they could simply seize it."

"You know that, but do they?"

"Ha, can you really see those dudes accepting a piece of paper for collateral?"

Dynamite, beginning to feel the wine and grass, giggled. "Neat trick if you could pull it off. They'd be getting fake papers to a boat that doesn't exist!"

"You're dreaming, both of you," Benjie stated flatly. "They'd never go for it."

"You're right," Josh said quickly. "But suppose we had a stash of gems to post as bond? Emeralds, for instance, for collateral?"

"Yeah," Benjie sneered, "a mere fifty thousand in emeralds. We just go out and pick them off the street."

"Don't make fun," Dynamite told him. "Necessity is the mother of invention. What have you got up your sleeve, Josh?"

"My friend, the jeweler, may be our provider. Emeralds of sufficient value but left in his safekeeping as an agreed-upon third party, a trust officer for all concerned. All that's needed is a little persuasive work on Señor Sergio, convince him our word is as good as a bond!"

"Ha," Benjie scoffed. "He'll want blood for security."

"Or maybe just Benjie's body," Dynamite snickered from across the table.

"Benjie the skeptic, the doubting Thomas," Josh hissed. "I tell you, it's doable just because it's out in left field. We won't be following the old rutted paths of the professionals. We're cutting our own road, insuring against double-crosses by tying the sellers in with our need to succeed. We're eliminating the middlemen and officials who need to be bribed. The pros can afford to do it that way but an amateur is crazy to try. They're the ten percent who get caught. We're not gonna end up as DEA statistics, friends. We're gonna score!"

"Bravo!" Dynamite clapped, already tipsy and stoned.

"My word on this, Benjie," Josh went on, seizing his moment, dark eyes sparkling like chips of obsidian struck from stone. "If everything isn't as foolproof as I promise, you can say no and we'll back off before the buy. But if I can fit all the pieces together, do I have your word you won't back out at the last minute for some chicken-shit moral or personal reason?"

Dynamite nudged him. "Absolutely! Tell him yes, Benjie-baby."

Lifting his glass, Benjie pondered his answer as he sipped the wine. Years of experience taught him how easily Josh carried others along with him. His enthusiasm was contagious, at times hypnotic. Sensing how cleverly he'd cordoned Benjie off as the only roadblock, he did it while simultaneously outflanking him on the ten-thousand-dollar investment capital, as if it was already in his hand and needed no further negotiating.

He knew he was at a crossroad. A "yes" would commit him to a gamble risking life and freedom but promising high adventure and enormous profit. A "no" would hold him to the same old rut of grubbing to eat and stay afloat. He was only beginning to see the sizable expenditures the *Gorda* required to keep her sixty feet properly cleaned and painted, engine and electronics maintained, sails repaired and lines replaced—a thousand and one little demands on the pocketbook. The *Gorda*, it was dawning on him, was indeed a fat lady, one with an enormous appetite.

"So…?" Dynamite urged.

"No hurry," Josh said, then added jokingly, "take ten seconds."

"I'll take a night and sleep on it!" he snapped angrily, sensing his reaction was only out of a need to assert himself.

There was no question where Dynamite stood anymore. The expensive boat, in part, dictated a certain logic and he couldn't fault her for that. Nor could he help marveling at Josh's scheming and his stubborn tenacity. He was even beginning to see what it was in Josh that wore down and finally won people over. His faith in winning, a refusal to let odds deter or dent his belief in swaying people to his will. He was the supreme egoist, emanating a certainty which Benjie, like most others, had long since surrendered to something resembling the collective good. A consensus was being asked for, but it was only the leader playing games with the faithful. He'd tell Josh "yes" in the morning.

It was a miserable sleepless night, his irritation accentuated by some of the things Dynamite said or implied. When she crawled in beside him, heated and high from the wine and smoking, he made no pretense of sleep when he turned away from her. Normally he was at his amorous best after a little pot-smoking, and so was she. It was one of the fringe benefits which gave an extra lift beforehand, knowing good sex was to follow. No matter that authorities often claimed *Cannabis sativa,* used habitually, led to lessening of the sex drive. So did alcohol, so did aging, so did a lot of things. All of them too many years off to worry about.

The wine had only dulled his senses without making him sleepy, and the expected euphoria of the pot failed even in lifting him out of his depressed state. So when Dynamite pressed against his back and groped his genitals, he pulled away with a shrug of annoyance. Her reaction was swift and bristling.

"Shit, you still sulking? You've been mad at me all day. Why?"

"If you don't know, there's no point in explaining."

Something in his tone, not as hard as his words, invited her to probe deeper. She moved closer and rubbed her cheek on his shoulder. "It's the decision that's bothering you. About whether to go along with Josh's scheme."

"No, that's already settled. I just didn't wanna give him the satisfaction of thinking he stampeded me into it."

"Then you aren't opposed? You're going along with it?" The surprise in her voice assuaged his ego.

"It's what you want, isn't it?"

"It's not just a question of what I want. It matters what you want too. But, damn it, beyond our sailing thing I don't know what you want!"

"Do I have to want something beyond what we're doing now?" He felt his mood darkening.

"Come on, Benjie," Dynamite pleaded. "When we're old and forty, you think we'll still be floating around like this?"

Her projection of an extended future together lifted his spirits momentarily, but not enough to offset the weight at the other end. "Why not? There's lots of folks puttsing around out there in their sixties and seventies. How about the Hiscocks, Eric and Susan? They're in their eighties now and they're still doing their thing."

"Bastard," Dynamite fumed. "You know what I mean. I'm talking money and how we're going to support this floating palace. It'll take one helluva lot of chartering just to keep this lady painted and in sails."

"And engine maintenance, parts and fuel, repairing and replacing," he added. "I know. But you never worried about such things before."

"We didn't have a gold-plated sixty-footer before! *Candy* was a toy compared to this big glutton. Just the paint we used on her hull...I still can't believe it! Wait'll we have to haul and paint her bottom at a hundred bucks a gallon!"

He was on the verge of forgiving her. Her cuddly efforts to make up were chipping away at his stubbornness. They both hated the necessity of having to spell it out and say, "I'm sorry." The simple gesture of holding hands, a wink or a laugh always patched up their quarrels. He felt one firm nipple graze his shoulder where she wiggled against him. The heat it caused raced like a flash-fire to his groin and ignited an instant erection. Then something she said threw everything in reverse.

"Imagine having a million dollars! Even if only a few hundred thousand. Does it excite you too?"

He could feel the shivers of excitement rippling across her skin. "We don't exactly have it in hand yet," he reminded her.

"Yeah but just the possibility of it, I mean. God, it gives me goosebumps thinking about it!"

"Me too, but for different reasons."

"Does it frighten you, baby?"

"Doesn't it you?"

She squirmed and snuggled closer. "Not really, not enough to turn me off. Is that stupid or juvenile or something? It just excites me, like embarking on a daring new venture. Even that little emerald uncorked something—"

"But you never wear jewelry. I thought you didn't even like it."

"I know, that's what's so crazy. I never did."

"You're not pregnant, are you?" he asked uneasily. "Isn't that when women go slightly ape with crazy cravings?"

"If I am, my uterus hasn't told me yet." Her fingers crept along his ribs. "Would it excite you or frighten you if I were?"

"Don't joke," he warned, feeling an alarm go off. "Haven't we got enough going for the moment?"

"Which means Baby-Ben is frightened—of what, competition or responsibility?"

"Oh for Godssake, Dyna!" He wanted to tell her to drop the baby names routine. It somehow emasculated him.

Dynamite's hand slid down to his penis, still half erect in its warm forest of hair. "Come on, Benjie-baby, fuck your momma and make us both happy."

Her four-letter words in bed never failed to arouse him. Though he seldom used them himself, he secretly enjoyed her using them. But now he felt demeaned and manipulated, and the words struck him as vulgar.

"It's just a piss hard-on," he grunted as he rose to crawl over her. "I gotta take a leak."

Out on deck he was forced to move to the stern so his stream wouldn't blow all over his legs on deck. The winter trades were kicking up. Even in the harbor where prevailing winds had to thread around mountain peaks and the city's walled fortifications, it was blowing a stiff twenty to thirty knots. Imagining its force offshore, out of the protection of land and buildings, he experienced the sailor's shiver, relief at his own safety and comfort mixed with sympathy for the unfortunates caught out in it. He knew what it was like out there on such nights, with seas running ten to fifteen feet in the swift current of the shallow continental shelf. Bashed by it once on *Candy*, they'd been forced to limp back to port to lick both the boat's wounds and their own. It occurred to him that the mechanics of transferring tons of baled marijuana from one heaving craft to another would be nightmarish, kissing hulls and squeaking fenders giving way to bent stanchions and cracked toe rails, opened seams and smashed planks. He shuddered.

Josh had no idea of the danger involved in an exchange of cargo between two small vessels at sea. With even the heaviest air fenders or rubber tires, with experienced skippers at the helms, it was still tricky and dangerous in anything but absolutely calm conditions. This was the winter season, when the intensified trades blew regularly twenty to thirty knots offshore, often much more. Josh, who couldn't know that, was frightened in the mildly stormy conditions in crossing the Florida Straits to the Bahamas. Dynamite, who should know, seemed oblivious to any worries other than getting caught. Even that she tended to ignore.

Disturbed by an ambivalence between his feelings and his decision to go against them, Benjie made his way forward against the strong wind to check that the anchor rope hadn't stretched and exposed the nylon line to chafing on the chock. It hadn't, but he got extra leather from the bosun's locker anyway and wrapped and lashed it around the line. His genitals, touching the metal deck plate as he stooped to his labors, reminded him they had anything but sex in mind that night.

Chapter Eleven

The next day brought new dissension and worry. Josh went dashing off to town in the morning as soon as he got Benjie's conditional approval of the smuggling venture, off and running like a greyhound from the starting gate. Benjie could only marvel at the store of energy Josh could summon when the right rabbit crossed his path.

The shipwright and his helper, due at eight o'clock, didn't arrive at the dock until after ten. To make matters worse, they forgot the tooled spokes for the taffrail, which they were to pick up at the cabinet shop the day before. The wood work, which should have been winding up by afternoon, would go on at least another day— more time and money down the drain. Benjie and Dyna had gone as far as they could with the painting and varnishing; their work was stalled until the taffrail was finished.

Benjie sensed that had Dynamite known the carpenters were going to be so absentminded, she might have dashed off with Josh, though he gave no indication he wanted either of them along. Her mood seemed to plunge at Josh's sudden departure. Only the presence of the workers kept her temper from exploding.

Shortly past noon a boater from one of the other anchored vessels dinked alongside and hailed him. Back from a mailcheck at the yacht club office, he handed up a small brown packet addressed to Benjie on Yate *Gorda*, c/o Club de Pesca, Cartagena. There was no return address, but the postal stamp was Bogotá. When he opened it, a key fell out into Benjie's hand. Inside was a note on a scrap of paper, written in the hasty scrawl of someone in a hurry.

It read: *Hey Benjie, you said you owed me a favor. I don't think so, but I'll ask anyway. Can you believe those bastards found me already? So quick I can't believe it. We took the first bus out and we are now in Bogotá·, la capital in case you don't know your geography. I don't dare go back to my room and that's why I got to ask you.*

My money is still there. In the coffee in the can in the refrigerator. More than three thousand, all the money I own. I didn't carry it on me because I got scared from your stories about the pickpockets on the street. Anyway, I left it in the coffee can at Hotel Panama on Avenida de la Republica by the big mercado. Room 32. I rented it for a month so nobody should be snooping yet—I hope. Bring the money to me here: Hotel Buenavista, Calle Lagrimas de Job (if you don't know what it means, I'll tell you when you get here and we'll cry together). Room 54. My name is Lopez. Juan Lopez.

Weeto

P.S. Tell me, friend, where can I go from here? I'm reaching the end of my rope but Chico still thinks it's a game. I'll pay the plane fares when you get here. Chico sends a kiss for Dynamite. Me too, if it don't make you jealous. We are at God's mercy—and yours. Make sure no gringo monkeys are following you.

"Just who the hell is after him and why?" Dynamite asked as she finished reading the letter. "What'd he do that's so awful they'd follow him all the way to South America? I can only think it must be the Mob."

"Or the FBI."

"The FBI!" she gasped.

"Ssshhh, even illiterate Colombian carpenters would know about them," he cautioned. "You might as well know the whole story."

Over cups of coffee he explained Weeto's predicament, summarizing the flights following the custody battle and concluding with an account of his own experience in the chase and escape in Lauderdale. When he finished, she was nearly as angry at him for not having told her sooner as she was at the vengeful wife and rich Texas daddy and the hordes of cops, private eyes and FBI agents making Weeto's life miserable.

Dynamite stared at him in silence for several moments. "Good God, and you let me think he was running away from the Mob."

"Wouldn't you rather it was? Who but the FBI would go to all the trouble of tracking him this far?"

"But I thought they only operated inside the U.S."

"So did I. Maybe they hire others to do it for them in foreign countries. The DEA guys operate everywhere, so why not the FBI? Maybe he only thought they were *gringos*. Maybe they were DAS agents doing the FBI a favor."

"Christ, how awful for him."

"For us too, maybe," Benjie added gloomily. "They must have gotten to his Cuban pals and found out about the boat. But how could they know where we went? And know it within a week of our landing?"

"You think they had a trace on the boat and knew where we were all along?"

He shook his head slowly. "No, nothing so exotic as that." But he knew there were so many secret homing and listening devices, satellites in the sky and so on, it wasn't farfetched to think a government, or an arm of it like the FBI, could do just that. "I think they merely circulated boat descriptions to all the entry ports around the Caribbean, and then got lucky."

"If they know about the boat, why haven't they swooped down and arrested us all?"

Benjie shrugged. "I don't know. Maybe they're only interested in getting the boy. A kidnapping is big news copy, especially if he's taken to a foreign country."

"Didn't some movie star do that a few years back?" she asked. "Sneaked his kids out of the country and took them sailing across the Pacific. Made a big stink in the news."

Benjie shrugged. He poured them more coffee and sat down to reread the letter.

"What's this do to our—to Josh's plans?" Dyna interrupted.

"They get put aside," he answered flatly, then looked up from the letter.

Dynamite raised her eyebrows. "You're gonna look after Weeto first?"

"How could I refuse?"

"I'm glad." She reached over and squeezed his hand. It said something about acknowledging the priorities. Postponing Josh's plan was one thing, but scuttling it completely would have meant something else.

Her approval caught Benjie a little by surprise. But when their eyes met in that familiar, knowing way, it was as if they had pipelines to each other's secret centers. For the first time in a week he felt they were on the same wavelength, and with it came a sweet ache to have her again. He might have suggested it were it not for the carpenters hammering on deck.

Stuffing two flight bags and a backpack, Benjie and Dynamite locked the boat and took the carpenters ashore, intending to leave a note and the boat key for Josh at the dockmaster's office. But as they edged to the pier, there he was, racing along the dock like a greyhound getting a second wind.

"My word, Bogotá! Exactly where I'm headed too!" he exclaimed when they filled him in on what was happening. "I was just going to let you know so you wouldn't worry."

"What's in Bogotá for you?" Benjie asked, suspicious that the scent of money in a coffee can might have caused the hound to make a detour.

Josh flashed a knowing grin. "An important person, a vital link in our little caper. Possibly the source, the fountainhead, if you get my drift."

"But you said there wasn't any one man or group in charge," Benjie said, "just a cottage industry with a bunch of competing entrepreneurs."

"So I did." Josh beamed with the pleasure of a teacher rewarded with proof of a student's mastery. "And so I mean. It's crawling with competition. But I'm bypassing the middlemen and going straight to a producer-wholesaler. Not that there—"

"It's on hold, Josh." It was clear to Benjie that Josh had missed the implication of Weeto's letter, that the pot plan was off— at least temporarily.

A pained look flickered across Josh's face. Then he launched his counterattack, insisting it was all the more reason to proceed swiftly, arrange a purchase and exit the country as soon as possible. With no indication the boat was under surveillance or ever had been, he argued, Weeto was the object of the manhunt. Whoever was after him either knew nothing of the boat and the others, or else had no interest in them or it. Benjie saw other possibilities.

"But if they know about us and the boat, as you seem to think," Josh adroitly countered, "wouldn't they be tailing us, hoping we'll lead them to him? For his sake, we're crazy to go anywhere near Weeto!"

"We're not going to ignore him," Benjie insisted. "Dyna agrees. The poor guy's begging for help. One way or another, we intend to get him his money."

Josh's head bobbed in agreement. "Of course we do the proper thing and play Good Samaritan, but let's do it with smarts and planning. No trips to his hotel. We get a message through and arrange to meet him in a popular, public place."

"All we need is a McDonalds," Dyna suggested, smirking. "Do they have a McDonalds in Bogotá?"

Josh nodded. "I'll go separately to the airport while you two finish your work with the coffee can. We'll stay apart on the plane too. If there's any indication you're being followed, switch the money to me. Just give me a signal which pocket it's in and I'll do the rest. We'll work the other details out as we go along."

They found the Panama between a public park and the mercado, on a street crowded with pedestrians and honking buses. The hotel entrance was sandwiched between two ground-floor cantinas with a set of worn wooden steps leading to a second floor landing directly in front of the clerk's desk. The latter was strategically located so that the comings and goings of the guests could be easily monitored. They had no choice but to rent a room.

Benjie managed to convey to the stout, beady-eyed woman
that they wanted a room on the third floor—his wife was superstitious and three was her lucky number. Once they had registered the
taciturn woman led them to Room 34, right next door to Weeto's.

"Un extranjero también, al otro lado," she nodded, smiling
amiably. The bill had been paid in advance and Benjie had just
handed her a generous tip.

He understood the word for "foreigner," and her pointing at
the adjoining wall clarified what she meant. Her courteous
"Bienvenidos" suggested she understood the need of foreigners for
company of their own kind.

It also meant Weeto hadn't passed for a native. At the same
time it removed another concern. If the desk clerk suspected he
skipped for good, she would not have mentioned him. There was a
good chance the room hadn't been disturbed. It was also reasonable
to assume neither the room nor the hotel was under surveillance.
Such activity surely wouldn't have escaped her attention.

The room was surprisingly clean for the tough neighborhood.
Its heavy wood furniture, the work of semiskilled local craftsmen,
looked sturdy, dusted and polished; the tiled bathroom and fixtures
were as scrubbed and shining as the small range and fridge in the
kitchen. Such housecleaning in a low-rent district bespoke a stern
hand at the top. Benjie visualized the stout matron checking the work
of her mestizo girls like a white-gloved admiral looking for dust.

They went straight to work. Satisfied no one was in the hall
or coming up the stairs, Dyna posted herself by the landing while
Benjie slipped into the room with the key Weeto had sent him. A
minute later he was out again, carrying the shopping bag and
Weeto's tool satchel.

"No point in leaving these," he said once back in their room.
"He may need his tools. And they can use the sweaters and clothes.
It gets cold in Bogotá. What's the elevation there, eight or nine
thousand feet?"

"What about the money?" Dynamite blurted out anxiously.

"Intact and aromatic!" He grinned happily, taking it from his
pocket and holding it under her nose. "Smells like the best
Colombian, huh?"

"How much is there?"

They counted it out, twenties and hundreds, still powdered with coffee. Three thousand, four hundred and forty.

"God, how lucky can we be?" Dynamite said with obvious relief. "It's a miracle the old hag downstairs didn't go snooping the minute they left the room. Wouldn't it burn her to a crisp to learn there was a stash of Yankee dollars right under her nose and she didn't sniff it out?" She held the greenbacks under her nose and savored the aroma. "Wow, I still can't believe it!"

But getting out with their own belongings and Weeto's gear posed somewhat of a problem. With effort, the tool bag was stuffed into the backpack. Dynamite jammed the sweaters and clothes into the flight bags and her shoulder purse. The fire escape outside by the landing looked far too unstable and using it would put them in plain view of people in the street. They were left no choice but to leave the way they came—past the old watchdog at the front desk.

"I'll play ugly American tourist," Dyna whispered. "Tell her there's a cockroach in our room and I refuse to stay another minute. Insist on our money back. That'll keep her too agitated to notice our baggage looks bigger than when we came in."

"I wish Weeto's tools didn't rattle so much," Benjie muttered.

"Ssshhh," Dyna hissed. "Just keep moving."

They descended the stairs, praying that the señora had been called away to some other duty. But only so much luck comes in a single day. La Señora was there alright, perched on her tall stool behind the grilled cage-front like a permanent fixture. To their surprise, she smiled at them when she looked up from her book.

In halting Spanish, Benjie stitched together enough words and gestures to get his point across. "My wife, *mi mujer no gusta cucarachas*." He pointed to the ceiling and the woman's eyes followed his finger, looking for the cockroach.

"No, no, aquí, aquí," he switched, now pointing to the floor, then back to the ceiling. *"Muy grande cucaracha. Is dirty, sucio. Mi esposa no gusta."*

The smile evaporated from the Señora's face like a midsummer's flash of lightning. In its place was the outrage of the dedicated housekeeper and the alarm of a businessman suspecting a swindle.

"Ah no, señor," She shook a finger as if they were naughty children, *"No, no, no, no, no! Es no sucio, no hay cucarachas."*

That was about all he caught before she exploded into a flood of words like popping firecrackers, denouncing them as liars bent on ruining her reputation and slandering her establishment. All he caught was the word *"limpia"* — clean — which she repeated endlessly, emphasizing with gestures the hundred ways she and her cleaning girls scrubbed and disinfected to make the rooms spotless.

Her indignation at being accused of dirty accommodations couldn't have been greater than if he had pointed a gun at her and demanded the cash. In her emotional state, she appeared to have forgotten about the return of the money and had to be reminded. She angrily counted the bills out of the drawer and shoved them across the counter in a flurry of paper and outrage.

"How to ruin a good woman's day," Benjie sighed when they reached the street.

"I feel rotten," Dynamite confessed. "She was so upset we could have walked off with the bed and the stove and she'd never have noticed. You feel like a heavy, too?"

"Mucho." He shifted his cargo. "Weeto's tools weigh a ton!"

Josh was in the small waiting room at the airport, propped against a wood bench cushioned by his bedroll, his face buried in a local newspaper. Benjie envied his facility with languages. The Spanish he picked up only a year or so earlier while bumming around Mexico was astonishingly good. He regretted not having tried harder to learn the language. He might have spared that poor woman the charge of being a dirty housekeeper.

Josh gave no sign of noticing them as they passed. But his plane ticket, openly displayed in one of the hands holding the newspaper, was easy to read as they walked by. Flight 44 was due to depart in forty minutes. Benjie bought tickets for the two of them.

When it came time to board, nothing suggested they were being tailed. It was a weeknight flight of tired businessmen and a group of red-eyed women in black returning from a funeral, a clutch of German tourists, three nuns and a talkative bunch of college students on their way to or from home between terms. Confident all was well, shortly after takeoff Josh stretched out across both seats and fell asleep.

When they arrived in Bogotá, they saw no reason to remain separated and walked together through the long corridors of the gleaming new terminal to the waiting taxis outside. Climbing into the back seat of one, they consulted the map Benjie unfolded in his lap. Lagrimas de Job was only two blocks long, near Plaza Bolivar and the government buildings, within walking distance of the city center where many of the hotels were located. Directing the driver to that part of town, they eventually settled on a somewhat seedy-looking but affordable hotel and took a room for three.

Josh, refreshed from his nap on the plane, was anxious to prowl the nighttime city. Benjie, unable to sleep on the plane and exhausted by lack of sleep the night before, was ready only for bed. He noticed Dyna's eyes brightened at the suggestion of a night on the town, and he wouldn't have objected if she wanted to go off with Josh. Instead, she decided to sack it out too, and do the town another time.When they tumbled into bed together, Benjie's fatigue fled before a wave of passion.

"And I was afraid we were coming unglued," he sighed contentedly.

"I know," she said softly. "But nobody promised it was all going to be roses. And even if it was, what would roses be without thorns?" Her voice became husky with desire. "After all—see how I bloom from your prick?"

His feelings were enhanced that night by a different note, a bittersweet tenderness directed as much at himself as at her, a sense of the fragility of human relationships and a marvel they survived so many threats. He loved her more than ever, if that were possible, and in a paradox he found he loved himself more too. Overcome by an exquisite sense of ascension, celebrating a union of triumph and surrender, he played over her more attentively and unselfconsciously than he ever had before. He had the feeling a circle was closing again and reinforcing itself in the rejoining.

Waking again with the first light of dawn, they made love

again. More playfully this time, less consecrated, invigorated by the night's rest and the good vibrations they took into sleep, they fell back laughing at the appendages nature had designed to trap them into the pairing game.

One of their jokes concerned Benjie's foreskin, saved from the knife not by his Protestant mother (who considered circumcision hygienic) but by his Jewish father, who called it a barbaric custom and a painful trauma for infant males. Dyna referred to it as his "blinkers," "blinds," or "curtains."

"Your blinker's opening," she might tease as he was rising to tumescence. Or as now, with his penis in exhausted retreat, "The curtain's closing. He's not shutting down for the day, I hope."

"Give him ten seconds," he laughed, confident even in satiety as his hand traced her contours. First a breast and nipple and then gliding down the slopes and across the flat valley into the rise where the silky forest of her Venus mound quivered gold and coppery in a shaft of window light. The carnal pleasure of sight and touch still amazed him, made him want to think they were unique to him and uniquely because of her. How could he ever want that smooth skin stretched, feel the curves marred by the swelling of pregnancy?

"Don't touch unless you mean it," she squirmed, tittering. "And from the looks of him, Junior could use a rest. So could Jane, she's crying 'uncle.'"

Benjie grabbed for her but missed.

They bathed together in the shower stall. Their first hot-water showers since leaving Florida, so deliciously invigorating neither wanted to leave. Laughing, pushing, tickling, they were like teenagers again, starting all over. They almost forgot anything could ever disrupt their harmony.

Deciding to find breakfast first and worry about Josh later, they dressed, left a note for him and hurried down to the street.

Chapter Twelve

A round the corner and down a broad cross street, Benjie and Dynamite came on a row of fashionable shops, most still closed except for a few restaurants. Feeling fresh and touristy, they splurged on a breakfast of poached eggs, scones and lemon tea at an expensive hole-in-the-wall with the façade of a Swiss chalet and the incongruous name London Pub. They laughed as they thumbed through some travel folders, almost forgetting the purpose of the trip in their eagerness to see the sights of the city.

"Look at this!" Dyna raved, showing him pictures of the Gold Museum housed in the national bank. "If we see nothing else, we gotta see that! Everybody says it's spectacular."

"How about the Salt Cathedral?" Benjie suggested, absorbed in his own research. "Only one of its kind in the world, carved inside a salt mine. It says it's still used as a church by the miners and their families."

"Far out! How do they keep it from melting? Oh, and look at this! A funicular almost in the middle of town. It takes you to the top of the mountain, nine thousand feet elevation. They warn you to wear warm clothes. Here we are practically on the equator and they're urging you to wear winter clothes."

"It's a city of museums, according to this. Bogotá is sometimes called the Athens of South America. Lots of schools and universities, culture all over the place."

"The emerald mines!" she shouted, reminded by the tourist brochure of her excitement in the emerald shop in Cartagena. "For sure, we gotta go visit them!"

"You don't imagine you're going to pick a few off the ground, do you?" Part of him still rankled at the defeat; the little green gift from the jeweler was now like a talisman in her purse.

"Who knows? Friends at Cal went panning in Mother Lode country once and came back with several hundred dollars in gold flakes."

"Enough maybe to pay for their panning equipment?"

"Don't be so pessimistic. Stranger things have happened. Wasn't the world's biggest diamond picked off the ground by a lucky native? How about Papillon? If I can believe what he says in his book, they plucked diamonds out of riverbeds here."

"That was in Venezuela," he corrected.

"So? Diamonds in Venezuela, emeralds in Colombia. It's the emerald center of the world. Practically all the world's emeralds come from here."

"Sure, from guarded mines. Tourists don't just pick them off the ground."

"Killjoy," she huffed, her hair like a slash of gold and platinum as she tossed her head back. "I thought you were on my side—you were all last night in bed."

He grinned with remembered pleasure. "Last night was pretty great."

"And this morning," she added with a leer. "Are your curtains going up?"

"Let's get out of here," he groaned, conscious of the stiffening bulge in his crotch, "while I can still walk erect!"

"I don't believe in Freudian slips," Dynamite said coyly. "But that's one if I ever heard it."

Taking a different street back, they crossed the plaza in front of the national bank where the Gold Museum was housed. It wouldn't open for another hour, and Benjie reminded her they still had to find Weeto and get him the money. They could play tourist afterwards.

Back at the hotel there was no indication Josh had been there or tried to make contact. There were no messages at the desk and the note was still untouched under an ashtray. After adding a post-script to their note telling Josh they'd be back in an hour or two, they dashed back into the street and headed for the government buildings and the old part of town. Hand in hand, they walked along cobbled streets and narrow alleys, past ancient walls and handsome Colonial villas, many converted to museums. Crossing the stoned expanse of the huge Plaza Bolivar, ringed by weathered venerable buildings aflutter with pigeons, they felt like newlyweds on a honeymoon for whom it was all staged: crisp air, warm sunshine and a bustling panorama of everyday Latin street life.

They stopped at an open-air coffeehouse patronized by students and ordered demitasses of the national drink, *tintos*. The thick black coffee was so rich in caffeine that one small cup could fray the nerves. While Benjie went inside to make his call from a public phone, Dynamite basked in the hazy sunshine and the appre-ciative stares of the men. She was the only female there. Her bronzed skin and blond hair, coupled with her good face and body curves, acted like a magnet among dark iron filings. But she didn't mind the attention, it was a morning for gazing and wonder. She pretended not to hear the whispered banter of the three students at the table behind her, though she understood they were mentally undressing her. That, too, seemed as natural as the weather.

One of the students finally dared to approach her table and, excusing himself in English, asked if she was the American cinema star. Recalling the tactics she had used in the cocktail lounge, her mischievous side took over and she admitted that Farrah was, in fact, her cousin. The boy's jaw dropped and his eyes widened. She winked at him. "How'd you guess?"

Stunned, the awestruck student scurried back to his friends when he saw Benjie returning to the table.

"Like bees to honey, huh?" he remarked as he eased into his chair. He jerked his head in the general direction of the students. "Who are your friends?"

"Admirers," she purred. "Did you reach Weeto?"

"He wasn't in. I left a message that I'd call back in an hour. No name, I just said *un amigo*. Want another *tinto*?"

"I don't dare, my hands will crack and fall off. See how they're shaking?" Extending a hand, she exaggerated a quiver. All eyes in the place followed her every move.

"It's from all the male attention. You're being scrutinized. I guess you know."

"So I found out. One of them thought I was a movie star! How about that?"

"Don't let it go to your head. They think that about every blond woman. Latins go ape over platinum. Enjoy it while you can."

"I am, I am!" She fluttered her eyelids, striking a glamour pose. "I feel like a celebrity. How do you feel?"

"Better, like I'm on a honeymoon. See what you're missing by refusing my marriage proposals? Come on, I'll treat you to the Gold Museum."

Like him, she felt a special tone in this day, as if the world was poised to touch her with magic—drop a diamond-studded tiara on her head, turn her sneakers into golden slippers, make her into a movie star. She had always laughed at such fantasies and could enjoy indulging them because she was so certain they had no hold on her. Or did they?

In the glass and marble cavern of the museum, padded like the velvet interior of a jewel case, the last relicts of the Inca goldsmiths reposed in isolated icy splendor. Polished flatware vied with delicate laughing animals, spun filigree so fine it resembled the gossamer of spiderwebs. The Royal Music Barge with its miniature figures still seemed to be gliding endlessly along some imaginary river, on its way to some brilliant state visit. Exquisite bracelets and necklaces, some studded with jade and emeralds, face masks for royal balls and funerals. Earrings of such pure gold with such large gems, Dyna speculated they must have stretched the lobes of their owner. Created in an ancient past, they glittered as if minted only yesterday. Dyna's breath stopped when she read what the Conquistadors did with such crafted artwork. They melted it into bullion for easy shipment to Spain. Only a tiny fraction of Indian art survived the Spanish melting pots.

Exiting the main salon, they were herded by armed guards through the enormously thick round door of a bank vault. When the room was filled to capacity, the door was clicked shut, leaving them in total darkness.

A few seconds later the room exploded with light, its intensity resembling beams of pure sunlight. From floor to ceiling, surrounding them on all sides, they stood like Pizzaros being offered a king's ransom—a roomful of gold and precious stones.

Everybody gasped. Dynamite trembled with excitement. Dumped unceremoniously like junk in a secondhand store, it had the appearance of discarded or overlooked loot—a prize for the taking. Her palms itched to reach through the bulletproof glass and feel the cold blazing metal and gems. She stood transfixed by the spectacle and Benjie had to nudge her when the guards signaled it was time to leave.

"That really got to you, huh?" Benjie asked as they were descending the stairs to the bank lobby. Before she could answer, a familiar voice called out to them from the main entrance. Josh waved to them from just inside the glass doors, then hurried over to join them.

"Just how did you know we'd be here?" Benjie asked as he shook his friend's hand.

"Elementary deduction," Josh joked. "The note said an hour or two and this was the nearest tourist trap. Besides, I knew Dyna couldn't resist the lure of gold."

"It's priceless, exceptional," said Dyna, still under the spell.

"You think Uncle Josh should take it in too, yes?" He wiggled his eyebrows. "If things weren't so pressing I'd do it now. But things are cooking and I've got to mind the store. Benjie, I need some dough. Three thousand snaps as a matter of fact. I've got two of my own but I need three more and I need it like right now. This could be a deal of a lifetime for us, so don't say no. We can use Weeto's cash temporarily and pay him back later."

Benjie frowned and shook his head, "No way, Josh. I've got a thousand of my own you can have, but not a dime of Weeto's without his okay."

"Great, friend, old buddy, just great," Josh muttered in disgust. "I'm set to meet somebody at the top of the funicular in a couple of hours with five thousand in cash. Just the most incredible deal anyone could hope to fall into, and you're telling me I have to forgo it for lack of a paltry two thousand skins? Unbelievable!" He glanced pitifully at Dynamite. "It's only a loan, for Chrissake, only for a few days!"

Benjie shook his head again, wondering if the pleasure he was feeling came from something more than fulfilling an obligation to Weeto. "Gimme the details."

"No time to explain. I've got another stop to make before I meet with my contact. What about Weeto, you tried reaching him?"

Benjie explained the phone call. Surprisingly, Josh no longer saw danger in contacting the fugitive and urged him to keep trying. If he succeeded in time, he was to get Weeto to meet them at the top of the funicular. Everybody knew where that was, even the one-day tourists. Having made his pitch and lost, Josh showed surprising calm in accepting Benjie's refusal to let him use Weeto's money. Benjie almost felt guilty.

"It's okay, good buddy," he said, taking the thousand Benjie handed him. "You're only forcing me to consider alternatives and I just may have a better idea. Just in case, though, try to get Weeto up there. We're not asking for his money, only to borrow it for a few days." He started off, stopped, then added, "No later than one-thirty. After that, it's no deal. Ciao!"

He went through the doors and down the entrance steps, taking them two at a time in his lanky stride, scattering pigeons and people like a scarecrow come to life.

Benjie phoned from the bank lobby and this time, after a single buzz, Weeto was on the line.

"Hey, am I glad to hear from you," Weeto said. His voice sounded relieved. "Everything go awright?"

"Like grinding coffee, man. We even saved Chico's sweaters and your tools. They weigh a ton, you know. I'm now the hunchback of Notre Dame from lugging them all this way."

"Jeez, and I was afraid you din even get the note. No problems, eh?"

"None so far, but no point in taking chances. Chico okay?"

"He's fine, can't you hear him? He wants to know who's calling."

"I hear, I hear," Benjie said, smiling at the high-pitched voice in the background. "Listen, Weeto, can you meet us within the hour at the top of the funicular? You know what that is and where it's at?"

"Oh sure, we been there twice awready. Chico loves it."

"There's a reason we need to meet there and it has to be before one-thirty. Better if you get there before one so I can explain, okay? You can make it all right?"

"No problem, we'll be there. And, hey, they got ice cream at the top for dessert. I owe you one."

"I accept if you buy for Dynamite, too. It took two of us to rescue your coffee can."

Weeto laughed and agreed.

"Hey, Benjie, one other thing. *Muchas gracias, amigo.*"

"*De nada*—that means for nothing."

Grinning, he hung up and grabbed Dyna's arm, guiding her to the doors. A crowd was gathered around two cameramen on a bench at the foot of the stairs.

Dynamite, suddenly recognizing the student who talked to her at the coffeehouse, saw him point at her and whisper to the cameraman. Her little joke had backfired.

"It's you they're after!" Benjie exclaimed in alarm. "Why?"

"Never mind, let's just make tracks out of here!"

If they'd been experienced paparazzi instead of student reporters looking for a scoop on the regular press, they might have anticipated a celebrity dodge and cut her off. But they weren't prepared for an athletic girl in sneakers who could feint like a halfback and run the hundred-yard dash like a track star. Benjie was hard pressed to keep up with her.

The reporters, with cameras awkwardly perched on their shoulders, were hopelessly outdistanced by the time they reached the alley. But other students, at first lagging behind the technicians, raced ahead now and were in full pursuit as the fleeing couple raced across the street, dodging traffic and threading through an open arcade of shops.

Emerging into the street at the far end of the arcade, Benjie and Dyna cut left and ran for half a block to the corner. A battered old taxi was parked at the curb. Tearing open the back door, Benjie called to the driver, whose balding gray head snapped around in surprise from the newspaper he was reading.

"Vamanos, pronto!" Benjie ordered in his most commanding Spanish. Down the street he could see the students rounding a corner.

He was just as startled by the speedy reaction of the old man, who started the engine and was screeching away from the curb as Benjie closed his door. The driver called over his shoulder in a thick British accent, "Where to, mates?"

"Just go, man, fast!" Benjie shouted. "Anywhere, just open it up!"

"Shaking somebody, are we?" The driver glanced in his rearview mirror, then turned and grinned impishly. "Here's how it's done."

"You're British!" Dynamite shouted in surprise.

"And you're American," he winked back in his mirror.

Tires squealed as they abruptly turned left, narrowly missing an oncoming car. The driver leaned on his horn in fury and shook his fist. In gleeful retaliation, the cabbie shook a fist back and grinned merrily at the open pavement of the broad carrera ahead of them. "Mind telling me who we're shaking?"

"Reporters," said Benjie.

"Photographers," Dynamite said simultaneously.

"Oh, goody," the driver responded enthusiastically, his eyes like bits of sea-blue flashing incandescent mischief. "Dreadful lot, news people. No sense of proportion or respect for anyone's privacy. Are you celebrities of some sort?"

"Christ, no!" said Dynamite. "But the idiots think I'm Farrah Fawcett."

The driver gave her a puzzled look in the mirror. "Should I recognize the name?"

"At least I'm not the only one," she observed. "I've never seen her either. A new television star in the States, I'm told."

"Ah well, if you'd mentioned stars from back a ways, I'd have known—Jean Harlow, Carole Lombard, Bergman, Grable, Monroe.

But, of course, you're much too young for that old crowd." He gave her another searching glance from his mirror and smiled appreciatively, "I must say, you're pretty enough to be a film star."

Flattered, she smiled back. "What's a Britisher like you doing here, hacking a cab in Colombia?"

"Like what's a pretty girl like you doing, running away from publicity?" He laughed appreciatively. "Actually I'm not British a-tall. Only went to public schools there and college when my father was in the diplomatic service. My mother was English but I was born here. I'm Colombian by birth and family, but until I was thirty I hardly knew my country except as a visitor."

They were on a highway leading out of town. Glancing back, Benjie saw a taxi in hot pursuit, arms waving wildly out of all four windows. And it was steadily closing the gap. Taking stock of the funny little car he was riding in, he saw it was an English hack, one of those small square high-roofed jobs which movies always showed tooling around in the London fog. Top speed probably fifty. How could they possibly outrun the other taxi in this farting little midget?

"They're gaining," he shouted at his inattentive driver.

"Just teasing," the driver winked saucily. Even so, it seemed to Benjie they were slowing down. "Want them to know they've been in a chase. We have a peasant saying here: .'*La cara del santo hace milagros,'* which means 'the saint's face makes miracles.' You believe in saints and miracles?"

Benjie gritted his teeth. "We're gonna need one to shake that taxi!"

"Or the right number of horses in a souped-up engine," the driver replied. He slammed the accelerator down.

The sudden acceleration was like a take-off, as if the old car had sprouted jets and wanted to leave the ground. He couldn't believe the horsepower hidden under that funny little hood—the "bonnet" as the Brits called it. Within minutes, the other taxi, fading like the sun sinking from the horizon, was out of sight. When Benjie signaled the driver to turn around and find a side road to take them back to the city, he wasn't sure he hadn't witnessed a miracle.

"Shook them we did," the driver stated victoriously. "Where to now, mates?"

"To the funicular, the tramway that goes to the top of the mountain," said Benjie. "You can drop us off there."

"Oh, a must, the funicular, for any tourist!" the cabbie proclaimed like a barker. "Best view of the city you can get, absolutely superb—twice a year when it's not fogged in!"

As he swept into a U-turn and headed back on the same road, the cabbie glanced over his shoulder. "Don't worry about running into the reporter chaps again. Not a chance they can catch us. Take my word."

As delightful and comic as the funny little car he drove, the cabbie radiated cheer to match the balmy mountain air and noontime sun. When he suggested hiring him for the rest of the day, Benjie might have said yes but for the depleted amount of cash in his jeans.

"Look, chaps, it's not like London or Paris," the old man explained. "We don't charge an arm and a leg like they do in New York. I'm an independent. I set my own rates. Ten dollars for the rest of the day—till six, that is. You owe me three already and another three to get you to the funicular. Might as well keep me for the rest of the day, only four dollars more."

He winked at them over his shoulder. "Never can tell when the paparazzi will pop out of the woodwork again and you'll need Barney Oldfield to shake them. As a young man I was a racing car driver. Raced all over Europe. Loved it, still do!"

Dynamite grinned. "So that's it! You're doing it for kicks!"

"Don't I wish!" he corrected. "It's my livelihood as well. Changes of fortune, you know. Latin politics is like gambling at Monte Carlo—winners one day, losers the next. There was a big revolution here in 1948. Lasted ten years, what we call the great Violencia. Murder and mayhem, property burned and confiscated. The sort of nonsense Latin America has become famous for."

"I'm sorry," Dynamite said quietly.

"Bless you, my dear, but you mustn't feel sorry for me," he chirped, looking merry and owlish at the same time. "I've had a fabulous life. Spent my childhood and youth in the best of all worlds—Europe between the wars, truly exciting! I've lived in your country as well. Spent the war years in New York. A fabulous city then, exciting time to be living there. Now I hear it's all gone to pot."

Benjie and Dyna looked at each other and snickered. The driver raised an eyebrow.

"Have I made a funny? Ah yes, it's what you young people smoke these days, isn't it?" He smiled, pleased with his own alertness. "Funny, we smoked it too, back in the twenties and thirties. Called it tea then, we did. Nobody made much fuss about it then. Don't know why your government chaps make such a fuss about it now."

Dynamite could have kissed the shiny bald spot that made his hair a gray-fringed halo and kept reflecting sunlight like one of the smiling deities in the Gold Museum. He reminded her of a philosophy prof at Berkeley, her favorite teacher, an old man who rummaged through Plato for revolutionary ideas and who, like Socrates, smiled at the antics of youth as necessary bulwarks against dogma and hypocrisy.

"Did you work when you lived in New York?" Benjie asked, intrigued by the old gent.

"Like a demon! Doesn't everybody in your country? Even the rich—harder than the poor. No wonder you're so powerful. Fantastic wealth, but it's hard work created it. I worked with General Electric as an electrical engineer. Loved it."

Catching their surprised expressions, he winked again. "Almost as much as I love motorcars and tinkering with engines. Don't be fooled by the appearance of this old tin Lizzie. It's what's under the bonnet that counts, or do I say hood for you Americans? I do my own mechanical work. I can outrace anything on the road down here. Wouldn't want to challenge some of your young chaps up there, however."

"Outta sight!" Dynamite's laugh was pure praise.

Benjie remembered Weeto's tools and clothes and had the cabbie detour to pick them up at the hotel. To make them less conspicuous he packed them in one of the flight bags.

As they criss-crossed the center of town, their driver kept up his lively conversation, pointing out the highlights. By the time they reached the station platform at the base of the mountain, he seemed more an old and trusted friend than a taxi driver. He warned of pickpockets, the street kids in particular, not to leave valuables in their room, to add restaurant and bar tabs carefully and count their money twice in a money exchange.

"Don't know why we're so rascally," he wondered aloud. "Many countries are poor but their people don't resort to thievery. We take sport in it. Outwitting the other fellow, especially the foreigner, and most especially if he's got more than we've got."

He sighed resignedly. "Well, it could be worse. Somebody may use a knife to threaten you, but nobody really wants to hurt you. They just want your money and valuables. We love taking what isn't ours. Maybe it reflects our origins, when we first took it away from the Indians. We love being sneaky!"

As they started walking away, Eduardo called out to Benjie. "Let me see your watch. Ah, that's all right, you have it in a buckle strap. If it were one of those stretch bands, any Colombian schoolboy could slip it from your wrist without your knowing it." He waved to them. "Cheerio, enjoy the view of the fog!"

"He's like a goodwill ambassador," Dyna raved as they headed for the ticket station. "Did you ever hear an accent more British than that?"

"Some opinion he's got of his own people, though. Maybe he's warning us to keep a sharp eye on him, too. Remind me to count my change twice when I pay the fare."

"How terrible!" she scolded, pinching his arm. "He's absolutely charming. I'd trust him with my life."

"Your life maybe, but not your body. I noticed he enjoyed giving you the once-over a few dozen times."

"Baby, that's the nicest thing you've said to me in the last ten minutes." She squeezed his hand. "I noticed he didn't miss any passing stuff in the street, either. So he's a sexy old man—it's probably why he's still so young in spirit. Pretty cool for a guy in his sixties or seventies."

Halfway up, entering the cloud cover that perpetually hung over the mountaintop, the air turned noticeably cooler even in the closed compartment of the metal sedan. Having forgotten to heed the warning of the travel folders, they were soon massaging exposed arms to bring circulation to their lazy, tropic-conditioned blood. Dyna dug out two of Chico's sweaters and, using one for each arm, tied the sleeves around her neck. She managed to stay warm and clowned her way to the top.

Whereas the city below was bathed in warm sunshine, on the mountain it was foggy, dark and cold. Clouds boiled above them and on all sides. Looking down the slopes they saw only grayish streams of more clouds. Collectively they resembled an avalanche of dirty cotton tumbling in slow motion down the pine and stone-studded hillsides. Occasionally tatters broke away on a wisp of wind and afforded hazy glimpses of the sparkling city below. In their holiday mood, neither Benjie nor Dynamite gave any thought to danger or remembered to watch for anything suspicious. Only when they got out of the car and stepped into the spooky pea-soup fog of the top were they jolted into remembering their mission and what Josh was up to. Dynamite had an added concern, which was as much anxiety as anticipation.

Chapter Thirteen

Waiting until the other passengers drifted off, they made their way slowly through ghostly landscape, eerie as an English moor in the movies. Josh was nowhere in sight. Nor Weeto and Chico. It wasn't quite one o'clock and Benjie knew they could still be on their way. They decided to check ahead, in the shadows where a cluster of shops loomed on both sides of the precipice like walls containing a narrow cobblestone street that meandered between them and ended at the door of a church. Making their way to the end, they glanced in the door of the empty chapel, then came back to where a path forked and a sign directed them to a fast-food restaurant at the edge of the mountain. Benjie raised an eyebrow.

"It's not McDonald's," she observed, "but it's the only eatery up here. Food for thought if not for Benjie's stomach."

He grimaced.

The open balcony, railed along the side overlooking the city, was lined with rows of empty tables. Too cold for outdoor dining, only two small boys playing some hide-and-seek game, occupied it for the moment. The bigger boy, pointing an imaginary pistol, was stalking a smaller companion who ducked behind a dumpster. There were only a dozen or so people inside, weekday tourists lost in the big barnlike room. Weeto was there at a table by the window, his back to them.

"Hey, como está, amigo?" Benjie called out when Weeto spotted them. "I might have known that was Chico playing cops and robbers out there."

Jumping up, he pumped Benjie's arm with two hands. "Oh yeah, he foun' a frien' awready." He turned to Dyna, beaming. "You look good as ever, Dynamite, even in that funny fur you're wearing."

"It's damn lucky we had Chico's sweaters along," she replied. "It's freezing up here!"

"You found out, eh? Hey, you guys, before Chico comes back, I wanna thank you for what you done. I really owe you." He looked from one to the other, his eyes glistening with emotion as he awkwardly grappled to find the right words. "Call me when your diesel needs an overhaul, eh? No charge."

Benjie felt guilty about asking for the loan. If Weeto suddenly had to run again, there might not be any way to get his money back to him. And in his present state, with no chance of settling down and making some money, he needed every dime he had. Still, Benjie had made a promise to Josh. When he finished relating the events leading up to the borrowing of Weeto's money, the stocky Puerto Rican rose suddenly from the table, visibly agitated.

"Jus' a minute, I need more coffee." He nodded at Dynamite. "I think you could use some too—your teeth are chattering. You want your ice cream now, or you wanna save it for a warmer time?"

"Save it for summer," she answered, shivering. "Just coffee for now, hot and black."

Weeto motioned Benjie to follow and the pair made their way towards the food line. "If you needed the money, Benjie, you could have it," Weeto told him. "Ask for whatever I got and it's yours, jus' so I got pocket money until I get settled. But you don' even know what that clown is up to. You said so yourself. I don' trust him. Could be gettin' you into a lotta trouble." He rested his hand on Benjie's shoulder. "Listen, just tell me it's you who wants the money and it's yours, Benjie."

Benjie smiled and shook his head. Weeto had just given him the way out he'd been looking for. "Don't worry about it," he said, extending his hand. The two solemnly shook hands. "No hard feelings, really."

"You sure? Because for you, anything I got. But your friend, Josh, he scares me like big trouble. What's he gettin' you into? No drugs, I hope."

A faint grin tugged at the corners of Benjie's mouth as he fumbled in his pocket to pay the cashier. Weeto stopped him with a frown and took care of it.

"Do me a favor," Weeto added as they made their way back to the table. "If you gonna smuggle, do clean stuff—emeralds or Indian artifacts or wild birds. You'll go to jail if they catch you but you won't be bringing poison or death to somebody's life, maybe innocent school kids. Don' let Josh talk you into crazy stuff like horse—heroin, you know?"

"They've switched roles," Dyna told them when they returned, her gaze fixed on the two boys outside the window. "Chico's now playing sheriff and the other kid's in hiding. None of that pistol stuff for him—he goes for the long rifle. Look."

Shouldering a long-handled mop, Chico was stalking his quarry whose jean-clad butt protruded from behind a mountain outcrop disguised as a stack of Coca-Cola cases. Closing one eye, he took aim down the long barrel of his imaginary buffalo gun and squeezed the trigger. Simultaneously, a loud report like a gunshot exploded outside and echoed through the stony hillsides. Benjie and the others stared in surprise at each other a moment, then erupted in laughter.

"Somebody couldn't find the restaurant," Benjie said playfully. "They've taken to the hills to hunt down their dinner. Probably not as good a shot as Chico though."

"I'm surprised he knows how to play sheriff," Weeto remarked. "He's used to playing the bad guy, you know? Hey, I'll go get him. He likes you two and—"

Dyna put a hand on his arm, "No, let him play. Don't take his fun away. Besides, even when he's tired, he still has enough energy to challenge us old folks."

Dyna fell abruptly silent as the door flew open and Josh rushed in. He gave no hint of recognizing any of them as he swept past their table and dropped a small leather bag into Dynamite's lap. So rhythmic was the move and so deft the drop, no one in the room would have connected the scarecrow with the startled blond *gringa* and her two companions. With their backs to the entrance, neither Benjie nor Weeto realized what was happening until Josh flashed by.

He disappeared through the swinging kitchen doors like a Halloween joke, followed almost immediately by the sound of crashing pots and pans and a series of shouts.

Dynamite gently squeezed the pouch as she slipped it into her purse. Rocks or stones. Guessing emeralds, she felt a flutter of excitement as her fingers probed inside the pouch.

Suddenly the entrance doors burst open again and three men, shouting and gesturing wildly, rushed in. The patrons, most of them out-of-town Colombians on holiday, sat in stony silence, volunteering nothing. Even the serving girls behind the counter and the cashier looked to the ceiling and at each other with innocent, glazed expressions when one of the men demanded information. The other two had dashed in opposite directions. One darted through the kitchen door. The other, a stocky black teenager in yellow raincoat and yellow track shoes, sprinted to the restrooms in the back corner. Surprised women and girls fled screaming from the ladies' restroom. The intruder reappeared a few moments later, a lascivious grin plastered on his pockmarked face.

At a signal from the man by the counter, he followed his partner. The two ran through the kitchen and out a back door. Reappearing on the veranda outside, the yellow-jacketed man began methodically kicking and overturning discarded boxes, checking behind stacked cases of bottles and poking inside the dumpster with a mop handle.

Moments later, Dyna saw Josh stroll into view on the veranda, an innocent-looking tourist going to scout the city below. The wig was gone and the beard, which normally went to his chest, was cropped short. He was wearing shades, the large face-fitting style. The cutoff jeans had been replaced or covered by full-length khakis and a long-sleeved shirt had taken the place of his poncho. The big leather bag which always hung from his shoulder was missing, replaced by an even larger black camera case. A small cheap Kodak hung from a leatherette strap around his neck.

Weeto, who raced outside to extract Chico from the bedlam, passed him with no sign of recognition. Dynamite drew her breath in sharply as Josh pointed his camera at the yellow-clad black who was continuing his search of the storage area. At the same time his companions reappeared from behind the building, looking puzzled and frustrated. They shouted back and forth angrily at each other.

Weeto and Chico had no sooner rejoined them at the table when more noise erupted outside. Eduardo, the taxi driver, came flying through the doors only a few feet ahead of a dozen or so young people pursuing him. Flashbulbs popped and cameras began whirring. Weeto was first to react, grabbing his son and the flight bag of tools and running for the exit.

"Come on, mates, here's how we lose them," Eduardo shouted in the confusion, pointing to the kitchen. Following blindly in a mad dash past potato sacks and boxed canned goods, they overturned a tub of cabbages, startling the poor cook and his female helpers all over again. Exiting the rear door, they ran through a vine-covered gate and down a narrow path between the backsides of the restaurant and a row of gift shops. Shouts from the reporters and the others followed on their heels.

Eduardo threw open one of the shop doors and motioned them inside. They raced through and out of the front, crossing the cobbled street to the door of the facing shop. They sailed through the open doorway, igniting the proprietor's shouts as they knocked over a stacked display of baskets on their way out the back. Eduardo led them down a dirt-biking trail to a switchback off the main trail, stopping finally behind a large rock outcropping. The faint clamoring in the distance suggested their pursuers were headed off in another direction.

Eduardo turned to Dynamite, "It's a few miles down on foot. The only way besides the car. They'll be sure to be waiting for you there."

"But how did they find..." It dawned on her that their taxi was one of a kind. A dead giveaway once it was spotted. "I'm not who they think I am!"

Eduardo eyed her dubiously. "Don't tell me you don't believe me either?" she groaned.

"Of course I do, my dear." His smile lacked conviction. "Of course it's possible they'll have chaps posted at the bottom as well. We'll just have to slip by them."

Voices crescendoed along the trail below them. The trail they were on dead-ended farther up the mountain. To reach the main trail leading down to the foot of the mountain, Eduardo explained, they had to backtrack and sneak along the ridge to the other side of the cable car station before they could begin descending. His focus for the moment was simply to stay hidden until the crowd dispersed, allowing them to cross enemy lines undetected.

Talking excitedly in Spanish, a few pursuers passed along the lower path beneath the spot where they were concealed. The only word Dyna understood was *"ladrones,"* thieves. Whether part of the press crowd or merely innocent spectators swept into the excitement, she couldn't tell. As their voices faded away down the trail, Eduardo motioned them to move out.

Dynamite shivered in the cold, thin air as they ran crouching along the path, wishing she'd grabbed another of Chico's sweaters. She'd lost one in the escape from the restaurant and the other had gone over her head, turban fashion, to hide her hair as Eduardo had suggested. Goosebumps covered her bare arms.

As they neared the top of the ridge, a piercing shriek abruptly rose above the din of their pursuers. Voices babbled excitedly and somebody shouted for the police to be called. *Un muerto!* A dead body had been discovered on the trail.

"Now! Before the mob finds us!" Eduardo shouted hoarsely. They tumbled over the top and dashed left along the edge of the cobbled street.

Voices called after them but they kept running, hoping the grisly discovery on the trail would draw attention off them. Approaching the tram station platform, they saw it was empty except for the ticket-taker. If some of the press horde had been stationed there earlier to block their escape route, they'd obviously been drawn off by the smell of blood.

Eduardo seized the opportunity and herded his charges unnoticed into one of the cable cars. A young Indian couple with their two shy children and two elderly men were the only other passengers. After a few tense minutes, the warning bell sounded. A second before the doors closed, Weeto rushed aboard with Chico in tow, his other hand gripping the flight bag. He'd been hiding behind one of the steel support columns, waiting till the last moment before daring to board.

Spotting Benjie and Dynamite, Chico began to shout a greeting. But Weeto clapped a hand over his mouth and, half-lifting him, hustled him into the back seat, whispering in his ear. Weeto looked furtively around as the tram began its descent. The Indian family and the pair of professors seemed interested only in the scenery outside. He leaned forward and spoke in a low voice into Benjie's ear.

"What's goin' on? What the hell happened back there?" After Benjie explained, disgust washed over Weeto's face. "All that runnin' and chasin' just to get a picture?"

"Que pasa?" Chico asked his father.

"Ssshhh, quiet," Weeto eased him back into the corner. "Don' talk Spanish. Now's the time to speak English."

"What happened, Poppi?" Chico persisted. "Who killed the man?"

"Not now, later! Like not a word, *nada.*" He turned to Benjie. "The man killed back there—can it have something to do with what your friend was up to? He was running around up there like a madman."

Until then, Benjie hadn't connected the discovery of the dead man with Josh. Too much had happened too quickly. He always believed Josh was in it strictly for laughs. In the end the gun would only squirt water and Josh would pull off his disguises and leap to the floodlights for the plaudits of his audience. Now, he was forced to see some connections.

He realized the shots they all thought they heard when Chico was squeezing the trigger of the imaginary buffalo gun had been for real. Gunshots only minutes before Josh burst into the restaurant pursued by three angry men—the timing seemed more than merely coincidental. His reappearance minutes later in disguise proved he anticipated events requiring an elaborate change of clothes.

Dyna suddenly nudged him and motioned to a figure on the trail.

Josh in his new disguise, looking like a tourist with the big camera case hanging at his side, strolled down the path as casually as a Sunday hiker. As the cable car broke out of the cloud cover and they turned heads to stay with the figure on the trail, they saw him stop and aim his camera at the descending cab.

Dynamite's hand flew to her mouth. "There, the yellow jacket!" she whispered between her fingers.

A hundred yards farther down the trail, the three who had chased Josh through the restaurant trotted along the narrow path, glancing nervously over their shoulders. Weeto tapped Benjie's shoulder.

"The guys who were chasin' him. They took off the same time I did. When they heard people callin' for the police, they really made tracks. Are they the guys he was supposed to meet, the ones he needed the money for?"

"I don't know," Benjie answered thoughtfully, glancing at Dyna. If she shared his misgivings about Josh, she gave no indication. Sitting erect and attentive under the knotted wool sweater covering her head, she had the relaxed expression of someone immersed in her own thoughts. Her hands, tightly clutching the top of the purse in her lap, gave the only clue of tension. Her knuckles were turning white.

Approaching the station at the bottom, Benjie saw a dozen or so people were milling about on the platform. There were no signs of cameras or press people among them. It looked like a safe walk home as they got off. But as they neared the old taxi, someone shouted from an unmarked van parked across the street. Two men, one shouldering a camera, bounded out of it. Several young men piled out of the car parked in front.

Eduardo's racing days had conditioned him to fast pit stops. The doors had barely slammed before he had the engine in gear and tires spinning in the shoulder gravel as he cranked into a U-turn.

The college boys dove back into their white Mercedes and screeched out of park in an attempt to block the road.

Wildly shouting and honking his horn, Eduardo accelerated, seemingly bent on hitting them broadside. In this dangerous game of chicken they blinked first and veered off just as Eduardo cut to his right, braked momentarily, then zipped past their rear, missing them by a hair. Arms with clenched fists sprouted from the Mercedes' open windows. Regaining his nerve, their driver floored the gas pedal and sped off in hot pursuit. Behind them, the van carrying the television crew pulled away from the curb and followed.

As they rounded the first curve of the downgrade, Dyna shrieked from the front seat. Ahead a band of scrawny chickens had wandered onto the pavement to scratch in the loose gravel in some potholes. In a flurry of white feathers and hysterical clucking, they skidded honking through the unfortunate flock.

"Aaiiy, mas rápido!" Chico shouted, snapping his head around to peer out the back window. Weeto glanced at Benjie, his eyes wide in astonishment.

Screeching around another corner, they headed down an industrial street of warehouses and truck depots. Too late Eduardo saw the road ahead was blocked by a truck and trailer backing into a loading dock. A stone wall on one side and a chain-link fence on the other prevented any means of detouring the temporary blockade. Braking almost to a stop, he veered right and over a low curb, grazing the fence as close as he dared before swinging sharply into a U-turn.

But the maneuver had cost him his lead. The Mercedes and van had turned into the street and, seeing their prey headed back their way, moved to seal off the street. At the last instant, Eduardo spotted a gap in the chain link fence, cranked the wheel hard, then shot through the opening.

Still followed by the van and the Mercedes, Eduardo roared into the open freight yard, past forklifts and stacked pallets of cargo. Chased into the warehouse area, he raced around and between buildings, weaving through stopped trucks and startled stevedores, some stopping their work to watch the mad scene of the vintage taxi outrunning and outwitting the shiny new vehicles in pursuit.

Several times the van and Mercedes split up and angled off in efforts to outflank and corner the taxi. Eduardo always managed to slip past their flanking movements at the last second or by a hair's width, nearly causing them to collide head-on or into stacks of cargo. At one point, bouncing over the crossing of a railroad spur, a piece of the taxi's rear bumper was jolted loose and clattered onto the pavement.

The pursuers might have been puzzled at their inability to catch the old taxi, except the chase thus far had been more a matter of tactics than speed. Sharp turns, dodging objects, pedestrians and moving forklifts, braking, accelerating, slowing. At last the taxi found an exit at the far end of the yard and went careening out into the street that led to a major highway.

For some distance both vehicles confidently continued the chase. About the time the taxi was swinging onto the *autopista*, however, the van was rolling to a stop on the shoulder. Only the shouting college boys in the Mercedes were still in the game. Only a few car lengths behind, a mile later as they were entering the *autopista*, the gap had mysteriously widened. And it kept widening. After ten minutes on the straightaway they lost sight of the taxi altogether. But an occasional feather, drifting erratically in the wind drafts, told them the taxi was still ahead somewhere in the widening distance.

Benjie had Eduardo drop Weeto and Chico at their hotel first. Still shaky from the wild ride, Weeto could only roll his eyes, gulp and shake his hand. Dynamite kissed him on the cheek. Chico allowed her a hug before he bounded off to where a vendor was peddling mechanical animals performing on the sidewalk.

"*Buen suerte,*" Benjie called from the taxi's window. "Don't let them catch you, *amigo!*"

"*La cara del santo hace milagros,*" Dynamite shouted, showing off her first Spanish aphorism.

"All I need is a saint!" Weeto shouted back, laughing. "Don' forget, I owe you one. Jus' call me. Anytime!"

Benjie considered for a moment going back to look for Josh but too many people had seen the souped-up taxi. In any case, he reasoned, Josh was doubtless down from the mountain and out of the area by now. He decided to ditch the taxi two blocks from the hotel and go the rest of the way on foot.

Eduardo showed obvious disappointment at the extra two dollars Benjie handed him as a tip. Dyna guessed he was still convinced he'd been hauling around a celebrity and, in the end, his extra effort would merit a reward commensurate with the risk. Two dollars wouldn't begin to pay for the damage to his bumper, he complained.

Benjie's explanation as to why he couldn't afford more was met with the skeptical gaze of the entrepreneur who's heard it all before, but is too civilized to trade manners for a brawl.

"Well, then, that's all to be said, isn't it? We're all of a piece, nobody hurt, and didn't we give those chaps a race?" His impish smile returned as he dipped a salute to Dynamite. "Cheerio, young lady. Good luck—as if you didn't already have it all."

"It's true, Eduardo, what he's telling you," she fumbled as she dug in her purse. "I'm not who you or those reporters think I am. I feel bad about your car—the bumper damage, I mean." She pressed a small tissue packet into his hand. "This should pay for it. Good luck to you too, and may your saint continue protecting you with miracles."

Benjie was surprised she was so willing to part with the emerald. She'd been carrying it around with her like a charm ever since Josh gave it to her.

Dyna felt no loss in parting with it. The leather pouch in the bottom of her bag was full of emeralds, as an earlier inspection had revealed. Nor did she vacillate in her resolve to keep silent about the cache, knowing how it would alarm and upset Benjie. In no way was she willing to connect the emeralds with the man found killed on the mountaintop. The timing of the shot and its possible connection to the trio chasing Josh were coincidences even she couldn't overlook. But she couldn't for a second believe Josh would ever resort to violence. The shooting was part of some bizarre collusion of events which Josh, if he was connected at all, could not have anticipated or prevented. She could hold onto the gems without guilt or fear of getting blood on her hands.

Chapter Fourteen

Back at their room, Benjie and Dynamite had barely opened the door when the phone rang. Josh. He laughed at Benjie's anxious tone.

"Don't ask me to explain anything on the phone," he instructed Benjie. "What was all that business with the press and television people? They nearly blew my game plan."

Benjie hastily explained, adding, "Even the taxi driver thinks she's that Farrah girl. I think she's beginning to believe it herself."

Josh asked to speak to Dynamite.

"Listen, Farrah, you haven't let your boyfriend in on what I dumped in your lap, have you? Just answer yes or no, and laugh when you say it. Good girl, I knew I could count on you. I'll explain why later. But for the moment, you mustn't tell him. Our little secret, yes? For now, just tell him I was ribbing you with an offer to go to Hollywood as Farrah what's-her-name's stand-in, okay? Keep those green things safe and hidden. Ciao, baby. Put Benjie back on."

Benjie took back the receiver.

"About the money I asked you for...stop fretting," Josh said flippantly. "I didn't need it."

Josh's carefree air took some of the edge off Benjie's concerns.

"Listen, friend," Josh continued, "be ready to move out on a minute's notice. You two can play around for a couple of hours, but after that stick by the phone. If you go out, tell Dyna to cover her hair and rub burnt cork on her face? We sure as hell don't need the press corps on our tails. Ciao!" Before Benjie could reply, Josh hung up.

As soon as it was dark, Benjie and Dynamite slipped out to eat at a small restaurant around the corner. The décor was decidedly Russian, with icons and samovars, dim lights on framed reproductions of the Winter Palace and the onion domes of the Kremlin. A musty atmosphere, like a closed house in winter, pervaded the place. They had hot borscht and stroganoff with noodles.

"I wonder if Russians eat American food when they're visiting Rome or Paris," Dynamite speculated. With her hair swathed in a white towel, she looked less a movie star than the cleaning girl just in from dusting the furniture. After the hectic events of the past few hours, the sudden quiet, almost church-like atmosphere, the flickering candles and the scent of incense were a balm to their nerves. They had ice cream for dessert and coffee afterwards to fight the sedation of the wine.

The phone didn't ring until nearly nine o'clock, when they were both dozing on top of the covers. Benjie was instantly awake.

"What have you two been up to?" Josh asked in astonishment. "Dynamite's a cause celebre! On the evening television news, prime time. They're linking her to the shooting hoax on the mountaintop. They really think she's the Farrah girl, and that the whole thing was some kind of publicity stunt."

"Stunt? Was it a hoax?"

"Call it a diversion," Josh cackled maniacally for a moment. "But who could have guessed we'd have the Associated Press of Colombia breathing down our necks? And the TV news medium and the gossip columnists…" He sighed heavily. "We don't dare go out of here by plane, everybody's looking for her. Even if they've phoned Hollywood by now and found out Farrah's been in Palm

Springs all week, they're still gonna want to find the mystery girl and determine what the joke was all about."

"What was it about?" Benjie asked irritably.

"What you don't know can't hurt you," Josh told him. "I'll tell you when you get here. Grab a cab and meet me at the Linea Expreso Brasilia bus depot. That means Brazil Express Line, in case your Spanish isn't so hot. Quick as you can, and I do mean pronto. Bring everything, we're moving out for good, and fast. Tell Farrah to strap her chest flat and cut off her hair—or at least hide it under a babushka. *Hasta la vista,* chum."

They barely made the last bus out for Medellín. For once Josh was on time and hustled them along with hardly a word. The moment they climbed aboard, the doors hissed closed and the bus lurched ahead. Luckily it was less than half filled and they had a section of seats in the rear all to themselves.

The overland trip between Bogotá and the coast was a grueling business at best. Three mountain ranges, the Cordilleras Oriental, Central and Occidental, intervene like giant serrated backbones which have to be scaled and descended in a seemingly endless series of loops and switchbacks, along narrow cuts of two-lane pavement exposed to falling rocks on one side and sheer drop-offs on the other. Vehicles stay mostly in low gear, grinding up the steep inclines or holding back to save brakes on the downslopes. Slower-moving trucks, barely able to creep along some of the steeper grades, slow everything down and compound the problem of both time and danger. Caught in their wake, irritated drivers eventually start passing on curves and blind spots, magnifying the odds of an accident. Combine Latin temperament with a dash of machismo, and driving in Colombia begins to resemble Russian roulette.

Having started their journey at night, the trio were blind to some of the thrills of unrailed drop-offs and recent landslides. But, nearly eight hours later, the spectacular dawn revealed what they'd been missing. Despite the dangers of their journey, they all knew they'd come too far to turn back. Besides, there was too much catch-up talk to notice road hazards.

The dead man had been a hoax, Josh explained over the noise of the grinding gears. A store mannequin with a dash of ketchup on the forehead placed on a ledge where it could be seen from the trail above. The shot was real, but it was a stage blank fired by one of the men they saw chasing him. The three actors were street toughs he'd hired for the day.

"Start from the beginning," Benjie complained. "Who were you meeting up there and why?"

"Remember the collateral I said we needed? Reason one. The other was to work out terms and make a down payment with Número Uno, someone called Don José, who's both a grower and wholesaler. Obviously most amateurs never get to him, they get siphoned off by all the middle dealers around the harbors and airfields. By getting to him we shaved a big chunk off the price and eliminated a lot of potential squeezers and squealers. Like I said, it pays to go to the source—"

"How come you were so lucky," Benjie asked suspiciously, "if most others never get to him?"

"Good looks and charm, what else?" Josh grinned, running a languorous hand over the stubble beginning to sprout on his head again. "I made them think I was after bigger game than pot, like coke or horse. Many little dealers aren't into that so I got pushed up the ladder. My good friend, Sergio, graciously opened a few doors—"

"Good friend?" Benjie mocked. "You haven't known him a week."

"It's not time that counts, it's trust—and the smell of money. Don't forget, he thinks I'm a screwy branch of the Vanderbilt tree. He's our..." he paused to emphasize the magnitude of his coup, "our sponsor for the collateral, fifty thousand dollars in emeralds."

He saw Dyna's eyes widen in surprise, then slide away.

"He brought his emeralds for examination," Josh explained. "Naturally Don José brought along his own expert jeweler to verify their authenticity and value."

"The two professor types on the funicular who went down with us," Dyna interjected, "could they have been your Número Uno and his jeweler?"

"Could be," said Josh. "Both white-haired, in dark business suits?"

Dyna nodded. "But why wasn't your friend, Sergio, with them?" she wondered aloud. "He wasn't in the car and we didn't see him on the footpath either."

Josh stroked the stubble on his chin. "Well, you see, he ran into a bit of trouble up there and got delayed. Fortunate for me, it happened after Don José had examined the emeralds and concluded the deal with me. Sergio pledged the jewels as collateral but holds them in trust until the operation is completed. If we get our pot safely to Florida and fail to pay the balance, he surrenders them to Don José. If we proceed as proper gentlemen and pay what we legitimately owe, Sergio keeps the gems and gets a handsome commission from us to redeem our pledges."

"What pledges?" Benjie asked, his head spinning from all the financial finagling. "What're we providing Sergio with to induce him to risk his emeralds on our behalf?"

"The boat papers. I convinced him a free-and-clear documented vessel worth half a million is a sizable piece of collateral. Enough to make it worth his while to hire a lawyer in the States to seize the vessel if we renege."

"He believed that?" Benjie asked.

"So far, yes."

"And if he changes his mind and the deal's off, we're out the three thousand you shelled out this afternoon?"

Josh shrugged. "The price of doing business in a high-profit field. When you don't have sufficient capital to cover your margins, you have to be prepared for occasional losses."

Dyna knew, of course, what he was leaving out, which explained his indifference about the down payment. But how the jewels came into his possession and how he intended using them in the transaction—if at all anymore—were more puzzling than ever.

"You mentioned Sergio ran into some trouble up there," Benjie reminded Josh. "Explain."

Josh cleared his throat and took a breath. "Well, it seems my hired actors were more thieves than thespians. Not satisfied with the thirty dollars each I paid in advance and the hundred promised if they performed as instructed, they were carried away by greed. When they took possession of Sergio's emeralds, instead of turning them over to me as the scene called for, they pocketed them and tried to hold me up as well."

Dynamite began laughing. Benjie looked aghast.

"You mean," he almost choked, "you mean you planned on stealing them?"

"Borrowing," Josh corrected. "And only for a short time. After my thieves relieved him of his valuables I, devoted friend of the man, would make a foolhardy pursuit. I catch the thief, wrest the gun away and retrieve the gems. Only to return them to the rightful owner for what I hope will be a commensurate reward—his trust and affection."

A sigh seeped from his lips. "Unfortunately Colombian street toughs are no less untrustworthy than their American counterparts. Once they had the bag of stones, they turned the gun on me. Why settle for a hundred? Keep the nuggets and take whatever else I had on me. But I was luckier than Sergio. My three thousand was in the pocket of Don José, who was already gone. Secondly, I knew the pistol was a stage gun with blanks, having bought and loaded it myself. And third, as you probably noticed, I can run like hell when I have to."

Just then the bus found a level stretch of highway and the sudden absence of low-gear grinding as it shifted into high was almost like absolute silence. Josh's voice carried like a megaphone and all three glanced around to see if anyone was listening. But at one o'clock in the morning everyone was asleep—or seemed to be. An Indian woman two seats ahead was the nearest passenger and they were confident she couldn't have understood their conversation.

"The change of clothes," Benjie asked, a perplexed look on his face. "How could you anticipate your street boys would double-cross you and you'd have to make like Houdini?"

"I didn't. The fast change act was planned for others—for the cops or DAS agents, in case I was being set up. Colombia, land of intrigue, remember? The cross and the double cross. At least three people knew I'd be arriving with five thousand Yankee dollars. Two knew Sergio was coming with a cache of precious stones. Tempting loot even for the least greedy. How could I not anticipate surprises and try to prepare for them?"

Josh yawned. Dynamite saw more than fatigue in the gesture; she saw an anxiety to get through Benjie's questions and lay them to rest. But his answers still left her with doubts. She decided the answers were tied up in the leather pouch in her purse and, until he explained that part of the scam, she'd have to settle for a half-solved puzzle.

She was not to get any explanations until they reached Medellín near noon and taxied across town to another depot for a bus to Cartagena. With time to kill before their bus was to leave, they searched for a place to eat and stretch their legs. While Benjie was in the toilet cleaning up, Josh told Dyna what she hoped to hear.

"We're keeping the stones. I mean we're taking them all the way to the States, *entiende?*"

She nodded vigorously, though still puzzled. "But I thought you needed them for the collateral?"

"I did. And I may need them again. But not this collection. Think about it. As far as Sergio's concerned they're gone, filched by that trio of street thieves."

"But how, who? You don't expect him—you do!" she sputtered, amazed at his gall.

"Exacto!" He beamed like a Latin bingo caller. "He has to trust me. He's out a sizable chunk and he's miserable. I'm his only way of covering his loss. I've already jazzed him about doubling or tripling his commission and how bad I feel he got robbed—all because he was trying to accommodate me." Suppressing an urge to laugh, he leaned closer. "Why not? What's fifty thousand when we're talking millions? Chicken feed, right? Crumbs from our banquet table."

The spiraling figures and his enthusiasm worked their special magic on her. She sipped her glass of *agua minerale*. "How do you know he doesn't suspect you were behind the caper?"

"Because I was with him last night, commiserating with him before I phoned you two. He's the one who told me the whole thing was on the seven o'clock television news. He saw it on his hotel set and it turned on a light bulb. Who else but Don José? Only a big organization would have the nerve and manpower to arrange such a scam." He smiled confidently. "Why suspect me? Didn't they point the gun at me too? And didn't he see me running for my life?"

"Then your actors didn't double-cross you like you said earlier," Dyna surmised, her head spinning from the complexity of his plan.

He wagged his head, laughing deliciously. "That was for Benjie's benefit. We both know how he'd react to stealing, even from a big jeweler thief like Sergio. Which is why, Dyna-baby, this is our own little pact. Closed lips all the way back, okay? For safety's sake, you keep the stones. Hide them on the boat somewhere. Our little insurance policy. If all else fails, if we have to dump the pot or get torpedoed, there's still a chance we can salvage the emeralds. Our secret?"

She nodded, anxious only to hear she wouldn't have to give up her latest talisman. It helped to cut the tinge of guilt she felt at agreeing so readily to keep secrets from Benjie. Since it was for his sake as well, she didn't feel she was conspiring against him. The theft itself was made tolerable by assurances they were only stealing from a much bigger thief. But something else troubled her.

"If they're all so untrustworthy, how do you know this Don José won't just pocket the three thousand dollars and thumb his nose at us?"

"Because he needs me," Josh assured her. "To make a delivery. A message which can only be delivered person-to-person in Miami. Okay? Please don't ask any more questions about it, and please don't mention it to Benjie. Our second secret, okay?"

On the second leg of their bus ordeal, Benjie still had questions. But laundered through Josh's convoluted answers, they came out faded as the worn jeans he wore—barely an itch, so well had they been stretched and curved to fit what had to be covered.

The raging river they crossed and recrossed reminded Benjie they would have to cross the Magdalena on their way to the rendezvous with the delivery vessel off the fjords. Sea lore had it that in flood stage the river's mouth extended twenty miles out to sea with turbulent waters and vicious crosscurrents. Boaters reported tree trunks and other large debris moving fast enough to stove in a hull. That was enough to divert Benjie's attention from financial manipulations to the more practical problem of how to take on tons of baled grass in heaving seas.

He had earlier given Josh a crimped idea of how much cargo the *Gorda* could carry. If they gutted the interior, stripped it of fixtures and partitions, more could be squeezed aboard, but he wasn't about to allow such desecration. Besides, too much weight would put them low in the water, impeding passage, and make them suspicious to every passing boat. Scaled down to a few tons, they weren't talking multi-millions anymore as Josh was inclined to do. But even at half a million the figures rained on Benjie like confetti. He couldn't believe the numbers, nor the absurdity of a system which converted an innocuous plant into an expensive product. An ordinary weed, able to grow almost anywhere, had been trans-formed by laws and sanctions into one of the world's highest-priced commodities.

Josh's meeting with Don José had also eliminated another problem. As a major dealer with international connections, he required a sizeable and reliable delivery system to where buyers normally accepted delivery, harbors and airfields. He even owned a few coastal trading schooners which could make deliveries to vessels offshore. They wouldn't have to make side arrangements, thus eliminating a prime source of leaks. A further benefit came in the timing. In response to pressure, the Colombian government was going through the motions of an official crackdown, arresting some street dealers and a few minor officials who were a nuisance to all concerned. In the U.S. a genuine anti-drug campaign had been initiated, with seizures of cargoes, crews and couriers, pinching the traffic to a trickle. Colombian distribution points were bulging. It was a buyer's market on the shipping end.

"And a seller's market in the States," Josh crowed jubilantly. "Nothing's moving, everybody's waiting for the heat to come off. Our timing's perfect, with anxious people on two continents."

Don José even provided a buyer. One of his Miami customers was willing to take whatever they could deliver at a guaranteed $100,000 a ton for a Bahamas drop-off. With their own fleet of fast powerboats, they'd arrange to meet at one of the isolated keys and run the cargo across themselves. Josh was letting Benjie know he was honoring the pledge not to re-enter U.S. waters. But skepticism still gnawed at Benjie.

"What's to keep them from cutting the price when we get there?"

"Competition, or the threat of it anyway." Josh smirked with devious pleasure. "I didn't say no and I didn't say yes to the offer. I let him think I had some New Jersey connections I wanted to talk to first. I'm to notify his boat agent in Santa Marta if we want to avail ourselves of his Miami contact. We will, of course, but first I'll try to bargain for more. It may boost our stock as professionals, dispel the notion we're a gaggle of smackheads or rube amateurs."

"Why the need for collateral then?" Benjie asked, a puzzled frown on his face. "If we're selling to Don José's Miami connection, why not have them withhold the balance due and send it directly to him? Why the need for guarantees?"

"Ah, there's the rub. I didn't learn of the Miami deal until after I dragged Sergio in with his emeralds. Now that he's lost them to the thieves, he can't be very happy. He doesn't know about the Miami connection or that it might eliminate any need for collateral guarantees. But I don't let him know that, do I? Hurt feelings turn easily to vengeance in this trade. I don't want his to be the tongue with the anonymous tip to the nearest U.S. consulate about a pleasure yacht on its way north with contraband cargo."

He glanced out the window as if needing the perspective of distance to see the woof and warp of the design he was weaving. Staring at the river in the gorge below, he mused aloud, "We've got no choice. We have to make him think we still need his bag of stones and he's part of the enterprise, if only to protect ourselves from any surprises."

Benjie still didn't have a firm handle on all the intricacies of the deal. Despite his concerns at times, he admitted to a certain admiration for the wizardry of the scheme. He was comfortable letting Josh call the shots on the business end of the deal. He'd take care of the sea part. The rest was fate.

Chapter Fifteen

If any of the fugitives on the bus had seen the televised version of events on the mountaintop, their plans would have been scrapped, or at least altered. Certainly Weeto, totally unaware of it, wouldn't have stayed roosting like a chicken in plain sight of the foxes trying to sniff him out. A miracle of sorts occurred that day, in that a wracked and ravaged world was relatively trouble-free for twenty-four hours. No new wars broke out, no flare-ups on the Arab-Israeli border, no terrorist bombings or hijackings nor political assassinations, no droughts or monsoons or earthquakes threatening new famine and epidemics or mass destruction of lives and property—not even a newsworthy death of an important leader or celebrity.

Like nature, the news media abhor a vacuum. What would otherwise have rated no more than a few lines in the gossip columns of *El Tiempo* got instead a full minute of prime time television, in glorious color, with intriguing blurred shots of the new American film star caught startled with her friends at the table, in headlong flight through the restaurant kitchen, and later fleeing in the funny old taxi that oddly outran everything on the road. Interspersed were shots of the dead body on the trail, arrival of the police and discovery that the body was a store mannequin with a fake head wound. The commentator mentioned reports of gunshots, the presence of thieves reported robbing a man of his wallet and chasing a foreigner.

The question was asked whether it was the American film star in their midst and if her flight, the fake body, and the thieves chasing the bearded scarecrow were all part of a stunt, a publicity effort to promote a film in the making. Or was it, as the commentator asked tongue in cheek, a charade staged by a group of university students, reportedly first to know of the actress's presence in the city and first to give chase in their cars?

Whatever, it was a pleasant departure from the winter gloom and the usual daily diet of crime, drugs and violence. Most Bogotanos responded with their characteristic appreciation for pranks, but a few viewers saw something else in the scenes flashing across the screen. Among these were José Lleras Gomez, or Don José as he was generally addressed, one of the two distinguished-looking white-haired men on the cable car whom Dynamite mistook for a pair of professors. Hardly known for his letters in a city famous for its degrees and universities, he began life at the lowest extreme of the social ladder—as a bastard and orphan. As a boy bootblack he survived on cunning and thieving until he could connive his way out of the street life of the gamines into a variety of employment which led to land acquisitions and enterprise, the extent of which only a few close associates even vaguely knew.

In comparison to the oldline landed families and industrial merchants, he displayed little evidence of wealth. The bulk of his income was invisible in the form of foreign currencies in banks outside the country. His only visible assets were a modest villa in town, a vacation home on the north coast and several large fincas dotting the broad savanna surrounding the capital where he reputedly raised a variety of plants and flowers for export. As everyone knew, for decades Colombia has been the world's principal supplier of blooms and bulbs, with the United States its prime customer.

It was not surprising, therefore, that he often traveled out of the country, principally to the U.S. and occasionally to Europe and Hong Kong. His frequent trips to Peru were explained by the presence of family there. His wife was a Peruana, they had relatives in Lima and Cuzco.

Having just returned from Miami the week before, he had reason to be astonished by what he saw on the television set. The Miami man, one of his most valuable customers, was agitated by more than the current trafficking crackdown which had virtually brought his operation to a standstill. A lawyer representing a number of his associates had died suddenly while on a mission to Switzerland. Important papers were missing. The gravity with which he viewed the loss was underscored by his unwillingness to specify its nature, hinting only that in the wrong hands it could ruin lives and destroy careers, possibly undoing much of the protective apparatus of the organization he had struggled to develop.

He had reason to think the papers were hidden on a pleasure yacht stolen the week before and believed headed for the Caribbean, possibly Colombia. Handing Don José a stack of duplicate pictures of the boat, he cautioned it was doubtless renamed and otherwise altered, but asked that his coastal crews be alerted for a boat of that size and description. A second stack of prints pictured a full frontal view of a husky Latin holding the hand of a small boy in swim trunks and sailor cap, waving an American flag.

The color screen had just flashed the startled face of the same man scooping up a young boy and dashing out of camera range. For Don José, trained to remember faces from the time he shined shoes in the street and honed to perfection by all the years of his lively enterprise since, recognition was instantaneous. He went to his desk drawer and studied the picture. *Confirmado.*

Even identified, the matter of locating someone in a city of five million people would still be a daunting task. But the tail end of the film clip had shown a battered old cab pulling away, the camera zooming in on the taxi license and the boy's face grinning out the back window. It was only a matter of a few phone calls, first to a contact at the television studio to secure the vehicle's license number. The second call went to an acquaintance in the agency responsible for licensing taxis, for the driver's name and address. The last went to Miami, seeking further instructions.

At the same time Don José was watching the film clip, another viewer elsewhere in the city concluded that the world was indeed shrinking. The American had played a hunch and caught an overnight flight, catching the news at his hotel room while he waited to change planes the following day.

An ex-cop turned private investigator, he worked for an agency in Houston, innocuously named Pathfinders as a cover for the nature of the highly secretive and exotic work they normally engaged in. His legal name was Jefferson Dalton, but as his specialty was ferreting out corporate embezzlers and industrial spies, he often went by other names for long periods of time. His involvement in the routine tracking case he was currently working on was as coincidental as the airing of the film clip he had just watched on his hotel television. He never would have even known Juan Rodrigues Ordaz were it not for his strange relationship with a crusty old man named Gene McFarland, the father of Weeto's ex-wife and thus Chico's grandfather.

As the startled faces of father and son leaped from the screen in the Bogotá Hilton his recognition was instantaneous. When the shot of the old taxi came into view he was ready for it, committing the license number to memory before it faded into the face of the commentator.

For a few seconds he sat back in his chair, weighing duty and conscience against his own self-interest. The case was closed, wasn't it? A routine tracking job when McFarland first requested his help, it was sent out to California, Oregon and Washington firms when the trail led in that direction. Enforcement agencies would help in state, but once they fled across state lines it became a game with new rules. The police avoided involvement in long-distance parental fights over children. Once traced and located, someone would have to snatch the child away from the father and get him back to his mother.

It was a sense of debt that had prompted him to get himself assigned to the case when the pair turned up in Chicago. Afterwards he blamed the weather: it was so cold and snowbound the city was nearly shut down. Unless he waited a week for warmer weather and factories and schools to reopen, he had to abandon plans for taking the boy at his day-care center. Instead the element of surprise was turned on him; the man and his son already gone when he reached the deserted apartment.

Returning to Texas empty-handed, he flew first to Abilene, then made the long drive out to Forty Acres to report his failure in person. McFarland had brought in his first wildcat well there fifty-some years earlier and still lived on the property. It was Dalton's first time in the house and the first he'd seen of McFarland in years. The house's interior was like the outside, big and sprawling but otherwise lacking in pretentiousness, its furnishings dusty with neglect. McFarland, who had always seemed old even when he was young, looked quite old now and had taken on the same faded look of his surroundings. In his mid-seventies now, repeated attacks of gout had him on a restricted diet and the arthritis crippling his joints had left him permanently stooped and gnarled, cramping his spirit even more than his frame.

"Alice Gene's dead, Dalton," McFarland growled before Dalton could launch into his report. "I got word of it this morning."

Dalton began to express sympathy, but the old man waved away his condolences. He asked McFarland if that meant they should close their file on the case.

"On the contrary, I want you to work harder than ever to find them." His eyes glowed faintly with inner resolve. "The boy's come into a small inheritance from his mother's estate. He and that Portareekin father of his ought to be told of it, don't you think?"

"Yessir," Dalton agreed. "If only to let them know they can stop running." A certain respect for the man they were chasing was already in the reports of those who had preceded him. It had wormed its way into the detective's own feelings even while he was being outwitted in Chicago.

"I'm glad you didn't catch him for her," McFarland said, taking him by surprise. "She was hardly a fit daughter, much less a good mother."

His eyes drifted, as if looking beyond his physical surroundings. "A man that determined about his boy can't be all bad, can he?"

"No sir." He might have cited additional qualities but the old man's reputation for not being conned remained even in what appeared to be his last days. Rumors had it he took heroin regularly to block the pain.

"One thing I won't tolerate, howsomeever, is foreign ways." His eyes focused on Dalton, reflecting codes too embedded ever to be eradicated, like brands on cattle hides. "If anything comes from me, the boy's got to be raised here where the McFarlands have been since the time of the Alamo. If he takes that boy out of the country and turns him into some kinda Spic-speaking hoodlum, I won't ever care to see either of them. They can stay down there in Portareeka or whatever and keep that palaver to theirselves. Forty Acres has always been true blue Texas, one hundred percent American. I won't have spics or wetbacks taking it over, whether they claim a bloodline or not."

He shook one bony finger to emphasize his point. "I'd rather my money went to the state than fall into the hands of foreigners. You find he's fled the country, taken the boy to Portareeka or wherever, and you can stop the chase right there. They're on their own. That clearly understood, Dalton?"

"Yessir." At the time it struck Dalton as an unusually harsh and ludicrous sentence. Perhaps confusion caused by the dope. Nothing indicated the runaways had any thought of fleeing the country, nor did they possess the means for doing so without taking on the burdens of living and working as illegals in a foreign land.

But when Dalton reported they were presumed to have gone off in a stolen boat, probably headed for the Caribbean or South America, the reaction was instant and crystal clear.

"That's it then, Dalton, close the case. He's made his choice for the two of them. Let the sins of the father be visited on the son as the good book says. He thinks he can find a better life among foreigners, let him go try. Let him see how well they treat wetbacks down there!"

An absurd piece of logic, and politely as he could Dalton tried to point it out. "Sir, we hardly left them a choice."

"Choice, Dalton?" The glazed eyes suddenly blazed with fervor. "Who's talking choice? Destiny is what it's all about, the timing of place and opportunity. It's why an old skunk like me is worth millions while millions of other harder-working folks have got nothing. Destiny brought me those wells, just as it made you a cop and got you embroiled in the politics I rescued you from. The same way it decided I wasn't to have a son, only a wastrel spend-thrift daughter!"

He massaged the gnarled knuckles of his hands like a wizened old shaman probing for auguries. "Now destiny is telling me I'm to have no blood heir—"

Remembering the shock and fear in the faces of the father and son on the screen, Dalton wondered about his options. He was developing a growing respect bordering on admiration for the determined Latin who had twice eluded the traps set for him. It seemed a cruelty far worse than a crime to let him go on thinking he was still a fugitive.

Quickly dialing before he could change his mind, he made three calls before he found the dispatcher who controlled the cab he wanted. Señor Eduardo, he was told, went off duty at six o'clock. Could they send another? No, only he would do, his favorite driver whenever he was in town. If he could be reached at home and persuaded to pick up a fare, there would be a reward for the dispatcher and an even bigger bonus for the driver.

The droning voice on the other end suddenly changed pitch. *"Sí, sí, señor, a sus órdenes!"*

As he climbed into the taxi, Dalton's first question brought out the driver's testy side.

"Funny you should ask if I speak English. Matter of fact, I do." Eduardo's craftiness was evident in his voice. "Mind telling me what's this all about? I've never had you for a fare before, have I now?"

Dalton liked the patrician old man with the stand-up manners of a grandee. What he was doing there, driving an old hack in his grizzled years, was an oddity he preferred unelucidated. He answered with another question, "Are you always so sure about repeat customers?"

"Never forget a face, not when he's a big tipper." He turned in his seat. "You've dragged me away from my board and bed at a most uncivilized time of night. I don't suppose it's to take you on a sightseeing tour of the city. It's too early for nightclubbing. Besides, this is a city of bureaucrats and academics who don't much go in for nightlife anyway."

Dalton smiled and studied the old cabbie's eyes. "I noticed you're missing part of your rear bumper."

"Ah-ha, so that's it! Something to do with this afternoon's little road race. You're an American newsman looking for that lovely girl everyone's been chasing all day!"

"Something like that." Dalton was enjoying the fencing. "Only it's the man and boy I'm after. I have good news for them."

Eduardo's eyebrows arched. "Good news?"

"Yes, his wife died and he doesn't know it yet."

The puzzled expression on the cabbie's face faded into amusement. "Ah yes, that sometimes is good news, isn't it?"

"Very good in this case." He found himself imitating the older man's voice and guile. He didn't have to give a lengthy explanation. Four tens, extended fanwise so the numbers showed, were inducement enough. Impoverished grandees had the same weaknesses as most taxi drivers.

Dalton hadn't decided how much he was going to tell the fugitives. The impulse to act stemmed from his need to let them know they could stop running. Nothing more. But as they drove along the broad carrera in the flickering drizzle, his options steadily dwindled to nothing less than the whole and unqualified truth. If he turned away from recognizing the full rights of the runaways, he was worse than the aristocratic old gentleman chattering next to him. Forty dollars bought his soul. An impulse to deny is no less than to take. A *mordida* is a bite, is a bribe, is a theft, his conscience persisted. Even a senile old millionaire with one foot in the grave deserved some final piece of loyalty.

When Weeto responded to the knock on the door by asking who was there, Eduardo replied. Weeto opened the door a crack, the security chain still in place. When he saw it was the old cabbie, he hurriedly undid the chain. Instantly, the door burst open. Before he could react, the big Anglo had him locked in a bear hug and was making him listen to a lot of nonsense too good to be true. He immediately recognized the blond hair, moon face and bull neck as belonging to one of the phantoms from his past.

"Come on, you tellin' me she's dead?" he said skeptically as the big arms relaxed their hold on him. Middle-aged or not, he was strong as an ox, and Weeto wondered if in a showdown he could outmuscle him.

"A year already, right after you gave us the slip in Chicago. Your father-in-law or rather your ex-father-in-law, hired me to find—"

"He's dead too?" Weeto didn't believe that anymore than he believed Alice Gene was dead. It was a trick to get him to go back voluntarily so they could grab him without a lot of international red tape.

"No, he's still alive. At least he was two weeks ago when I last spoke to him. He'd like to see his grandson before he dies."

"I bet. Like I bet you're not with the FBI."

"Ever since the Lindberghs," the big man laughed, opening his wallet and thumbing through plastic windows to display his credentials, "people think the FBI comes in whenever a state line is crossed. Not so. There's no federal statute covering parental custody. The FBI isn't the least bit interested in you. I'm sorry if you thought they were."

Chico appeared in the bedroom doorway just then in his jockey shorts. Spotting the taxi driver, he pointed and squealed. *"El chofer, el chofer!"*

"No, no, monkey, back to bed you go!" Scooping him up, Weeto carried him into the other room. He glanced past the beds to the double windows. They looked like they couldn't be budged without a crowbar. As if his thoughts were being read, the Anglo stood in the doorway when he turned around.

"Juan, Weeto—what should I call you?" Dalton asked quietly. "Believe me, nobody's chasing you anymore. She's dead. We've been trying to find you to tell you."

"Who's dead, Poppi?" the boy's voice called after Weeto as he turned off the light and started to close the door.

"Jus' somebody I used to know. Go to sleep now, Chico."

"Myself and a local P.I. were hired to find you," Dalton explained a few moments later. There was something sincere and reassuring in the big man's manner. They sat down at the modest kitchen table. "We didn't do so hot, did we? That was the second time you left me red-faced and frustrated."

Who were the tails in Cartagena then, Weeto wondered, if they weren't private eyes or the FBI? Dalton could only suggest they were figments of his suspicion—street thugs or money-changers sizing him up for a touch or a take.

Weeto got up and brought bottles of beer from the small refrigerator in the alcove. It was a locally brewed beverage called Bavaria. "Maybe not so good as Dos Equis," he said, expecting the Texan would know the popular Mexican brand. "But not bad."

"It's good," Dalton agreed after tasting it. Then he began explaining what had happened, going back to his first encounter with Gene McFarland on the highway outside Abilene. He included some of his own impressions of Alice Gene and indicated how in the end the old man saw her as undeserving of the child and wanted only to keep tabs on the whereabouts of his grandson. Coming to the part where he had to explain McFarland's reaction to their flight out of Florida, he hesitated.

"You don' have to esplain," Weeto interrupted. "I know what you mean. He don' want no spics in the family."

Eduardo snorted in disgust. "Sounds like any bloody good Englishman back in the days of empire. School ties and proper blood lines, no tolerance for inferior breeds infiltrating good family trees. Not at all like you Americans, I shouldn't think."

Dalton smiled, reminding him he didn't know all Americans if he'd never been along the Tex-Mex border. He looked back at Weeto. "You have to understand he's a very sick man, in pain much of the time or so doped up with painkillers he doesn't much know what he's saying." If a shred of sympathy could be salvaged for the dying man, why should either side be deprived of its grace?

Weeto was only just beginning to realize the import of their good fortune. He felt a pang of disdain at mention of the small estate—$18,000—left by Alice Gene to Chico. But now Dalton was talking about something big coming from the father's estate if he could get over his hang-ups about "spic" blood and foreign ways. "How much?" Weeto asked. "A couple hundred thousand?"

"Oh my, yes!" the big guy chuckled. "I'd say a hundred times that or more."

As he started enumerating some of the more obvious assets, Eduardo's eyes widened in astonishment. Figures on wealthy Americans were positively disconcerting at times—they sounded more like the gross national products of many small countries. Weeto listened halfheartedly, not yet willing to let go of his first sensations of freedom for fear it would suddenly vanish.

"You know I'm here illegally," he said, then glanced inquiringly at Eduardo. "We din esactly come through the front door."

"Good heavens, don't look at me," Eduardo admonished. "It's no skin off me. If I had my way, there wouldn't be any borders."

"I guessed as much," Dalton grinned at Weeto. "Your Cuban friends tried to be helpful once they understood my true purpose—"

"You know about the boat then, the one we were supposed to scuttle...?"

Dalton allowed his eyes to wander toward the ceiling at this new and unanticipated piece of information. Still, there might be a way out of that, too.

"There's nothing to prevent others coming along after a botched scuttling job and claiming it for salvage," he advised, tongue in cheek. "Could you go back the same way you came?"

"Maybe. I have to talk to my friends on the boat first." He sipped his beer. "You saying I shouldn't go back through normal channels. We could get into trouble."

Dalton tried to guess the old man's true intentions and couldn't. If Weeto returned trailing proof they left the country, if only for a few weeks and for urgent reasons, would it matter? Impossible to think McFarland could hold to his fanatical notions of what was true-blue Tex-American and what was beyond the pale.

"Your in-law can be a very determined man," Dalton cautioned. "A stickler for details when he wants answers. Yes, I'd say you're taking a chance on a plane out of here, not to mention what Colombian authorities might do if they found out you entered illegally."

"And get my friends in trouble too, eh?" Weeto mused aloud. "Okay, I get the picture." Eduardo supplied the name of the hotel where Benjie and Dynamite were staying. They tried reaching them by phone only to learn they had already checked out.

It was decided they would go overland back to Cartagena and Eduardo would take them by taxi rather than risk plane or bus transportation where officials might get picky about their faked identification papers. Once safely back in Florida, Weeto would contact Dalton and "allow" himself to be found.

"Good luck," the big Texan said, looking suddenly tired when they shook hands.

"You awready brought it," said Weeto, squeezing his hand. Then he winked to Eduardo. "*La cara del santo hace milagros,* eh?"

"*Claro,* truly!" Eduardo sighed.

As Dalton left, a high-pitched voice called from the bedroom. "*Que pasa,* Poppi?"

"*Milagros!*" Eduardo shouted at the boy and they all laughed.

Chapter Sixteen

The following morning, postponing a planned trip to one of his flower farms to await the arrival of the Americans, Don José received word shortly after nine that they were checked into the Hilton and ready to begin work. Learning from the dispatcher that the driver Camargo had phoned in sick that morning, they circled the block of weathered old apartment buildings where he lived. Seeing no sign of the taxi in the courtyard or in the surrounding streets, Don José sent his assistant to check with the landlord.

He knew nothing, he said, prefacing his remarks with the usual Bogotano disclaimer. He had seen, or rather heard Señor Camargo drive off in the morning—the car was in need of a new muffler and made a lot of noise.

"When was that?"

"Oh, not much after seven," he recollected. "I was having my first *tinto* and reading the newspaper when I heard him go off. Surprised me, I can tell you, because he's never about before eight. A true Renaissance man with a wide range of interests. Speaks flawless Castillian and just as fluent in English, French and German, I'm told."

The short fat landlord was a retired history professor who

easily became loquacious when he had an attentive ear. "Perhaps that funny thing on the news last night had something to do with his early morning departure. He went out last night also at an odd hour, before I had a chance to congratulate him on his car's fine perform-ance on television. I was waiting for him to finish dinner. He always dines promptly at seven-thirty and resents any intrusion before eight, so I waited. Then, to my surprise, I heard him speeding off right in the middle of his dinner!"

"You heard him return?" the assistant interrupted, glancing impatiently at his watch.

"No, strange—I didn't," the landlord wondered aloud. "Odd, yes. I was reading Cicero's *Orations* and perhaps I fell asleep. Obviously he returned, otherwise I wouldn't have heard him go off again in the morning, would I? Are you from the newspaper? Ah, I thought so! Still trying to catch that North American film star? Is she so famous? I never heard of her before but then they're all— yes, well, you're most welcome. I'll get your card to Señor Camargo when he returns."

The Americans fumed as Don José translated the assistant's conversation with the landlord. An odd, mismatched pair to Don José's trained eye. The younger man, in his late twenties, was modishly dressed in the newest Miami fashions—pinstriped beige suite with wide lapels, tie and vest, matching two-tone tan and brown shoes. He had an intolerable habit of cracking his knuckles when he was nervous. For a big man, powerful-looking through the chest and arms, he was surprisingly fidgety. He was called Vincent, not Vince or Vinnie as he pointed out in introductions, and his self-centered air created instant barriers. He was the muscle for the pair, Don José concluded and guessed that he probably worked with his bare hands.

The older man, Harry, was obviously in charge. As laconic and undemonstrative as the other was nervous and excitable, he had the glazed look of a haggard traveler. Fortyish and balding, with a ragged fringe of gray hair, he had a face as emotionless as a death mask. Except for the eyes. Faded gray-blue in color, they were quite alive behind the heavy-lidded sleepy gaze he showed the world. His rumpled dark suit looked like he had worn it on the plane. The impression he generated was so average and ordinary, he could well have passed for one of Don José's florists from Denver or Des Moines arranging purchase of a shipment of orchids.

"Shit! Damn it all to hell!" Vincent exploded on hearing his quarry was out of reach. He slapped the steering column so hard the passengers felt the vibrations. "Where's our luck, Harry? Even these fucking Mexican wetbacks give us the slip!"

He was an import from Phoenix, Don José learned later, to whom everyone south of the border all the way to Tierra del Fuego were lumped together as Mexicans or, pejoratively, wetbacks. He had another annoying Americanism, an arrogance in saying whatever he pleased in a foreign land, even among natives who understood English.

Unperturbed by his partner's raving, Harry turned a tired look into the back seat and asked sleepily, "Any suggestions, José?"

Another annoying indiscretion, the American habit of calling strangers by their first names from the moment of introduction. He could accept it in the States, where it seemed suited for the pace of American business and society. But in the setting of older, more traditional cultures and structured ways, it was an effrontery bordering on insolence. For one who had risen from the lowest ranks by determined effort, a respectful prefix had nearly as much meaning as money. No one, not even his wife in the privacy of their bedchamber, called him by his first name only.

"It's not so hopeless as all that, is it?" He pointed his question at the fuming fashion plate behind the wheel. "We've established his pattern. Home at night at six, dines promptly at seven-thirty. Probably he's been hired again by that actress woman for the day. Is it so urgent you can't wait until evening?"

"Like it shoulda been done yesterday or last week!" Vincent flared, flexing his hands and cracking his knuckles again. "Yes, damn it, it's that important!"

The excessive reaction revealed more than just the violent nature of his undisciplined guest. Even the matter of locating the taxi driver wasn't to be entrusted to anyone outside their ring. He considered keeping them under surveillance all night, to ensure they didn't leave or simply wander off without him knowing. Their impatience pointed to something so extraordinarily important that they didn't want anyone, not even a trusted ally like Don José, to discover their secret.

Earlier he gave the Americans a summary of the television show which provided the lead to the taxi driver. Harry now asked if there was any way of locating the actress Camargo was connected to.

"Apparently only the taxi driver knows that too." He could say it with certainty, since he took the liberty of phoning his contact at the television studio earlier that morning, only to learn the girl's whereabouts were still a mystery. He had reasons of his own for wanting to know the connection between the actress and the man and boy Miami wanted so desperately. He wondered if they had any connection with the tall hairy savage he dealt with on the mountaintop—that *nadista*, as they used to call them before everybody started calling them hippies.

"Could we just drive around town and hope to run into that oddball taxi?" Harry wondered aloud in his monotone voice.

"Be my guest. Only remember, it's a city of nearly five million people and it sprawls like Los Angeles." Don José stared out the window impassively. "I could have my dispatcher alert all the taxis in town to be on the lookout for him, but are you sure you want that kind of general alarm sounded?"

"No, no," Harry said quickly. "We want no more attention on him than we do on us."

By the following morning, with no indication that the taxi or its driver were still even in the city, the impatient Vincent was acting as if someone had conjured up the disappearance as a personal affront to him. The knuckle-cracking took on the ceaseless rhythm of a newly caged animal. Don José had arranged for an around-the-clock stakeout of Camargo's apartment house, not so much to spare the Americans and allow them their sleep as to ensure they didn't blunder and cause a scandal, which could reflect back on him. Neither of the idiots spoke a word of Spanish. How did they plan on communicating with Camargo? He knew from his dispatcher and his assistant's talk with the landlord that he was fluent in English, but they didn't know that. The world of business might revolve around the English language, which is why he had honed and polished his from the time he was on the streets, but this was Colombia. American laziness in languages would eventually be their undoing as world traders, he often thought. In the interim, it might provide him some insight to the secret they guarded so carefully.

Though only one of a number of growers and processors of marijuana in the country, Don José was certainly one of the biggest, with an ambition to become even bigger. By Colombian standards he was doing exceptionally well, but measured against the Americans who were dependent on him for products they merely resold, his income was only a fraction of the end price. The middlemen, as always, were gobbling up the lion's share.

For some time he'd speculated on possibilities for setting up his own operation in the United States. Nothing openly controlled, that could bring trouble from those already operating there. Besides, he was already the principal supplier for some of them. But new organizations were a sign of the changing times and his recent trips to Miami were in part scouting missions for his larger ambitions. Properly fronted by local lieutenants, he might then claim his fair share of the profits and, as he was fond of seeing himself as a risk-taking entrepreneur, enhance competition in the marketplace.

He thought the time had come and opportunity was ripe. With recent seizures in the U.S. and crackdowns in Mexico and Colombia, with supply lines reduced to a trickle and existing supplies in the U.S. dwindling, if he got his "message" through to his man in Miami they could launch a new operation that would be a sweeping coup. It amused him to imagine the surprised look on the face of his new American partner when that shaggy dog, the *nadista*, turned out to be the delivery boy.

He sent his assistant back to Camargo's landlord for a more detailed interview. More background was needed, where his family lived, his hobbies and interests. Were there friends or relatives outside the city whom he might be visiting? But all the possibilities drew blanks. Camargo lost his parents in the period of the Violencia following the assassination of Gaitan in 1948. An only child, there were no siblings. There were cousins living in the department of Antioquia, outside Medellín, but they never visited each other. Political differences made them social enemies.

"Señor Camargo is an Anglophile and a Conservative," the landlord explained with the delicate precision of a historian. "His cousins are on the political left, supporters of the Linea Dura. No, no, from what he said to me a number of times, it's quite out of the question he would have gone to visit his Antioqueño relations. As for distant friends—too many to count, but mostly abroad in England, France and the United States. Many friends here in Bogotá, of course, but he would hardly have gone overnight. Not with his apartment close by and all the things he loves. Like a Renaissance museum, his room is full of collectibles he brought from his travels abroad—astrolabes and perpetual motion machines, miniature replicas of Bleriot's airplane, copies of Da Vinci's drawings of—"

"And lady friends?" the interviewer interjected. "Were they ever much in his life?"

"Oh my, yes! Still are, you know. Can you believe it?" he tittered, blushing with lascivious delight. "Passes them off as nieces of old friends or students of his professor acquaintances. Friends, mind you! Just what an old roué would say. Yes, yes, of course I'll tell him how anxious you are to talk to him. I still have your card with the number."

For three days they waited for the return of the taxi driver. Long distance calls went back and forth to Miami and Don José's watchdogs kept twenty-four hour surveillance on the apartment building. It was as if he had vanished and the cab with him. The same was true of the actress woman, as his studio contact kept reporting. If she went out by plane, they would certainly have spotted her at the major airports. But what was so frustrating to the Americans, enraging to Vincent whose knuckles were popping like castanets, was to Don José's Machiavellian mind an intricate puzzle he delighted in deciphering.

Toward dusk on the third day, when even the jovial landlord was beginning to worry, the old taxi came rattling down the street and rolled to a stop in the courtyard. The driver, nearly as dusty as the car from his sixteen-hundred-mile round trip, emerged in leather helmet and goggles, a white silk scarf loosely knotted about his neck. He smiled absently at the landlord's importuning and accepted with indifference his show of concern as the card was pressed into his hand.

His happy mood of fatigue was still with him as he undressed and climbed into his steaming bath. The Puerto Rican had been more than generous. A holiday from fear and his anticipation of the fortune he might be coming into made him reckless with his money. He forced a thousand dollars on Eduardo and declared him the other half of his lucky charm, the face of the saint they'd all been joking about.

He wasn't often so praised. More often he was the object of contempt from those who knew his family background—all over a label which, in truth, never had meaning for him nor ever warranted his allegiance. It was as if society denied the validity of being truly liberated. Free spirits whose allegiance was planetary, to the race of man rather than cults, tribes or nations, were consigned to a limbo of indifference, if not open hostility.

He was still soaking in his tub when the Americans and the assistant rapped at his door. Half dozing, he didn't hear them at first. When a number of knocks brought no response, Vincent put his weight to the door, splintering the frame as he smashed it open.

They found the old taxi driver sitting erect in the tub, his head resting against the tiled wall. The startled expression on his face was that of a gentleman caught in flagrante delicto. His heart had stopped.

Had he known he was being chased, he might have gone out with a smile on his face. He had slipped across borders and through political and religious nooses so often just in the nick of time, his checkered life had the quality of a road race—and the luck of never having been caught. Even dying, he managed to stay a step out of reach.

The enraged big fellow, unwilling to be so cheated, grabbed the body by the throat and lifted it out of the tub. He shook it like a rag doll, as if he intended to force it back to life. Harry restrained him finally and put him to work searching the apartment while he went through the pockets of the discarded clothes on the chair. He found the thousand dollars in U.S. currency and the emerald in the tissue packet, but could find no stubs, tickets or receipts—nothing to indicate where he'd been.

When the landlord came running to investigate the noise, his opening salvo of shock at the sight of the dead body sprawled alongside the tub quickly turned to unbridled terror. A powerful hand had seized him by the throat and was shaking him for answers.

"He only said he went for a swim!" he shrilled, choking his answer past the vise on his windpipe. "That's all he said. He seemed quite happy—"

"Where did he go for the swim?" Harry's question was promptly translated by the assistant. Then the reply came back in English.

"He doesn't know. Camargo never said."

"And the fucker never bothered to ask!" Vincent's rage went out of control again. While he was shaking the landlord with one hand, his other hand walloped the wall with such force lamps went crashing to the floor. The landlord's face blanched white as the bathtub.

"That was his way," he rasped. "He often spoke in riddles. A tricky and devious type, I needn't tell you." He spoke quickly and passionately, certain his sincerity would shine through to the Americans even if they didn't understand his words. "Slippery and underhanded, one could say. True to his origins, if I may say so. He was here only out of Christian charity, understand. I felt sorry for the man, doomed like his race to wander the earth for eternity."

He pointed a twitching finger at the naked body on the floor. "As you see, if you need proof, the man was a Jew!"

A search of the dusty taxi in the courtyard yielded no further clues about the journey. Only when they rejoined Don José and he heard their story were they given a trail to follow again. The three-day absence and the U.S. currency pointed to a long trip with American fares, going overland the hard way to avoid notice or detection. The driver's sly joke about "going for a swim" meant they drove to the sea, probably the north coast—Santa Marta, Barranquilla, or Cartagena. The emerald was an additional clue which, however, he didn't share with the Americans.

All the same, time was running out. Even if the taxi driver had lived to bend to the physical persuasion of the muscle man and revealed his passengers' identities and destination, the trail would rapidly vanish at sea. At that very hour, in the anchorage off the Club de Pesca in Cartagena harbor, the white sloop *Gorda* was hauling anchor to use the remaining daylight to thread her way along the winding channel which led to the Boca Chica opening to the sea. She was on her way to a rendezvous off the fjords above Santa Marta.

Chapter Seventeen

Aboard the *Gorda*, Benjie's preparations for departure underwent some novel twists and mounting tension. Almost all the rest of their money went off with Josh the day of their return to finalize the marijuana purchase, though he wondered what guaranteed delivery once the cash was handed over. Rounding up his carpenters, he finished the taffrail by noon the next day and was starting the varnishing when the taxi driver appeared on the dock with Weeto and Chico. When Weeto offered all the money he had left for passage back to the States, or the Bahamas if Benjie feared entering U.S. waters, he felt obliged to reveal what they were up to.

Weeto's disapproval was so direct and caustic, Benjie was all set to call it all off until Josh returned the day after with a sealed deal and an operation already in motion. His reservations were cut short by Josh's warning they could be in far worse trouble than merely losing their money if they backed out now. Collateral pledges would have to be redeemed, one way or another.

Adding to the tension was the matter of a stolen sail and the arrest of a Colombian merchant acting as a fence, events occurring in their absence which culminated in a flurry of police activity on the docks when they returned. The story, as told by others, involved an American skipper who went looking to replace a sail stolen from his boat weeks earlier. A merchant in town offered him one for a thousand dollars which turned out to be his very own, with his sailmaker's name still stitched in a corner. Arranging for the sail to be delivered to the dock, the American brought in the police and had the man arrested when he arrived.

On the pretext of providing protection and preventing further thievery, police and DAS men were maintaining twenty-four-hour watches of the area. Two young Americans were arrested on marijuana charges the first day. In their zeal, agents boarded vessels without permission. Some testy skippers got into big trouble when they asserted the age-old sea captain's right to order them off. One had his boat seized and his crew arrested. A matchbox of coke was allegedly found aboard. The story claimed they were innocent, the cocaine planted by the agents. The Americans made trouble for a prominent local citizen—time to give them a dose of their own. Whether in this instance the young skipper and crew were innocent or not, it pointed to how easy it was to victimize anyone you had it in for.

Rumor had it the Colombians did it mainly for the shake-downs, threatening arrest unless they were appropriately paid off. Josh scoffed at such chauvinism, claiming the same thing was happening in the U.S. Entrapments, set-ups or stings by agents and vice detectives designed to shake down their victims or merely enhance their arrest records, were a problem in many countries.

"There's more of that goes on than the moral squares wanna believe," Josh snorted in disgust. "When the head of the DEA admits his biggest problem is keeping his agents honest among all those windfall profits, you know there's beaucoup shit going on!"

"How about the kids in Mexican jails?" Dyna reminded him. Hundreds of young Americans, innocent of wrongdoing, were rotting in Mexican holding tanks as victims of dragnets aimed at pleasing its powerful neighbor to the north who was constantly pressing for action. They provided statistics for the politicians on both sides of the border.

Anchored out, the *Gorda's* crew escaped most of the hassle. Still they worried about what could happen if they vexed the wrong official and he decided to make trouble. American fanaticism over drug traffic had reached out to people and governments across the world. Suddenly awakened to opportunities afforded by harsh sanctions, they soon learned to use them in their bag of tricks to put the bite on visiting foreigners.

The illegal activities aboard the *Gorda* heightened their unease. And Josh's hints of what could happen if they tried to back out added to Benjie's sense of entrapment. For one who avoided confrontation even as a kid, the underworld threat hung over him like a malevolent specter, more terrifying than the official threats of any government.

Now at dusk, as they nosed through the narrow Boca Chica opening and plunged into the chop of open waters, relief surged with the thought of putting aside at least one set of dangers. They hadn't been arrested or waylaid by any official traps or squeezes. What was still waiting at the fjords was like the fortune riding on a successful run to Florida—a fate on the horizon too distant to warrant his attention.

Somehow they lucked out on weather. The intensified trades of the past week had tapered to a comfortable fifteen knots as they headed out. The current, less hurried by the wind, wasn't so forceful. Waves didn't climb aboard, keeping them doused in the cockpit. A decent dry passage might be in store for them.

"Good sign, eh?" Dyna commented, taking first turn at the wheel.

"Don't count on it. It's a fluke getting it so smooth this time of year." Benjie sounded grumpier than he felt. Getting out to sea again was like a tonic, but he wasn't ready to let her off the hook yet for her changed behavior since Bogotá.

"Why so pessimistic? We could have had yesterday's winds," she chided. "What's our plan for taking the Magdalena?"

"Early morning, close in." From his charts, Benjie knew there were two favored ways of crossing the river mouth. Close in, at its narrowest point with "one foot on the beach," and gunning the engine to get across in half an hour or so. The other was going way out, twenty or thirty miles offshore, in a wide detour to avoid its strong crosscurrents and floating debris. Anything in between would punish boat and crew alike. Time dictated taking it close in for the passage to the Santa Marta fjords; comfort required doing it in the calmer morning hours before the easterlies gathered strength and set the sea and river currents to fighting. He timed it for an all-night sail, following the coast a few miles off, arriving at the river's mouth off Barranquilla at dawn.

"Early birds not wishing to catch the worm—or the overturn?" Dyna punned, grinning. Benjie saw the sea was working its magic on her as well. He started to make his own amends, but Josh came stomping up the ladder with a peevish complaint.

"What's with that Weeto," he whined. "Every time he gets me in a corner, he lectures me on the evils of my habit. You'd think he was over fifty and had never seen the scene before." He took a drag from his joint and offered it to Benjie.

"Nope. No dope, not tonight." They'd be close to shore all night, and there were dangers he needed to stay alert to.

"It's the kid," said Dyna. "He'd rather Chico wasn't exposed to the stuff, and I can understand that."

"Balls! Think my old man hid his cigarette habit from me when I was that age?" Gingerly he fingered his left earlobe, which he had pierced a few days earlier. The delicate gold earring that hung down glinted in the sunlight. With shaved head and a bristling beard he looked more than ever like one of Captain Morgan's crew.

"Well, he's got a point," Dyna argued.

Josh laughed. "What's he gonna do tomorrow night this time, with a hundred bales of the stuff on board? Pretend it's hay we're carrying to the Hialeah racetrack?"

"Well, why not? Or if not that, why not say it's tobacco?"

"I'm not out to scandalize kids, but on the other hand I don't see giving up my pleasures just to satisfy a daddy's whims. If he's so concerned about setting bad examples, why doesn't he give up his cigarette smoking?"

"Now there's a really bad habit, compulsively nasty," Dyna declared in a schoolmarm's mocking tone.

"Filthy," Josh bellowed, encouraged. "Ruins lungs, attacks the heart and the circulatory system, causes emphysema and cancer. Yet the dumb shits go on puffing. Nicotine's as bad as heroin. And just as hard to kick the habit once you're hooked."

"How about alcohol?" Dynamite added, her voice crescendoing. "Attacks the liver and kidneys, cooks the brain and causes more damage and ruined lives than all the other bad habits combined. And that's like okay, at least it's legal."

"And the government thinks we're idiots who have to be protected from the perils of grass."

"You two sound like partners on a debating team," Benjie observed. "Who're you trying to convince?"

"A word to your friend wouldn't hurt," Josh suggested. "At least you can talk to him. He thinks I'm a smackhead, an acid freak or something. Just because I smoke a little pot and he heard me say I dropped acid a few times."

"And sampled all the rest too, if I know you," Benjie concluded.

"Who hasn't, kiddo, if he's been to where it's happening for the past twenty years? Sure, I've tried nearly everything at least once, even horse. And I'll bet there's damn few you haven't tried somewhere along the line too."

"I missed horse and a few other things, and I plan to go on missing them," Benjie stated bluntly.

"So what's Weeto got against grass?" Josh repeated just as Weeto's head popped up out of the hatch.

"What I got against grass," he answered, glaring at Josh as he plopped himself on the seat directly across from him, "is that it leads to all that other crazy stuff."

"Oh man, that makes as much sense as blaming alcoholism on a kid's first cigarette. Oranges and horseapples." Josh had lost his cool.

"I seen too many crazies growin' up in New York. Guys who did nothing but scrounge and steal for only one thing."

"Right, crazies! Freak-outs! Crazies naturally, whether they're on something or not. Bad homes, bad schools, bad genes! Crowded tenements and ghettos breed crazies like rats in a cheese cellar!"

"No, I mean crazy on drugs! On pills and powders!"

"Don't leave out booze!" retorted Josh.

"Yeah but that don't kill them like drugs!"

"Oh man, check any Skid Row. Check the morgues!"

The argument continued at length, each side defending its own evil and attacking the other. In the end nobody won. Benjie suspected the same thing applied to drugs—nobody ever won.

Just before dawn the lights of Barranquilla came into view. Dropping some sail they glided along silently, waiting for the morning light to read the water and inch closer to shore for the river crossing.

When they crossed around seven in the morning, the muddy brown stream was almost a disappointment, relatively free of debris. They saw no floating logs or trees and were safely across in fifteen minutes. In another month, with the advent of spring rains, it could be a different story. Now the only thing that concerned them was the gray-hulled vessel Benjie spotted anchored in the harbor off the town docks.

"Navy or Coast Guard?" Josh asked as Benjie studied it through his binoculars.

"Official, anyway. U.S. surplus now serving Colombian interests."

At present, Benjie felt no great concern about being stopped by a Colombian gunboat. Their *zarpe*, required of all departing vessels, showed a destination of Aruba with "ports intermediate." This allowed stops at harbors and anchorages along the coast as weather and other conditions such as equipment failures, resupplying or crew fatigue might require. Sailing to Aruba from Cartagena was normally a terrible beat against wind and current. Not many sailboats made it. More often they finally gave up, even if they weren't severely damaged, and headed north for Jamaica and an island-hopping circle of Caribbean islands that eventually trickled down to Aruba.

The coast between Santa Marta and the tip of the Guajira Peninsula was inhospitable, wild and uninhabited but for a few Indian tribes. Still, it offered shelter from storms and a chance to rest and cook a hot meal. That it was also notorious for smuggling and piracy was a proven fact among visiting yachtsmen. Few yachts put in for refuge if they could avoid it. Too many vessels and crews were rumored to have vanished in these waters, never to be seen again. Piracy of the old-fashioned sort, that was to say boarding and killing the crew, stripping the boat of valuables and then sinking it, survived and flourished.

The *zarpe* was usually enough to satisfy the curiosity of boarding officials. But if they asked for boat papers, he had only a photocopy of the license. Josh had turned the original over to Sergio as collateral for another stash of emeralds he was holding in trust. Still skeptical about how he duped the jeweler with worthless paper, Benjie pressed for an answer again.

"You have to get inside the man's head," Josh said with exasperation. "Whatta you wanna bet he tries to hold me up when I fly back down to pay him off and redeem the papers? He thinks he's got us by the short hairs and we'll pay *mucho mas* to get them back."

"Are we coming back to pay off obligations?" Dyna asked innocently.

"Better believe it, momma!" Josh howled, his eyes widening incredulously. "We don't go back on our word, not when somebody will come looking for our heads if we cross them."

"What was the other thing you were going to use for security if you couldn't sell him on the boat papers?" Benjie asked.

Josh pawed a foot on the floorboard grates, hesitant. "Well, I didn't have to use it...so what's it matter?"

"I'd like to know is all. Call it idle curiosity."

"What you don't know, etcetera, etcetera..." Josh grinned teasingly.

"Yeah, Josh," Dyna said, leaning forward, "just what was that last ace in the hole?"

Josh rocked back and forth, a nervous grin tugging at the corners of his mouth.

"A hostage, what else?" He stared pointedly at Dynamite. "You if they wouldn't take me."

A tension-filled silence hung in the air for several moments. Then Dyna began laughing and Benjie followed, and Josh knew he had survived yet another gamble.

The day turned gorgeous and the weather, which could really be *malo* along that coast in winter, turned exceptionally fine. The normal easterlies that swept the Guajira and churned it into a maelstrom on the shallow continental shelf had given way to a southerly flow promising at least twenty-four hours of good sea conditions. They could hardly have ordered a better day. Then Chico crowned it by catching a flashing dorado, which Dyna sautéed for lunch. The *Miraflores*, the vessel scheduled to meet them, took on a special comic irony when Josh learned Don José was also legitimately in the flower export business. Look-at-the-flowers. Benjie had been along the Colombian and Panamanian coasts before and seen the big planked native schooners like the *Miraflores*. Tarred at the seams and usually painted black, they could pass for those notorious ships of another century. Because of piracy rumors, pleasure yachts tried to steer clear of them. Not equipped to sail fast, they couldn't head into wind like a properly rigged yacht and were generally underpowered, relying on economical one-cylinder engines, 'one-lungers' as yachties called them, to get them where they needed to go without breaking any speed records. Still, for Mom and Pop on their first retirement cruise, the sight of one approaching over the horizon was enough to start the adrenaline flowing. Most, he knew, were engaged in the innocent business of commerce. Fishing, trading, hauling cargo. He'd seen them in the San Blas Isles off Panama buying coconuts from the Indians, and later in Cartagena selling them. Still, seeing one close up, with its crude gear and scruffy crew, didn't erase the image of what they might resort to if business got really bad.

Chico was first to spot the vessel, still barely a speck against the tall cliffs of the fjords. But a look through the glasses confirmed its identity. A long ten minutes passed, establishing it was headed their way. Anxiety mounted until they spotted the prearranged signal flying at the masthead. A white flag with black crossbars. Josh ran a matching flag to the *Gorda*'s spreaders and, dropping the sails along with their fears, they waited for her to come alongside.

She was no longer than the *Gorda*, but her bigger beam and high freeboard, built for cargo rather than speed, seemed to dwarf them. Especially in the way she lumbered up like an awkward elephant in her improperly ballasted condition. They hadn't bothered to hide the cargo below decks, it was all topside. Although it was wrapped in black plastic, anyone could see they were bales of something, and in that area, not likely to be mistaken for cotton or hay. Either they were sure about the isolated location or they had paid off the right officials.

"Hey, how about that? Right on time," Josh cried out jubilantly.

"Fantastic," Dyna echoed.

Benjie felt some of the same excitement as the black vessel rolled in a slow circle and inched alongside. The crew on deck, blacks and mestizos, waved and grinned with the camaraderie of co-conspirators. Stripped to the waist for work, in ragged pants and cutoffs, barefoot, they beamed with the pleasure of holiday cruisers. Rows of rubber tires were strung like festive wreaths along the port side. The *Gorda*'s own row of white air fenders was lowered over the side to further cushion contact. The skipper of the *Miraflores* shouted instructions.

"Poco motor, adelante!" A twirling hand motion accompanied his shout over the noise of the engine.

"He wants you to move it a little forward," Weeto translated though Benjie had understood and already engaged the gearshift. Even without any knowledge of Spanish, the hand motion communicated the meaning. Benjie did a double-take, as did Weeto, seeing the skipper was one-handed. While his good hand did the signaling, he worked the tiller with the stump of his leather-covered wrist. Forgetting his objection to the cargo coming aboard, Weeto appointed himself translator for the skipper's shouted commands. A man in the bow signaled his intention to throw a line and Josh ran forward to catch it. Again the helmsman ran a string of rapid Spanish and Weeto, in turn, yelled to Josh.

"He says don't snub his bow with that line. Leave plenty of slack." To Benjie he added, "He wants you to stay in low rev, enough just to match his forward motion."

In addition to the captain, the *Miraflores* carried a crew of seven, and as the vessels closed four of them swung across to the *Gorda*'s decks. The other three had already started raising a net of bales on the boat's cargo boom. One operated the winch while the other two prepared a net for the next lift even as the first was being deposited on the *Gorda*. The four on the *Gorda* waved away any help and went swiftly to work storing the bales below. Rectangular in shape, weighing less than forty pounds, the sisal twine around them provided handles for easy lifting and carrying. An inner burlap lining was beneath the plastic wrapping. Benjie was surprised they came so professionally packaged. One of the stevedores explained it was to keep moisture out of the product and provide buoyancy in case any landed in the water. Don José, it seemed, was every bit the professional Josh had claimed.

Working with the rhythmic skill of a team familiar with a particular task, hardly a motion was wasted and the transfer proceeded at a lively pace. The three tons purchased, the maximum Benjie thought they could safely carry, would lower them a few inches, but still not below the waterline. Purposely, he hadn't topped off the fuel or water, anticipating the buoyancy of the half-empty tanks would help offset the cargo weight.

Three tons of bulky bales nearly filled the space below decks. The entire aft cabin was crammed sole deck to ceiling, including the passageways connecting it to the main cabin. Most of the main cabin was similarly filled, though not so high it showed through the ports. Being low in the water could attract the attention of passing boats, thinking the *Gorda* might be sinking. One could draw equal interest with closed curtains covering all the windows and portholes.

Even the dining alcove went for cargo space. They'd have to eat in the cockpit or standing in the galley. Only the enclosed head and the galley were clear and free of cargo.

Chico, enthralled by all the activity, had to finally be physically restrained to keep from being stepped on by the stevedores. When Weeto trussed him in his harness and safety line and clipped him to an eyebolt, he pouted dourly over his humiliation for about thirty seconds. Quickly forgetting what he was unhappy about, he began shouting at the men working the boom and nets on the other boat. Surprised at his Spanish and amused by his inquisitive questions, they good-naturedly shouted back to him. The one-handed skipper in particular was apparently willing to play his part. He simultaneously joked and manipulated the leather-covered stump with incredible dexterity at the tiller and the winch. Roars of laughter erupted from the skipper and his men. Benjie understood some of it, but much of the rich local dialect had to be translated by Weeto. Even he was sometimes lost with the double-entendres of the local patter, though he obviously enjoyed the humor and camaraderie. Like Weeto, Benjie was enthralled by both their humor and their seamanship.

As the last of the cargo was stowed below, he saw Josh count out a bundle of bills to the crew boss before they leaped aboard the *Miraflores* and hauled in their lines. They waved, laughing and shouting as the vessels parted. The *Miraflores* went chugging off on its noisy one-lunger in the direction of Santa Marta while the *Gorda* circled and headed out to sea.

Benjie felt lifted by the experience in more ways than one. He could hardly have hoped for a smoother transfer, hardly even a scratch on the paint. The skilled crew of the *Miraflores*, able to celebrate even in the meager circumstances of their material lives, had put them all in good spirits. It hardly bothered him that Josh had obviously lied about the money. In a way it restored his confidence in his business acumen, which had been shaken somewhat when he tried to justify payment of the money in advance.

Even Weeto seemed changed by the encounter with the *contrabandistas*. They were not the drug thugs he expected but hardy laborers he could relate to. As snippets of conversation had revealed, most were illiterate, unschooled men but with uncommon seamanship skills. Like the captain, whose hand had been blown off using dynamite as a fishing aid, they were all ex-fishermen or dockhands who had been frequently out of work until recent years brought them a new kind of steady employment for which they were obviously grateful.

Josh and Dynamite were ecstatic, and for a change Benjie shared their excitement. Josh cut through the wrappers on one of the bales to examine its contents. Putting a cupped handful under his nose, he breathed the aroma in deeply. "Gold, man, Santa Marta gold! Triple-A quality and we've got a mine full of it!"

"The proof is in the pudding," Dyna remarked. "Let's try some and find out!"

"My very own thoughts." Josh gloated like a kid who just inherited a candy store.

Benjie reminded them they first had things to do. Get the sails up for starters. Put a meal together. Plot their course and do some chart work.

By the time the sun's last yolky edge was melting into the horizon, the *Gorda* was gliding north through tropic waters at a respectable six knots. The breezy southeasterly coming over her shoulder was an idyllic caress, beckoning the coming night with sounds of streaming water and the flutter of telltales. Dinner finished, Josh broke out his newly-purchased ukulele and his freshly-rolled tin of smokes. Dynamite brought up a jug of dago red, one she had hidden away for just such an occasion, and a songfest started up. Even Weeto joined in the singing and tried a few puffs at Dyna's coaxing.

Benjie, for once unwilling to surrender the moment of euphoria—in spite of Dyna's new interest—told himself it was just her natural openness and outgoing personality in action.

Chapter Eighteen

Don José's Machiavellian mind delighted in deciphering as well as weaving webs of deception, so connecting the long-haired nadista to the vessel Miami was so desperate to find gave him one more piece of the puzzle. The delay in waiting for return of the taxi provided the margin of safety he needed. Unable to pry from the Americans anything more specific than what he first learned in Miami, he began to doubt his first suspicions. Perhaps it was only some papers they were after. Still if they were as politically incriminating as was implied, they had their uses also. Silence sometimes had the same cash convertibility as gold.

The pieces began falling even more rapidly into place soon after they arrived in Cartagena on a flight with the Americans. He chose Cartagena as starting point for the search, he told them, because it was the favorite port of visiting yachts. This was true enough, though it was actually the taxi driver's emerald which provided the pinpointing clue.

Sending his assistant off with the Americans to the yacht club to check the vessels docked and anchored there, he called on the jeweler. He wanted to verify that his "collateral guarantees" were still intact and properly safeguarded. He had the tissue-wrapped emerald taken from the pocket of the taxi driver as proof he had reason to be concerned.

The office of the jeweler, located behind a cavernous iron door at the back of the shop, reminded him of a chapel in a prison where he once spent time in his teens. The smell of incense, tinkling chimes and flickering candles reinforced the memory. In keeping with the design of the seventeenth-century fortress-like structure, tapestries and dark religious paintings, faded and cracked with age, hung from the whitewashed walls. Persian rugs covered patches of the stone floor and a candle sputtered homage in a red glass holder in a niche containing a carved wooden Madonna. This obvious respect for the past appealed to his personal sense of nostalgia, generating emotions only one deprived of elements of his past could feel.

He allowed himself a moment's reverent pleasure before returning to business. He began to pick out the room's salient features. It was a high two-storied stone chamber, the only opening a small window next to the ceiling, more for ventilation than light. Beyond the recess of the foot-thick wall, it was grilled with heavy iron bars serving more than a decorative purpose. In a chink of the plaster next to the casement was an exposed wire, doubtless part of a primitive burglar-alarm system. Theft had been long since relegated to a past repertoire.

After being shown the emeralds which were kept in a wall safe behind a lacquered Florentine screen, he was offered a seat on a cross-legged Roman stool facing the jeweler across a baronial desk from the Spanish Colonial period. Such an eclectic display of furnishings made him wonder if it was mere pretentiousness or the trappings of centuries of accumulated wealth by an honored family line which traced itself back to before the Discovery. He noticed the subtle distinction in elevation between the stool and the elaborately carved chair the dealer sat in and saw it had a practical as well as a psychological purpose. The lighting had been skillfully arranged to reveal every line of the customer's face while keeping the jeweler's profile in shadows.

Almost immediately the subject of the television newscast of the incident on the mountain came into the conversation, and he learned for the first time the jeweler had been relieved of more than his wallet and a few pesos as the police reported. He didn't have to guess why the victim felt it wiser to keep the matter of the emeralds to himself. But it threw new light on the question about the source of the emerald found on the taxi driver.

"I can tell you this," said the gem dealer from his shadowed recess behind the desk. "The thieves were no lucky trio of street *gamines* who happened on the scene by accident."

It amused him to think the jeweler probably thought him and his associates responsible, but fear or good manners kept him from even hinting at any such suggestion. Adroitly, he sidestepped any such inference by appealing to Don José's intimate knowledge of what went on in the capital.

"I'd be much obliged if you'd pass on any rumors circulating about a sudden fencing of emeralds in quantity."

"Of course, *por supuesto*," Don José assured him. Both understood he would not have waited so long if he believed his appeal would be taken seriously. He was simply playing diplomat.

When the jeweler mentioned the actress woman in a manner suggesting he knew her, the last pieces of the puzzle began to fall in place.

"Certainly I know her," he replied quickly to Don José's question. "She's a friend of that man, Vanderbilt, that you're doing business with. She's not that actress girl at all. She has nothing to do with the entertainment business. She comes from a fabled wealthy family, an heiress in her own right who abhors any sort of notice or publicity, as you saw for yourself on those news clips. And she has reason to—"

He leaned out of the shadows across the desk, his voice lowered. "She was kidnapped as a child and only redeemed by a considerable ransom. All very hush-hush, Vanderbilt tells me. Not even the police or the news people learned of it. She always travels incognito now, on false papers. Even the yacht she arrived on is licensed in her captain's name for security purposes. She's deathly afraid of being taken hostage for money."

"I see," said Don José, feigning idle curiosity. "I didn't catch her name—is it one I would know?"

"Oh, I'm sworn to secrecy about her true identity." The jeweler's retreat to the shadows carried the hushed tones of a government minister prevented by codes of state from revealing secrets even to a trusted colleague. "But for a slip of the tongue, I wouldn't have known either. Vanderbilt is not only her friend but closest adviser, a closeness that goes back to childhood. Neighboring vacation villas in that Rhode Island town, Newport, where the rich Americans spend their summers."

"Forgive my naivete," Don José entreated, "but is the *nadista* really so different, financially, from what he appears to be?"

"Haven't you guessed?" The jeweler clucked his tongue. "It's hard to believe it from the man's wild appearance and those awful clothes he sometimes wears. But who can predict anymore what the rich Americans will do for amusement? When money's no longer the point, what's left? And what better sport for rich young Americans than the one provided by their own government?"

Don José wondered whether he missed something crucial or he was talking to a fool. "Well, it's you who stands to lose if he's not what you think," he told the jeweler. "What makes you so sure of him?"

The jeweler smiled graciously. "It's kind of you to be concerned but you needn't be. I've seen pictures of some of the family homes. One's a castle in North Carolina called the Biltmore. The yacht they came in—it alone is worth half a million. By accident I saw a bank book of his—over seven hundred thousand in one bank alone. He could have a courier fly the money down in a day!"

"I see," Don José replied flatly.

They were interrupted by the entrance of an employee, the same dark, handsome youth who'd been with the jeweler in the juice bar the day Josh pulled the money switch. The coiffed gray head leaned out of the shadows with a scowl, a manicured hand waving the young man away.

"Not now, Juanito, can't you see I'm busy?"

The young man frowned in return, then turned on his heel and strode angrily out the iron door, slamming it noisily behind him.

Rising, Don José made his excuses and shook the jeweled hand, repeating his assurances to convey any rumors of stolen emeralds. He started to leave, then spun around abruptly, catching the jeweler off guard as he came around the desk.

"She's a DuPont heiress, isn't she?" He pointed a playful finger and flashed the smile of one already privy to the secret.

"I gave my word," the startled man whispered, a finger tapping his mouth. "Let it come from other lips."

Hard pressed to keep from laughing, Don José hurried from the room. So it was the scarecrow who staged the charade on the mountaintop and made off with the merchant's emeralds, he reflected. All that business of the press and television people was diversion, the girl a clever part of a smoke screen contrived to create confusion and cover their escape. What audacity! Behind all that hair the shaggy *nadista* had some brains and imagination to match his nerve. Not satisfied with pulling it off once, he had the gall to come back and twist the poor man's nose a second time.

He was still chuckling as he made his way to the nearest public phone. He got in touch with his man in Santa Marta, manager of his small fleet of trading schooners. The *Miraflores*, he learned, was out to sea on a delivery. Glancing at his watch, seeing it was after three, he knew delivery was likely in progress that very moment. He told the manager he would call back in the evening and to hold the skipper until then. He had a few questions to put to him. Inconsequential questions, really, concerning the length and rig of the *Gorda*, intended only to confirm something he was already certain of.

Elated and a little out of breath, he turned the corner and sat down at one of the empty tables in the juice bar in front of the plaza. Ordering a *chino*, he turned to the wall and sprinkled a bit of powder from a vial onto a peso note and sniffed it up each nostril. The white powder was one of his little luxuries in life. He didn't use tobacco and, except for a little wine and beer, hardly ever touched alcohol.

The cocaine cleared his head and sinuses and made him feel vitally alive, the sensation akin to being in his prime again with all the juices pumping and his mind like a dynamo. Well aware of the artificial nature of the powder and the problems its abuse could create, he allowed himself only occasional use and had never increased the dosage since he began the habit thirty years earlier. Moderation, Aristotle's "golden mean," had always been his practice.

The *nadista*'s gall made him chuckle again and reminded him of American excess. He could admire the excess that put a man on the Moon, but what about the excess that imprisoned young people for using a relatively harmless weed? The zealots' belief that laws could instill morality produced a predictable backlash, best exemplified by what happened when they turned the screws on hapless heroin addicts at the turn of the century. The ugly business of shooting up intravenously was a recent innovation—the result of vigorous law enforcement and skyrocketing prices. Addicts mainline because it's quickest and cheapest, often the only way to forestall withdrawal symptoms. Who would risk infection and embolism, sticking a needle in his body, if he didn't desperately need to?

American hysteria had created a self-sustaining monster. It supported armies of border patrols and undercover agents working around the world to stop the illicit drug flow. Billions were being spent in the mistaken notion that it could be stamped out—as naive an idea as the Prohibition experiment with alcohol. Predictably, enforcement agencies become self-serving instruments of the trade, perpetuating myths and half-truths even when they're not partners in action or sharers of the spoils. Each side sustains and engorges the other. Don José saw nothing surprising about it. As air rushes into a vacuum, humans are sucked into a space offering profits. Enormous profits attract enormously. Agents and officials are only human too.

"When the clever Americans figure that out, you'll be out of business," he told himself.

"Ah well," his mercenary side answered as he recalled the political implications of the boat papers Miami was so desperate for. "Smart money says change will be a long time coming."

There was excitement on the docks when Don José met again with the other three. Vincent, nervously cracking his knuckles, was talking excitedly about hiring a helicopter to search the coastline for the missing boat. The picture of the boat they first passed around got no results. No one remembered seeing it. But the snapshot of Weeto and Chico hit home. It seemed nearly all the docksiders remembered the boy. As he described the boat he left on the day before, the *Gorda* suddenly emerged as a match for the *Dragon* in the picture. The taffrail and figurehead had been changed and some remembered that being done while the boat was in harbor.

Some volunteered they heard it was headed for Aruba. Others, picking up on the Aruba destination, laughed and said they didn't have to go chasing it—they could wait right here for it. No one made it to Aruba against the winter trades! In a few days it would come limping back for repairs and new sails.

Don José's anxiety mounted higher than the coke euphoria. Official attention to the presence of a stolen boat in the area was nearly as bad as giving the Americans a lead on it. Fortunately, as his assistant hastened to explain, they had scuttled any implication of a stolen boat and said only they were trying to catch up with the vessel to report a death in the family.

"I hope you had sense enough to stay away from the port captain's office," he admonished, turning his back on the Americans and speaking swiftly in Spanish. The idiot would undo everything if he didn't keep a tight rein on him.

The younger man blanched. "We only phoned. They wanted to confirm the port of destination."

"Blockhead! And what reason did you give the port captain?"

"The same, Don José. A death in the family and we needed to get the information to the people on board."

"Are you quite sure you gave the port captain no reason to suspect it's anything but a bona fide yacht on a pleasure cruise?" His displeasure hissed through gritted teeth.

"Yes, Don José, quite sure. It was only some clerk I talked to, and only for a minute. It was all quite routine."

"You had better hope so. Because that is the vessel making my delivery to Miami. Three hundred pounds of powder, a kilo hidden in the middle of each bale!"

"Madre de Dios!" The younger man's face flushed red, then paled to the color of the powder his patron sometimes snorted. His eyes could find no cover.

"Yes, Mother of God! You'd better pray. Millions of dollars at stake and you could be the cause of losing it!"

The sloppily dressed American with the sleepy voice and blank face was, in fact, fluent in Spanish and understood every word he spoke. He had been carefully selected for the mission for that reason and one other indispensable skill. He was an expert cryptologist.

Even the burly fashion plate who had been sent along as his muscle had no idea Harry spoke or understood a word of anything but English. Nor could he have guessed that before the day was over, Harry would unleash him and finally put his meaty hands to work.

Chapter Nineteen

For three days the *Gorda* streamed north on a patch of perfect weather unusual for midwinter. First a southerly eased them off the continental shelf, then prevailing easterlies came back the next day with intensified twenty-knot winds that sent the long-keeled vessel scudding along at a steady seven- or eight-knot clip. Not once did Benjie crank the engine on, a fact which pleased his rag-sailor heart beyond any considerations of cost and fuel consumption. Resorting to the iron horse in open waters offended his sailing ethics.

Taking noon sights the first two days, he found he had been overcompensating for the current and altered course accordingly. On the third day the coast of Haiti loomed on the horizon off the starboard bow. Five hundred miles in less than three days, a feat he could never match in little *Candy*. Second boats like second mates are sometimes better, he mused. This one was a beauty. With her long keel she could move smoothly in the Caribbean's boisterous conditions. Flying on her big sails she was like a graceful lady, wedded to the water but in love with the wind. He was hopelessly enraptured—her performance thrilled him.

As usual, Chico was first to spot land. Something about a first sighting after a few days at sea always brought with it the irre-

sistible urge to celebrate. Josh was first to light up. Passing the joint
to Dynamite, he lit a second and handed it to Weeto, who was
taking a turn at the wheel. To everyone's surprise, he took it without
hesitation.

"It's not my first time," he said, trying to sound gruff when he
saw the others staring. "I smoked before a few times. No worse
than some of that other stuff, eh?"

"Enjoy, don't apologize," Josh ribbed.

"It's not addictive," Dynamite added. "It won't hook you like
cigarettes. You can quit anytime you like."

It was a form of proselytizing, no matter how they cloaked it
in humor, and Benjie didn't approve. One didn't have to play
missionary to convert others to one's vices—enough came of their
own accord. Still, in this case, he had to admit it brought a bonus.
Since the evening of merrymaking when he took a few tokes at
Dyna's urging, Weeto's voiced objections to the cargo had ended
and his animosity toward Josh had noticeably subsided.

He was aware of changes in himself as well. In the smooth
transfer from the *Miraflores* and the shared boat chores, he and
Dyna drew closer again. It even seemed her interest in Josh had
reached saturation and was beginning to flow in another direction,
evidenced from the ribbing she was subjecting him to again.

Following that first night's festivities, after Weeto had taken
Chico to bed in the forward cabin and Josh was on wheel duty,
Dynamite had stretched a beach towel out on the stern deck in the
privacy of the raised doghouse of the aft cabin and invited Benjie
to make love under the stars. Their quarters stacked with cargo, he
thought they'd have to forgo such pleasures for the duration of the
trip. She had other ideas.

She was, if that were possible, hotter than he. Her straightfor-
wardness in diving into sensuality was like plunging into a pool or
attacking a steaming meal after days at sea on cold canned rations.
In this too, she seemed more liberated than he—the archetypal
hedonist aimed at pleasing herself first. By daring to be herself and
open about her own pleasures, she helped undo his inhibitions and
freed his own deepest desires. Hardly a part of her body went unex-
plored by all the sensors of his being. Dynamite enthusiastically

reciprocated. "Wow," she sighed when finally they parted, both still breathing heavily as they turned to stare at the winking sky. "There were some firsts there, for both of us. I didn't push you too far, did I, sweets?"

"Why do you ask?"

"Oh, it's just you're an innocent in some things. I mean it as a compliment," she added, then snickered. "And I'll bet you're blushing."

"You'd lose the bet. It's all made for enjoying, right?"

"Even Josh's jeweler friend with the boy young enough to be his son?" she asked coyly. "Or that lascivious old cabbie, Eduardo? I just know he has a thing for young chicks."

"I can only speak for myself," he said, squeezing her hand. "Whatever pleases thee, pleases me."

"You know what that could lead to with me—total depravity."

"Yeah, like Weeto says, from marijuana to heroin. There's no stopping once you start, right?"

She leaned forward, her words forming lusciously on her lips. "There's one thing can keep us from going off the deep end."

"What?" He expected her suggestion would yield even more devious pleasures.

"A baby."

"A baby?" Benjie's upper body shot back in shock, pulling away from her.

"What a gross reaction!" she retorted hotly, snatching her hand away.

"In the middle of a pot run—" He reached for her hand again. "We'll talk about it when we finish this run, okay?"

"Sure." Dynamite withdrew her hand. "You're the skipper. It's a nutty idea anyway—we're not even married."

She shared a joint with him while they lay in silence, peering up at the stars. "What's that cluster of small stars ahead of Taurus?" Benjie asked after several minutes passed.

"Easy," she answered. "The seven sisters, the Pleiades."

"Good girl. Now name the navigationals you see."

Dynamite glanced sideways at him, then lifted her eyes. "In Orion there's Rigel, Betelgeuse, Bellatrix and Alnilam. The two B's are his shoulders, Rigel is his right foot and Alnilam is the middle star in his belt buckle. That long thing dangling between his legs isn't a sword at all, you know, no matter what the book says—"

Benjie cut her off. "Don't think dirty talk will get you dismissed from class. Name the navigationals in Taurus."

The pretty pout on her lips switched to a smile. "Aldebaran," she continued, "the bright star on his snout. There's another one, on the horns…I can't remember its name."

"Elnath, you land lubber!" he teased. "What am I going to do with you? I buy you books, provide schooling and still you won't learn."

"Tyrant! You didn't tell me it was gonna be a school session. I thought it was supposed to be fun time on the fantail." She drew her finger along his rib cage, her eyes challenging him. "You know what you can do with me."

He caught her wrist and rolled to meet her. Their lovemaking moved in a long lingering rhythm, unhurried as the stars in motion, synchronized with the lightly rocking vessel riding the waves. Night breezes caressed them while ancient gods looked on from above, unabashed.

The following night a series of little squalls dogged them through the hours before midnight, and their turns at the wheel prevented any repetition of the previous night. Now, with Haiti forming on the horizon, Dynamite teased him.

"Meet me on the fantail at ten, I've got another trick to show you," she whispered, then added aloud. "Beautiful navigating, luv. Right where you wanted to get us."

"How can you be sure it's Haiti, Skip?" Josh queried. "I mean, why not Jamaica?"

"It's on the wrong side of the boat to be Jamaica," Weeto snorted from the wheel, "unless somebody's been doin' some bad steering."

"Where's Chico? He spotted it first, let him name it," Dyna suggested.

They were suddenly aware of his absence. Sea conditions the past three days had been so perfect they had relaxed the rules about the harness and lifeline and allowed him to roam the cockpit untethered during daylight hours.

Weeto called out his name. No answer. Benjie ducked below and checked the head and forward cabin. He cringed at the thought Chico might have slipped overboard.

Then Dyna yelled, pointing at the aft cabin where wispy smoke was curling out of an air vent. She got there first and rolled back the hatch cover. A cloud of familiar-smelling smoke billowed skyward. Inside, the bleary-eyed youngster was engaged in a private experiment, imitating adults. Apparently, it was not at all to his liking. Weeto hauled him out of the narrow cranny on top of the bales where he'd hidden himself. There was no point in punishment, he'd meted out enough to himself already. Grabbing him by his belt, Weeto held him over the low side taffrail while he heaved and vomited, alternately crying and gagging.

"Monkey, you could have set the boat on fire!" he scolded. "You din think about that, hah? Why din you ask me first? You din have to go sneaking off to do it." Chico stared up at him dizzily. "I don' care now if you have to be sick, but I care you almost burned us all up! You don' see anybody else smoking down inside the boat. Don' you know why, dummy? The boat could catch fire and then we all go down in the water. You lucky you only sick and not drowning in the water right now."

"No, I wouldn't," he said between heaves. "I can swim."

"Sure you can, monkey. Twenty miles, all the way to Haiti there. With sharks swimmin' in the water too! I couldn't swim half that far. How come you think you can?"

"I did it too at his age," Josh offered, "with cigarettes."

Dyna had a Minnesota version. "We tried it with corn silk when we were kids. Now that's a real gasser, guys—guaranteed to put you off smoking for life."

"We setting him a bad example," Weeto frowned. "He sees us smokin' and liking it, so why not sneak off and try it too? At his age is he goin' to have some kind of trip or something."

"Don't worry," Dyna assured him. "Here's the joint he was smoking. He got about two puffs on it before his stomach protested. He'll feel queasy and have a bad taste in his mouth, that's about all.

No worse than if he sneaked one of your cigarettes."

"That's another thing!" Weeto ranted, launching into another lecture. "He took somebody's property that din belong to him. That's stealing!"

Dyna had a cup of water and a damp towel ready. When Chico finished vomiting, she wiped his face and gave him a drink. Propping him against the bulkhead in a corner of the cockpit, she kidded him in Spanish with expressions he taught her in their daily language lessons.

"No school today, the teacher is sick," she recited in singsong Spanish.

Minutes later, she had him unwound and relaxed. Soda crackers and milk settled his queasy stomach, but he played invalid long enough to divert Poppi's wrath and cloak himself in sympathy. Five minutes later, he caught sight of a leaping sailfish and forgot he was supposed to be sick. He began yelling for his fish pole, climbing on the coaming for a better look.

"I'd say our p-a-t-i-e-n-t has made a full recovery," Dyna observed, rolling her eyes at the others.

"Monkey, you think you gonna pull in one that size?" Weeto muttered, running the line over the side and handing him his pole. But his pride flashed as brightly as the leaping fish in the water.

Dyna felt her own leap of pleasure at seeing his and it wasn't confined to the paternal nature of things. Somehow reminded of the husky hunter who faithfully foraged the nighttime sky, the appendage she imagined dangling between his legs symbolized more than family provider—it was foremost the necessary first progenitor. She betrayed none of her feelings minutes later, however, when she was returning the cup and crackers and ran into him in the galley, drawing himself a drink of water.

"You're too rough on him sometimes," she told him, undoing one of the cupboard sea bolts.

"Maybe so. I don' always know where to draw the line." He paused to consider his answer. "It's not easy bein' both Poppi and Mommie to him, you know? Besides, I don' look much like a Mommie, do I?"

"No, I'd say not," she replied, grinning. "Did you ever think about providing him with another Mommie?"

Weeto shrugged. "I din have much chance or time to think about it, you know?" He smiled at her. "I wanna thank you, Dynamite, for what you're doin' with him. He really likes you and before he din used to like any women at all."

"Just put another star on my report card," she kidded. Her smile faded. "Don't think women are all the same. They aren't all lousy mothers."

"I know," he said, but there was a weariness in his voice. The flecked gray of his sideburns projected an older, more serious persona than his fractured English sometimes suggested. Too craggy-faced to be handsome, he had the hard-hat look of the solid provider.

"Was she such a bitch?" she asked abruptly. "I mean, he's a doll. Who couldn't enjoy him? I'll take one myself if you're handing them out free."

Not one to be easily embarrassed, Weeto blushed as spontaneously as the Freudian slip that had just escaped her lips.

"Not a bitch, not really," he said, modestly overlooking her remark, "though I used to call her that. She's gone now and it's not nice to talk bad about the dead. I feel sorry for her. She was, you know, like a sick person. Sick in the head, I mean."

Shouts and squeals rang out topside. Chico had a strike on his line and Weeto pounded up the steps to help him. Dyna stayed below to finish her chores. She put the crackers back into the lower food locker next to the stove where she kept the supplies. The storage space contained a series of graduated tins and large plastic screw-top jars she used for flour and rice. Since she had checked and reprovisioned before their departure from Cartagena, she knew the ones she had filled and the ones that should have been empty.

A squarish object in a brown paper bag, hidden until she moved the large tin to put the crackers in, caught her attention. Opening it, she found the big camera case and the small Kodak Josh had carried on the mountain top. An odd mismatch, it was an even odder place to be stowing it. Her pulse quickened.

Examining the space, she saw one of the plastic jars had been shoved into a back corner, behind a row of empties. Digging it out and unscrewing the lid, she found it contained two sealed plastic bags filled with a grayish-white powder.

Her skin went tight and prickly. Though she'd never seen either before, she knew that it was heroin or cocaine. She also knew who had put them there and how he came by them.

She recoiled at the obvious truth. The money Josh needed so suddenly in Bogotá wasn't for the marijuana at all—it was to make a separate purchase he was concealing from them. She thought back to the conversation in the restaurant in Medellín. Was this the "message" he was delivering for Don José to the Miami contact?

The excitement of discovery disappeared as she stared down at what she held in her hands. You couldn't stuff a million dollars into the jar but that, or something near it, was the street value of the powder which only half-filled the container.

Drawing her forefinger over the sealed plastic bag, she felt the cold powder within it. She shivered. Too many horrors, exaggerated or not, were associated with this powder.

Dynamite hesitated. Benjie would explode if he knew; she didn't dare tell him. Carefully replacing everything, she went to the forward cabin. She crawled to one of the upper bunks and opened the lazaret.

On their return from Bogotá, looking for a place to hide the emeralds, she had discovered a secret niche in the chain locker. A section of beam had a hollowed-out area with a cover plate and a notched groove that opened and closed on hidden brass runners. The small chamber inside was just large enough to hold the bag of emeralds.

Following the discovery of Josh's hidden stash, she felt a sudden need to verify her own was still intact. She hadn't told Josh where she hid them, and until then hadn't felt a need to check on them. She had hidden them away like a precious reserve—a last ace in the hole to save them in the event of a crisis. Sliding the plate open, she reached inside and squeezed the leather pouch. As she felt again the sensations of hot and cold as the stones rolled and clicked together beneath her fingertips, she experienced the relief of all secret hoarders.

Late in the afternoon, as they were entering the Windward Passage and came abreast of the southwest tip of Haiti, the wind flattened to a dead calm. Wanting to maintain a six-knot average for timing purposes, Benjie fired up the engine. A hundred and twenty miles ahead was the snouted tip of Cuba, a little east of due north, which he wanted to make before dark next day to ensure a course correction kept them out of Cuban waters. Once around Punta Caleta and Punta Maisi, they'd alter course again for a run up the Old Bahama Channel between the bank and Cuba, reversing the track of their passage down.

The calm lasted only until around eight that night, when the wind suddenly shifted from the west, throwing the sails in a whipping crack and reversing the heel of the vessel. Josh was on wheel duty when the others came topside to see what was up.

"I'm exactly on course," he shouted in self-defense. "The winds just shifted on me. Whatta you make of it, Skip?"

Sudden sustained wind strength ought to be welcome, but the direction caused Benjie concern. Coming during the winter months, it was often the first warning of an arctic mass on the way down. Pushing against the warm tropic air, it set off atmospheric turbulence which could generate gale-force winds and rough sea conditions. And on their current northern heading they were rushing to meet it. As the wind went clockwise with the weather front, shifting from west to northwest to north, its tendency was to increase in strength and violence. Finally, drawn out over the Atlantic, it would blow itself out from the northeast and the normal easterlies would take over again. Such was the typical pattern of a norther. Though he'd never experienced one, Benjie read about them and knew they could be fearsome along the north coasts of the islands of the Greater Antilles—Cuba, Hispaniola and Puerto Rico—and throughout the Bahamas and the Florida Straits.

"May be only a temporary williwaw or an offshore breeze," he said hopefully, reading sixteen on his hand-held wind gauge.

Weeto also knew something about northers from his work in Florida the winter before. Josh wanted explanations and the mechanic obliged, detailing with relish some of the more unpleasant stories he'd heard about being caught out to sea in such storms.

Benjie went forward to check the set of the sails and make some line adjustments. Dynamite followed after him.

"If it turns into a norther like Weeto thinks, what are our options?" Caught in the red glow of the port running light, her face reflected her worry and alarm. "We can't run for shelter, can we?"

"You know we can't—not with the cargo we're carrying."

"I don't mean a port. I mean ducking behind that long arm of Haiti. The Gulf of Gonâve, I think it's called on the chart. Not to go in anywhere, just to hide behind for protection—"

"If you're not close in, there is no protection," Benjie reminded her. "You should know that. Remember Tehuantepec?"

"Don't remind me of that." The boat lurched and she grabbed a mast cleat for balance. "It's just...we've had such a beautiful sail, everything's gone so perfect. It'd be crappy to have it all go bad now."

He'd been teasing her and now he was sorry. Her sudden panic, surprising in her, was real. She needed reassurance.

"Come on, Dyna, you're letting Weeto get you all worked up. Winds from the west at sixteen, what's the big deal? Could be just local shore winds coming from Cuba."

He doubted that. They were too far out to be affected by shore winds, and it wasn't the hot summer period when daytime heat on landmasses could generate locally contrary winds at night.

"If it was just the two of us—no sweat. You know I'm not a quitter, Benjie. But for us it was a choice. I'm not even counting Weeto. But that little kid—what choice did he have in any of this?" The rare look of alarm on her face was highlighted by an even rarer glimpse of her maternal instincts. "I swear, if anything bad happens to him, I'll never...ever forgive myself!"

"The great earth mother speaking?" Benjie teased, her momentary vulnerability drawing him to her.

"I mean I really dig him," Dyna went on. "I'd like for us someday to have one or two from the same mold." She drew back when he reached for her. "Don't fool around, I'm serious. I will feel personally shitty if...if anything happens to him. You didn't really want us to pull this off. Josh and I talked you into it. So if this crap we're carrying keeps us from seeking shelter and the worst happens, I'll feel personally responsible."

"You're getting all worked up for nothing," he told her. "This isn't *Candy*. This is a big mother with a good strong engine. Even in a storm it wouldn't seem so bad. And you can cut the crap about feeling responsible for talking me into this venture. It's what I wanted. What I still want. With no regrets, understand?"

Saying it made him realize its truth. She had unwittingly jolted him into an honest acknowledgement of his true feelings — he wanted the money for the freedom it could bring.

"If it gets rough," she said hesitantly, "if we get into a really bad storm, we'll just dump the crap and put into the first safe port. Agreed?"

"You know we will," he answered. But he knew it would have to be a life-and-death situation before he'd relinquish the valuable cargo. It was, after all, the key to his future.

For the rest of the night they went on double watches, one at the wheel and a relief standing by to assist if wind changes required sail adjustments. It turned out not to be necessary since the wind remained steady in velocity and direction. The engine was kept in low rev, just enough to offset the adverse current and maintain steady progress at six knots. It was also recharging the engine and house batteries. At six-thirty in the morning, while Benjie was on duty, the wind began intermittently shifting north of west but with no noticeable increase in velocity. It didn't even affect his sail plan. He had some easting to do anyway, to round Punta Maisi and stay well off the Cuban coast. Anticipating the wind shift, he had held to a course of due north, saving his easting for when he could put the wind to advantage. Now he used it.

During the night he'd picked up several Miami weather forecasts and knew a cold front was moving into the area. Already storm warnings were up for the Florida coast and adjacent Bahamas. By itself, the advisory was a relative warning since it was aimed at the smallest sail and power boats with a day sail or fishing trip in mind. A forecast of eighteen to twenty was enough to keep the little guys tied to the dock, and sensibly so. But for an ocean-going yacht that could represent ideal sailing conditions.

The advisory called for a wind shift to the north by late afternoon. If it held to that prediction, the timing would be perfect, permitting a reach along the three hundred twenty miles of Cuban coastline to where their course would turn north to follow the curve of the bank up to the Biminis. By then the wind would have eased east, once more allowing them to use it to advantage. Such calculating is ritual among rag sailors and Benjie was no exception. Even without contraband aboard, it's unlikely he'd have decided any differently, such as opting for shelter in Haiti or Great Inagua Island. Taking advantage of a storm's wind patterns, though it meant discomfort and some danger, was a big part of the thrill of sailing. Much as Josh was stimulated by mind games, Benjie got high juggling nature's inconstants.

Late in the afternoon, rounding the tip of Cuba, the weather lived up to the forecasts with almost uncanny timing. The wind shifted north with a sudden increase in force. Close-hauling the sails, on a pinched reach the boat began noticeably picking up speed. Benjie turned off the engine. The sudden absence of machine noise and vibration brought cheers from his crew.

"Abajo los stinkpots!" Dyna shouted, something rehearsed in her Spanish lessons.

"Abajo los stinkpots!" Chico echoed, jumping on the floor grates.

"Arriba los veleros!" she chanted, thumbs up.

"Arriba los veleros!" he repeated, imitating the gesture.

Together in rally fashion, the mismatched pair repeated their chant in the cockpit, hands pointing up for sails and down on power. Finishing, they fell into a tickling contest on the seat cushion. As on the trip down, the daily Spanish lesson was ostensibly for Dynamite's benefit, but she skillfully worked it into a two-way flow of instruction, with Chico learning to manipulate numbers and practicing his reading and spelling. Chico's distance with females was vanishing rapidly under Dyna's tutelage.

Watching their horseplay, Benjie could no longer dismiss her maternal needs as merely a whim she'd put aside the minute Weeto disappeared with the boy. Feeling no paternal urges of his own, he wondered if he lacked some vital core of maturity. He loved kids too, he told himself. And if he wasn't ready for any of his own yet, he knew someday he would be.

Glancing at the darkening sky, he easily shrugged off his abstract dilemmas. More concrete concerns were gathering overhead.

Chapter Twenty

Conditions the first night along the Cuban coast and most of the following day were what rag sailors regard as exhilarating. Winds eighteen to twenty-two knots, eight-foot waves with a froth of whitecaps, and enough sea spray blowing in the cockpit to keep them in oilskins whenever they left the cabin. It was button-down time for boat and crew alike, with hatches and portholes closed and lugged down and swimwear discarded for long pants, socks and shoes, sweaters or jackets and foul-weather gear. The sunny days when they could spend all their time topside vanished with the chill wind blowing down on them from the north. Except for the helmsman and his relief, the cockpit was generally empty while conditions below became increasingly crowded, monotonous and boring in the bale-crammed quarters.

The *Gorda* was making good time, however, averaging better than seven knots, as Benjie was able to confirm with the last of the noon sights he'd be getting for a few days. By afternoon the racing clouds had settled into a permanent shroud that dropped a curtain across any view of the coastline. With a forecast of worsening conditions over the next twenty-four hours, Benjie reefed the mainsail in the late hours of sunset.

Living up to prediction, the weather deteriorated steadily as the night wore on. At nine o'clock he was getting readings of twenty-six knots and gusting up. Steering became tiring work and he cut their shifts from two hours to one. By midnight it was pushing thirty knots, a borderline case for reducing more sail. In the narrow neck of the channel where the Cuban islands comprising the Archipelago of Camaguey are separated in spots from the Great Bahama Bank by no more than fifteen or twenty miles, he wanted to slip through in darkness as quickly as possible.

In that respect bad weather was a blessing. It wasn't likely the Cubans would have their gunboats out on patrol. As for their fishing trawlers, they had enough sense to stay buttoned down when northers were blowing. Not wishing to be sighted in their waters in any case, Benjie steered a course as close to the bank as he dared, the depth-finder keeping a continuous check on whether they'd gone onto the bank or were still in deep water. At three in the morning Dyna reported Chico was sick and running a slight fever. She handed up a bucket of vomit to be thrown overboard.

"Seasick or something worse?" Benjie asked, after he washed the bucket over the side and handed it back to her.

"Only mal de mer, but it may be catching," she chuckled. "Weeto's not feeling so hot either. Chico's retching reminded him of his own stomach. I've got him stretched out on the other bunk, but he looks a little green around the gills."

"How're you doing, babe?"

"You know me, iron stomach." She laughed, thankful for her strong constitution. Except for some mild queasiness, due as much to exhaustion and lack of food as motion during their ordeal with storms on the Pacific side of the Isthmus of Tehuantepec, she never suffered seasickness. Even the moans and vomiting of others didn't get to her, which was more than Benjie could claim. He had two wretched bouts during the Tehuantepeckers and once again in rough waters on the Colombian coast.

"Forget about your watch," he told her. "Stay below with the patients. We'll handle things till morning."

But when he turned and saw Josh's drawn face in the glow of the compass light, Benjie knew he'd given in to the power of suggestion. He grabbed the wheel as Josh rushed to the rail.

Knowing he'd be out of it for awhile, Benjie insisted he sack out on the seat when he was done. He protested at first, insisting he finish his shift, but when a fresh wave of nausea erupted, he obediently collapsed onto the cushions.

Rain began falling. At first it was only slashing mists, so intermingled with sea spray Benjie took it for that at first. But it soon became a steady drilling pattern exploding on the illuminated areas of the deck and cabin like a harvest of bullets, red and green puffs smoking from the force of impact. The seas accompanied it with mounting violence. Waves broadsided and repeatedly climbed the high side, thumping and breaking before they gushed in. One nearly flooded the cockpit, knocking Benjie sideways and nearly floating Josh away on his seat cushion.

"Jesus, we're going under!" Unlike people, nature was an adversary difficult to predict and impossible to manipulate.

"Not as long as our heads are above water," Benjie assured him. He knew he was flying too much sail for conditions, but conditions were now almost too much to allow him to rectify it. He couldn't just drop them. That would put them at the mercy of the storm and their engine power alone couldn't provide control. Conceivably the storm could drive them south onto the reefs and islands of Cuba.

The boat wasn't equipped with roller reefing. Any sail reduction had to be done manually with hand ties and line lashings. The head sail had to be removed entirely before a storm jib could be hanked onto the forestay, hazardous work on deck in such conditions—doubly dangerous at night. Though Benjie had done it before in other storms, it always took an act of will over all the forces of human instinct that told him to seek the security of the cockpit.

Another wave engulfed them just as the other had finally sloshed out and disappeared down the floor drains. Some of it found its way around the hatch frame and filtered into the cabin below. Dyna was opening it when Benjie felt the lift and hiss of another big wave coming in. He shouted for her to close it. She opened instead the small porthole next to it, reporting what he already guessed.

"Weeto feels he should relieve you guys." In the maelstrom of wind and rain he could barely make out what she was saying, or rather shouting, from less than ten feet away.

"Not now! Stay buttoned down. I'll let him know if he's needed!"

Josh seized his remark as further evidence they were in more danger than Benjie was letting on. Forgetting his queasy stomach, he sat upright. "You're pretending it's not as bad as it is, aren't you? Will it help if we dump some of the cargo?" Josh shouted. Another comber came hissing aboard and flooded them to their knees again. "This is no time to stand on principle!"

It shouldn't have surprised him Josh was first to suggest it. If it wasn't so solidly stowed it might present a ballast problem. It was dangerous only if the boat was rolled or pitchpoled, and if that happened it wouldn't be caused by the cargo. Weight might even be an advantage, a drag to keep speed down and the heeling less pronounced. Beyond the obvious danger of blown sails or snapped masts, the only disadvantage was buoyancy. Lower in the water, waves could more easily board. If enough water found its way below, that and the cargo weight would take them to the bottom that much quicker if they swamped. But swamping wasn't likely, as he tried to explain to Josh. They weren't dealing with the monster waves of open ocean waters which can take a boat under with two or three big ones boarding in quick succession.

They fell silent in the overwhelming noise of the storm. Taking stock of the situation, Benjie felt conditions were steadily worsening, but couldn't be sure how much his judgment was affected by his fatigue and growing fear. Since midnight he hadn't bothered with wind readings. Beyond a certain point it hardly mattered.

Below decks Dynamite's iron stomach was churning in a different tempest, brought forcefully to connection by crammed quarters and the storm-thrashed vessel. Exhausted by his vomiting, Chico succumbed finally to her ministrations and, cradled in one of her arms, fell asleep. Temporarily freed of her nursing duties but imprisoned below on orders of the captain, she eventually turned her thoughts to the silhouette of the fully clothed body stretched out on the bunk across from her, an arm's length away. She reached out and gently felt Weeto's forehead, checking for fever.

"You okay?" she asked in a whisper.

"If you mean, do I got any fever, no," Weeto muttered. Dyna's hand retreated at the first sound of his voice. "If you're askin' how I feel, the answer is terrible. How's Chico?"

"Out, completely. Finally. But I'm afraid if I move I might wake him."

"You're doin' more than you have to, Dynamite. I don' expect you should give so much time to him."

"It doesn't bother you, does it?" she asked quickly. "I mean, I'm not usurping your place, am I?"

Weeto shook his head. "No, no, I din mean that. I'm glad he's gettin' that kind of attention."

"He's pure joy."

"Sometimes," he granted after a pause. "But sometimes he's a pest too, and a problem. Havin' a kid is a big responsibility. Anybody should think twice before doin' it."

"You can't mean you'd rather he hadn't come along." Her fawning was instinctive, a way of pushing down the fire she felt gathering within her. Body heat filled the sticky clothes encasing her. Her mouth went suddenly dry.

"No, but..." Weeto shifted uncomfortably. He too felt the danger of intimacy and desire filling the closed cabin like twin vapors, the palpable presence of an emotion needing no messengers to announce its arrival. What he feared was true. His body made a customary and instant reaction, requiring no permission of him.

Silence followed, excruciating in the signals it radiated. Above the thump of waves and water sloshing on the thin skin of the hull, he heard or imagined his own breathing and hers, vibrant with rhythm. He heard her clear her throat to speak, then fall silent again. His own voice refused to obey him.

He was about to climb out of his bunk when Dynamite reached out and languidly rested her hand on his crotch. Beneath the folds of his trousers and shorts, his genitals throbbed their ache of long denial.

He froze, unable to speak or move. Mercifully she didn't squeeze, as he'd seen her do when she groped Benjie. The hand merely rested, cupping the throbbing bulge in patient invitation, letting him make the next move. He stopped breathing, but still his chest thumped to the beat of the throbs below.

"Like I said," she murmured in a throaty voice, "I'll take one if you're handing them out free."

Her attempt at levity didn't work this time, not even on herself. Her face flamed at the sound of her craven groveling, the offending hand torched by its tactile declaration. The satisfaction that came from his body's reaction was dwarfed by the massive mental resistance locking him in stone. His reply was heavy-handed, insulting. Downright vulgar.

"Are you talking babies now, or cocks and *huevos*?"

She made an effort to answer but couldn't. A sinking feeling of being over her head pulled her lower.

"You don' know what you're saying, Dynamite," he added, filling the gap as he subtly shifted his hips and rolled away. Only a few inches, but enough to separate himself from the burning invitation on his crotch.

"We're not married, you know," she excused herself.

"He thinks he is."

Dyna withdrew her hand. A dozen reasons reverberated in her head on why that shouldn't matter. Prior to Benjie it never had, neither to her nor least of all the guys she made it with. Why should it feel now like betrayal? She chewed her lip, speechless for once.

"We'd both be doin' him a really bad turn," Weeto said quietly, filling the vacuum with more of the same paternal tone he used on Chico. "He loves you very much, don' you know?"

The question hung for a moment in the hush between waves, then was deluged in a comber that raked the hull and thundered on deck like a cascade of hissing snakes. Desperately needing to break the bonds of her trapped feelings, Dyna rolled up from the bunk.

Before she went crawling away over the plastic bales, she found her voice and threw the only snipe she could think of: "A simple no would have done it, Weeto. I didn't need the lecture."

Benjie stayed on the wheel until the first light of dawn began staining the horizon behind them, feebly etching the massive gray weather front with a woeful air of defeat. It was then the jib sail split a seam and he had to call Dyna up to handle the wheel while he lowered it. His postponed decision had finally caught up with him.

Waves battered him as he worked in the pulpit to bring down the flogging remnants. Half-blinded by salt spray, he clawed against the forces battling to keep the tatters aloft. Twice he was swept off his feet and might have been washed over the side but for the harness and lifeline securing him to the anchor windlass. For one who couldn't stomach the sight of human violence, even on film, he was remarkably calm in conditions of natural violence, absorbed in the mechanics of the immediate tasks at hand.

After lashing the sail to its boom and the boom to its deck chock, he groped his way back to the safety of the cockpit. His arms and legs, taut from the strain of fighting the wheel for over four hours, were ready to give out. Dyna insisted on keeping the wheel when he tried wresting it from her.

"Don't play Mister Indispensable!" she shouted at him as Weeto scrambled up on deck. "Out of your wet clothes and into some dry things. You too, Josh! It's our turn now!"

"She's riding low up there since you dropped the sail," Weeto said to Benjie, pointing at the bow. "I think you got too much weight aboard. If it was me, I'd dump some of the cargo."

Benjie watched the bowsprit dig into another wave. It stayed down too long. It needed some sail lift, but he knew he wasn't up to the task of raising anything at the moment. Later, with more light, he'd hank on the storm jib.

"Weeto's right," Dyna seconded from the wheel where he could see her struggling with the weight on the bow. Josh was quick to agree.

"Let's dump some, whatever's necessary. Better potless and alive than dead potted," he quipped feebly.

Benjie studied the action a while longer, saw how the bow dipped in the troughs, then stayed buried for what seemed like an eternity. A wave curled over the pulpit and sent a geyser cascading over the slanted deck, nosing everything down for the next wave to pile into. Handling the wheel had turned into a contest. He watched Dyna struggle each time a comber struck and started to take the bow with it. He knew that the strain on the steering mechanisms could conceivably snap cables or gears.

"Nothing goes! We'll shift some weight aft first," he said. "Josh, you're elected to give me a hand."

Weeto started to join them but Benjie wanted him topside as lookout, and told him to alternate with Dynamite at the wheel. Wrestling forty-pound bales in cramped quarters was no easy chore either, the boat rocking and bucking in heavy seas. It took over half an hour to move and re-stow twenty bales. Some went into the galley, clear of cargo until now. Others filled the aisle between the main and forward cabins. With less than three feet clearance to the ceiling, traversing the main cabin had to be done on hands and knees. Emptying the forward compartment of all but a single layer of bales opened the two lower bunks for use again.

Chico awoke as soon as the men appeared and began working. He wanted to go topside but Benjie told him it was unsafe at the moment. He untied him from the upper bunk and strapped him into one of the lowers as soon as it was cleared. Expecting he was going to be freed, he began pouting when Benjie wouldn't allow it and soon found another way to show his displeasure. Mounted on clips to the wall behind the bunk were two long wood dowels, used as dipsticks for measuring water and fuel in the tanks. Removing one, he was using it as a spear to jab at the bales nearest his bunk.

Their work finished, Benjie crawled back for a final check. His attention was arrested by Chico's action with the stick. Plunging it into the bale like a master swordsman skewering an enemy, the boy then pulled it out and slashed at the top of the bale. White powder rained over the black plastic like a shower of dandruff.

"Por que?" he whined, dealing the surrogate enemy another good whack which set the white granules dancing.

"Mas tarde, Chico, a little later," Benjie answered absently, his attention focused on the powder. Without wrenching the dowel away, he grabbed and examined the end. Two or three inches showed white. Directing it back into the opening, he shoved until it stopped. Withdrawing it, he saw the tip was coated with powder. He wiped it clean and shoved it in a second time. Again it came out coated with powder. Sniffing it, he didn't recognize the scent, but he didn't know what he was supposed to smell in any case. Still, he was certain that his find was either heroin or cocaine.

"Que pasa?" Sitting up, Chico was trying to peer around him to see what he was doing.

"Nada, nothing." Benjie yanked the stick away from him. "You can't play with these. They're important, they tell us how much water and fuel we've got, understand? And don't poke holes in the bales—you'll damage the tobacco!"

Josh was in the galley as Benjie came crawling over the stacks. Separated by a counter, it was the only area of the main cabin where one could still stand, though one had to stoop to keep from bumping the ceiling. His wet clothes discarded, Josh was donning a suit of thermal underwear he found in one of the clothes lockers. Sized for a short fat person, the fit was all wrong for him, with leg ends halfway to the knees and sleeves almost to his elbows. The waist could fit two of him and the seat drooped like an unfilled balloon. A rope belt held it all together.

"What weird pear shape fitted into this?" he joked as Benjie eased down into the galley. "He must've had an elephant's ass to fill all this."

Grabbing the seat, he stretched it out a foot behind him. Benjie turned away without replying, seething with anger. Slipping his rigger's knife from the sheath attached to his belt, he slashed through the plastic and burlap wrappings of the nearest bale and began scooping out handfuls of the dried weed.

"Hey, hey, man, why damage another one?" Josh objected. "Why not take from one we already opened?"

"Come on, you bastard, you know why! You probably fixed it so it's the one bale without a surprise package inside!"

"Surprise what? What the fuck you talking about?"

Benjie ignored him and continued scooping a tunnel to the center, oblivious to the mess he was creating.

"Mind telling me why you're busting open a perfectly good bale when there's one already open?" Josh demanded hotly. "And why are you treating our precious weed like it was plain old grass or hay?"

Benjie continued digging. Then, his fingers touched something he was certain he'd find there. After a few more scoops and a forceful tug, he withdrew a two-pound plastic bag of powder from its hiding place like a reluctant newborn forced from the womb prematurely.

"For this!" he cawed with bitter triumph, shoving it into Josh's belly. "And don't tell me it's all a big surprise to you!"

Josh's shock lasted hardly longer than it took him to whisper a drawn out "Jeeesssus!" He stared at the bag wide-eyed, then looked at Benjie. "You mean every goddamn bale aboard has one of these surprise packages inside?"

"Don't kid me, Josh. Two out of two is a perfect average." Too shaken to say more, he could only glare at his friend.

"Holy Jesus cow! A hundred and fifty kilos of shit!" Josh almost staggered from the weight of the figures racing through his head. "Benjie, buddy, do you have any idea of the value involved? A street price of forty or fifty million, maybe more! We're rich as Croesus if we can get it to market! Even wholesaling it, we're talking a range of five to ten million. The grass is scratch, nothing compared to this—this bonanza!"

His enthusiasm bubbled too fresh to be contrived. Benjie began to realize that Josh's surprise was genuine.

"And we were gonna let the whole shipment go for less than half a million!" Josh scoffed derisively. He chided himself for being taken for a turkey and nearly outconned. It was clear now why that sly old florist, Don José, was so easy to do business with. After only a slight bargaining skirmish, the price of the cocaine was reduced a third. The pressures of government crackdowns and bulging warehouses, he'd been led to believe by the gentleman's hints. For the same reasons he was reasonable and accommodating in the marijuana purchase. Naturally. The old fox was using them as unwitting mules for delivery of a hundred and fifty kilos of heroin. The two kilos of underpriced coke was his little scam, his treat—the *boca* out front to distract them from what he was up to in back. It explained the care in packaging and the skilled crew of stevedores waving away any help, providing a Miami buyer and arranging the rendezvous in the Biminis. Appalled at his own gullibility, Josh wondered what other tricks he might have overlooked.

"How'd you come onto this?" he asked in a whisper.

Benjie jerked a thumb in the direction of the forward cabin where Chico was still protesting his quarantine. "Our cops-and-robbers kid, playing Robin Hood with one of the dipsticks." Josh's duplicity, by then nearly laid to rest, led to the worse dilemma of what to do about the strange new cargo aboard. Benjie had no qualms about trafficking in marijuana, but the powder represented a profoundly new dimension.

"It is horse or coke?"

"Horse," said Josh. It was the answer Benjie dreaded most.

"You sure? Absolutely?"

When Josh nodded, Benjie said he thought heroin came from Turkey and Afghanistan or at least via processors in Marseilles and Hong Kong. Josh admitted he thought the same, but was more willing to accept the proposition that business will find the path of least resistance.

"Why not?" he challenged, seeing Benjie still unconvinced. "They've had the French connection doped out for years, the Golden Triangle too. Why not slip it through a different door? Bolivia's been known to cultivate the poppy. Maybe Don José is processing their crop, or maybe he's growing his own flowers in plastic hothouses to guard against aerial surveillance. Don't imagine it's any trick growing poppies, either."

"Shit!" said Benjie, his feelings knotted in a single word.

"Yeah, that's what it is all right."

"This is no joke!" Benjie fumed, stabbing his index finger into Josh's bony chest.

"Don't push the panic button yet, old buddy," Josh counseled him. "Just remember, we didn't contract for it, it was dumped in our laps—"

"We'll dump the shit overboard!" Benjie sputtered.

Josh went saucer-eyed and pale.

"Oh man, no! Don't even think it. Imagine what they'd do to us if we deliver the grass and the powder's missing. Don't you see? The powder's the whole point of the shipment!"

They exchanged ominous glances.

"They got us boxed in, you mean," Benjie groaned, shaking his head. "Horse is the worst, Josh. Really addicting shit! I could take smuggling coke in, maybe, but—horse! It freaks me out to be part of that evil scene."

His woeful stare made Josh even more nervous.

"Yeah, well, just remember somebody's gonna supply them their bags. If not us, somebody else. Feel for the poor bastards who suffer when the supply's cut off."

"Don't give me that shit, Josh! You know as well as I do, they can get methadone or go on one of the rehab programs. They don't really have to suffer anymore." He wasn't sure that was strictly true and not more media fluff than reality. He knew in England heroin was legally dispensed, not only for addicts but as a painkiller for terminally ill patients. Josh found other arguments just as cogent.

"Maybe so, but obviously a lot of them won't or can't, or the stuff wouldn't command the price it does. In any case we've gotta think about us first. Número Uno. If we dump the shit and go in with just the pot, you can guess what's in our future." He made the motions of firing a pistol into his head. "And dumping us for shark food."

Josh's expression softened and he grasped Benjie's shoulder. "But why so glum, chum? Now that we're in on the secret, why not try turning it to profit? Let's do some more bargaining and pick up an extra few million!"

"And get our heads blown off, as you so graphically indicated? You're dreaming, Josh."

"You got a point. Perhaps there's no bargaining with them. If we weren't in such a hurry to unload, we could skip the rendezvous entirely and look for new buyers. Or..." He gave his beard few thoughtful tugs and grinned. "There's a better way of dealing with the situation and getting some sweet revenge at the same time. We might substitute a percentage of the bags with sugar and flour."

Benjie turned away without replying. Words failed him.

"We'll talk about it later." He threw Josh a weary look, sourly wondering how best to contain the vile secret. "For the time being, just the two of us, okay? Not even Dynamite."

Weeto was at the wheel when Benjie came topside to check the results of their effort. Dynamite was his glum lookout, gazing forward with her chin resting against her hand on the cabin top.

"Well?" Benjie grunted, eyeing the bow.

"Improved," Dyna replied laconically.

"Better," Weeto seconded, "but we could still use some sail up there. She still digs in too much."

He watched Weeto struggle with the wheel when the big ones struck, saw the bow dip too sluggishly and knew he'd have to get the storm jib hanked on. He got a wind reading of twenty-six, an improvement over the night hours but hardly noticeable in the sea conditions. The waves looked angrier in daylight than he imagined them the night before.

The rain had stopped but visibility was cut to less than a quarter-mile by spray and the heavy cloud cover. He reminded Weeto to pinch into the wind as much as possible without losing headway. He wanted to find the bank in daylight hours and hug that side, at least until nightfall. Without any sunsights, the bank was his only sure way of knowing they hadn't drifted too close to Castro's side of the channel.

If visibility improved, they might sight Guinchos Cay which would fix their position. Failing that, he could still get a fix of sorts where the bank made its sharp curve north. By late afternoon or dusk, if his dead reckoning was in the ballpark, they ought to be clear of the channel and in the wider Santaren Channel, out in the open with a clean shot north along the bank all the way to the Biminis.

The condition of the sails, his navigational calculating and the fresh air after the closed musty atmosphere of the cabin came like heady medicines dispelling a hangover. He almost forgot his targeted destination was no prize Eden, nor an experience to look forward to. He even failed to notice Dyna's subdued and cheerless air.

Chapter Twenty-One

No matter the storm, daylight is always a restorative. Chico's shouts jarred Dyna out of her dark mood and she went below to make coffee and scrounge up a hot meal. Benjie untied Chico from the bunk and, as he bounded topside, took the opportunity to stuff and repair the hole in the bale so it wouldn't show. He remembered he needed to get the storm jib, which was stowed in the lazaret.

As he stuck head and shoulders inside to pull out the sail bag, he noticed the cuts in the beam. His finger found the notch and the cover plate yielded to his pressure. Reaching inside, he withdrew a leather bag. Excited by his find, he jerked his head back abruptly, striking the side of his head on the beam.

Cursing and massaging his aching head, he wondered at the hollow sound the beam made. Examining it, he saw it was twice the thickness of its sister beams. The larger size wasn't unusual but a hollow beam was worse than decorative fakery—on a boat it was an invitation to disaster. Feeling inside the opening, he was relieved to find the backside solid. He tapped it with a knuckle. Only the front section appeared hollow; behind was four inches of solid oak.

Untying the drawstring of the leather bag, he saw the green stones inside and poured some into his hand. Josh and the jeweler, he speculated. Some kind of switch. It dawned on him that Josh might have lied about the cost of the pot. What if some of the money went to purchase the emeralds? He had no idea of their worth, but why would Josh conceal them unless it was his own private stash and he didn't intend sharing with them?

He took a closer look at the beam. Benjie listened intently as he rapped beyond the niche holding the emeralds and continued to where the beam butted into the rib at the hull. To the casual glance it looked a solid piece of wood, especially as everything was painted white inside the locker. Great pains had been taken installing a fake addition, scarfing it meticulously to the existing beam to hide any traces of the lay-on. Why had such care been taken in disguising it unless it was intended for a hiding place? He searched but couldn't find any mechanism for springing it open. Any other time he might have explored it to the end but there were more pressing matters requiring his attention. Get the storm jib raised.

Normally he would have called Dyna to take over the wheel while he raised a sail, but as she was busy in the galley and Weeto was fast learning the intricacies of sail handling, he let Weeto stay on the wheel. After he removed and bagged the torn jib and got the storm jib hanked on, he signaled Weeto to head up as he went to the mast to hoist it on the halyard. Then everything happened at once.

Weeto let the bow swing too far. He didn't rev up the engine enough to offset the grab of the wind catching the sails from the other side. With a sickening thud the booms whipped to the other side and slammed the vessel into her opposite heel. Benjie was taken by surprise and, but for grabbing hold of a mast cleat, might have been thrown. Weeto's yell echoed from the cockpit at the same time Dyna's screams erupted from the cabin.

When Benjie looked aft, no one was on the wheel. Both Weeto and Chico had disappeared from the cockpit. Then, catching sight of Weeto's lower torso draped over the coaming, head and shoulders out of sight over the lee rail, he guessed what had happened. Chico had gone over and Weeto was trying to get a hand on his lifeline.

With the wind in command of the sail, and the engine in gear, anyone being dragged through the water would take a terrible beating. He slipped the knot of the main halyard and freed it from the cleat, letting the mainsail drop as he ran for the cockpit and threw the gearshift in neutral. At the same time the cabin door swung open and he caught a glimpse of Josh frantically beating at flames with a towel. Smoke billowed around the corner from the galley. Josh's shouts accompanied the banging of the wildly swinging door.

Benjie flung himself over the coaming next to Weeto. Still hauling with both hands on the lifeline, Weeto had Chico alongside and nearly abreast. Benjie leaned down and caught him under one arm. Weeto released the line and grabbed him by the other and together they hoisted him aboard. Benjie noted he was very much alive, but dazed and coughing water. Turning, he dove through the open hatch.

Josh was on the near side of the counter, atop the bales in the dining alcove, beating flames with a towel which was itself ablaze. Dyna was trapped in the far corner of the galley, battling the fire with the wet clothes Josh had discarded there earlier. Their flailing efforts were only scattering and spreading the fires.

"Smother it!" Benjie yelled, unsnapping his foul weather jacket.

Cooking oil flamed in streaks over the plastic-covered bales, most at the base of the stove. Like little rivers, they ran mercurially with the boat's rocking motion. The plastic only smoked and melted but if it got to the burlap and dried weed beneath he knew there'd be no stopping it. Slipping out of his jacket, he threw it over the puddle of flames nearest him and dropped into the galley well. While he trod the jacket underfoot, he jockeyed one of the bales out of its slot, shouting more orders.

"Drop them!" he yelled frantically signaling Dyna to discard the clothes she was flailing the flames with. As she did so, he dropped the bale on the smoldering remnants of Josh's wardrobe. He wrestled another and a third bale from the stacks and dropped them on other burning patches. Small liquid pools were still flaming on the stove top but Dyna quickly smothered them with kitchen towels. A minute later the remaining fires were extinguished. Miraculously no one was burned or hurt.

"My poncho!" Josh wailed, spotting its smoking remains.

"Shit, Benjie," Dynamite snapped, "you might have warned us you were coming about."

She stooped to retrieve the pots and pans coated with broken eggs and grease. "They flipped right over the rails. Yuck!"

"No time to apologize," he called over his shoulder, heading for the hatch. "Just make sure it's all out while I check on Chico."

"What's with Chico?" she yelled after him. Till then neither she nor Josh was aware of any problem but their own.

Weeto had the boy half-stripped out of his waterlogged clothes. There were no signs of an injury. He was apparently more preoccupied with retrieving the fishing pole that had fallen overboard with him.

"Forget about your fish pole," Weeto scolded as he roughly lifted him and stripped off the pants and shorts. "That's halfway to the bottom by now!"

"No, no, Poppi, I see it, I see it!" he objected excitedly.

His pole floated where he pointed. No more than a few boat lengths behind, its acrylic red and yellow was the only shiny contrast in the dull froth of gray and white. Benjie threw the engine in reverse and moved slowly towards it. Dyna stood by with the boat hook and dragged it in to the cheers of the naked boy on the seat cushions, his modesty momentarily overlooked in his joy at retrieving a prize possession. If there had been a fish on the end earlier, it was gone now. Even the bait was gone. The hook came up clean.

"That's twice you went overboard," said Dyna, withholding the pole a moment. "Three times and you're out. Know what that means?"

"*Si, beisbol,*" he answered seriously, then grinned as he held out his hand.

"What she means," Weeto interjected, giving Dyna a wink of appreciation, "is that if you go over again you might not be so lucky. Maybe no one will be around to hear you or save you."

Anxious to get the sails up and back on course, Benjie let Weeto take another crack at it, but not without warning him to rev the engine as necessary. Any other time Dyna might have stayed to proctor his handling of the wheel, but this time she ducked below with Chico in tow to find him dry clothes and make another start on breakfast. This time the adjustments went without a hitch. The small storm sail gave just enough lift to peak the bow over most of the rough stuff and they rode the better for it. Steering was easier, too. Benjie stayed with a single-reefed main. Conditions called for double-tucks but he was betting on a general improvement. Back on course, he took another wind reading and felt reassured. It was the same as before, but without the sudden gusts.

Returning below, the sight of Josh in the galley, still cleaning up the mess, rekindled Benjie's anger. Seeing Dyna in the far corner atop the bales in the dining alcove, dressing Chico, wouldn't stop him from saying what he had to get off his chest. If might even help her to see things more clearly.

"Jesus, a fire at sea!" Josh grumbled when he saw Benjie coming down into the galley. "Is there anything more dangerous to life and limb?"

"Falling out of an airplane, maybe," Benjie offered. Remembering the fire extinguishers positioned around the boat, buried now under cargo, was a reminder of the risks that accumulated when you loaded up with too much greed. "Why were you hiding the emeralds from us, Josh?"

Josh squinted up at Benjie. "Which one?" Dyna silently observed them from her perch in the corner.

"The ones you got stashed in the lazaret. Or do you have other bags hidden somewhere else on the boat?"

"Don't I wish!" Josh guffawed. "For all our sakes! Know what that little bag of nuggets might be worth in the States? Between fifty and a hundred big ones if we don't panic-sell and find the right fence."

"Where'd you get the dough for them, and why were you keeping it secret from Dyna and me?" He looked for her reaction but she didn't look up. Dyna fidgeted with a button on Chico's shirt.

"They didn't cost us anything," Josh explained. "To the second charge, I plead guilty. I kept it secret knowing that you'd disapprove. I didn't plan to say anything until we got safely ashore and cashed them in." He blinked innocently. "I had no intention of cutting you out of your rightful shares. I've never considered this anything but a joint venture involving a three-way split of all the profits."

"Who's talking shares or profits!" Benjie raged. "The emeralds are chicken feed compared to—" He checked himself. He didn't want Dyna and Weeto more involved than they already were. "It's the lies you tell, and your way of doing things behind our backs."

Josh remained calm. "Subterfuge is second nature to me. You know that, old buddy. And lies, you ought to know, are only my way of helping life's farce along. For fun and laughs, a bit of enter-tainment—is that so bad?" The pained look faded, and he stared at Benjie impassively. "But dishonest in trust or affection for friends—no, never!" He glanced at Dyna. "I did not use your money to pay for the emeralds."

"Then how?" Benjie exploded. "And don't tell me they were another gift from your faggot friend, that old-auntie jeweler!"

"No-no's, friend, unless you want others to judge your sexual intimacies," Josh cautioned, wagging a finger. "No lie. In a way they were like a gift from my merchant friend, though I tend to regard it more in the form of a loan which, God willing, when we get our cargo of goodies safely delivered, I have every intention of repaying him in full."

"You mean you stole them!" Benjie exclaimed in dismay. "All that stage play was to set him up, not by the street boys but by you!"

Josh feigned a hurt look. "My, you put things severely when you choose not to see all sides. What if I said I merely relieved the thieves of them after they stole them from Sergio. Would you believe me? Or would you insist I should have returned them? Ask yourself, could I?" He shot an inquisitive glance at Dyna before answering his own question. "My plan required split-second timing. Without their cooperation, it was dead. I'd have blown everything if I returned the stones later."

"I don't know what part of your stories to believe anymore," said Benjie, shaking his head.

"The important part. The only part that matters—our relationship." Josh grasped his arm. "My esteem and affection for both of you. Consider that it may all have been done to shield and protect a couple of innocents I happen to like and care for very much."

"Yeah, well…we're none of us so innocent anymore," Benjie said as he headed for the hatch. "If we ever were."

Dyna's cheeks burned from the possible import of what he said. Propping Chico up in the corner, she covered him in a blanket and crawled over the bales to the galley. "What was that all about?" she asked Josh.

"God knows," Josh said uncertainly. "You know him better than I." His eyes narrowed almost imperceptibly. "How'd he find out about the stones?"

Dyna held his gaze. "Probably the same way I found out about your powder in the sugar jar—by snooping."

"Oh you found my little white message, did you?" he said smugly. "Of course, as I've told you before, I'd rather you didn't know. It could lay you open to additional charges, in case—in case we don't make it through the blockade. I didn't want to hang that on either of you. Let's pretend you still don't know anything about it, okay?"

Dyna was in no mood to be dismissed so lightly. "What is it?" she demanded. "The big H or little c?"

"God no, not H." He cast a look in the corner where Chico was perched. "Just a batch of c for the Miami contact."

"That's why you needed the five thousand on the mountain, isn't it? How much will it sell for?"

"Remember what I told you—don't ask questions. What you don't know can't hurt you—"

"How much, Josh?"

"I haven't bargained on it yet. Maybe a hundred G's."

"Per kilo, and you've got two kees there." Even so, the figures were hardly enough to impress her anymore.

"No, for both! You see, you're getting wholesale and street prices all mixed up. And you're thinking horse, which commands a higher price." He studied her face. "You're not going to tell Benjie, are you?"

"No, I won't tell Benjie," she promised, enjoying besting him for once. "As for the rest, I'll let you know when we divvy up profits. Like the cabbie warned us, I intend to count my money twice."

She laughed loudly, then planted a kiss on his cheek. "I owe you one for protecting me. I could have come clean and backed you up with Benjie but the timing didn't seem right. I'll drop it on him later."

"You don't have to. In fact, I'd rather you didn't."

"Why? Because our stories might conflict?"

"Something like that." But his evasiveness suggested more elaborate reasons. Dyna flared again.

"He doesn't own me, you know. If he gets ballsy because I share some secrets with other guys, that's tough. He'll have to live with it, or else without me!"

"It's your rap, momma. But don't think you need to, to save my skin. I'm callused all over."

"The truth now, about the emeralds," she said suddenly. "How'd you really latch onto them?"

Josh chuckled. "Would you believe me if I repeated what I told Benjie a minute ago—an unplanned and accidental theft?"

"No. No more than I believe you intend to repay him."

"You see? Why ask then?" He grinned with the confidence of a man in complete control again. "You'll just have to wait and see, won't you, momma?"

Chapter Twenty-Two

That afternoon the weather eased and the wind began to shift direction as Benjie had hoped. To his relief, shortly after three they came on the bank, easily visible by its pale color even in the flurry of whitecaps frothing the surface like beer foam. Poor visibility still prevented sighting Guinchos; he'd have only the bank curvature to estimate their position. For the next two hours he looked for the point where it made its pronounced curve north. Just before dark, he spotted it. Then he went below to finish his evening chart work and set the course for the night.

Because of the cargo he had to do his charting in the head, on the counter extension of the washbasin, the only flat area where he could lay a chart on a firm surface and work the parallel rulers and dividers. The charts needed for this trip had been stowed on a shelf in the locker under the counter. As he stooped to leaf through them, looking for a more detailed one of the Bahamas, he noticed cuts in the beam bracing the counter top. They were the same as the pencil-line slits which framed the niche where the emeralds had been hidden.

The notched groove, when pressed, caused a cover plate to slide open on brass-lined channels. The space inside was empty and as small as the one in the lazaret. When he tapped the surrounding wood, it sounded hollow. Glancing underneath, he saw it was more a case than a beam, at least two feet wide and extending to the skin of the hull, six inches thick. No structural purpose suggested such a support. He felt inside the niche for knobs, protrusions or spring mechanisms. He pressed a finger around the inside surfaces. Nothing happened. Checking underneath again, he saw electric wires running along the hull and disappearing inside the false compartment. Was it wired to open electrically?

He recalled the snap switches in the control box on the galley bulkhead. He knew what they operated; stamped plastic tags spelled it out next to each button. He knew that the bottom button was tagless and appeared newer than the others. Dynamite was in the galley when he stepped into the passageway. He asked her to throw the bottom switch.

"And I wanna talk to you when you finish in there," she called out to him, then reached out and flipped on the switch. Slotting the plastic dishware into place, she threw the cupboard seabolt and spread the towel over the stovetop to hasten drying. Then she climbed out of the galley and across the stacks to the passageway, to have it out with Benjie.

Pushing on the door, Benjie's back blocked it from opening more than a foot or so. When Dynamite peeked inside, the reflection in the mirror of the medicine cabinet made her head spin. Diamonds mounted on black velvet trays glittered on the countertop like animal eyes spotlighting at night. Hundreds of them winked back at her. Benjie was still pulling trays out from under the counter. She gasped and Benjie leaned forward to let her in.

"My God! Whose? How?" She staggered to the toilet seat and sat down.

"At least I know it wasn't your doing," he laughed, giddy from the astonishing discovery.

"You don't think Josh...do you?" she asked, barely able to formulate a thought.

"No, for once I can't blame Josh. This is the work of someone who planned it very carefully. Look at the craftsmanship— beautiful joiner work, precision cabinetry, electrically operated switches. Somebody went to great pains and spent a lot of money preparing this home for the diamonds."

"You think they're the...the real thing?" she stammered breathlessly.

"I can't see anybody doing all this expensive camouflage for glass or zircons," he mused. "I haven't even checked the other hiding place, where Josh hid the emeralds. No telling what else we might find—"

"Where I hid the emeralds," Dyna corrected. "He was leveling with you but trying to protect me at the same time. I knew about the emeralds all along. We were only keeping it secret from you until we got ashore." Her eyes ravaged the diamonds. "Who put them there?"

"Why is what's bothering me," he replied pointedly, still sliding out trays of the precious stones. "A prior owner or skipper rigged all this, but why? You don't smuggle diamonds out of the U.S.—you smuggle them in."

"Unless they were smuggled in, on her last voyage or—"

"And they forgot they put them here?" he scoffed, smiling wryly.

"Maybe only one person knew and he was killed or something." She lifted one of the trays and saw an Amsterdam tag on the bottom. "At least we know the trays came from Amsterdam. Isn't it likely the diamonds did too?"

"She's never been to Europe, at least it's not logged in."

"Don't tell me you're logging in our passage to Colombia and back," she derided him with a laugh. "Are you detailing the kind of cargo we're carrying, too?"

"Don't get cocky. Yes, I'm logging it, in a new logbook I started. If we're going to be the *Gorda* we better get some history under our keel in case we're ever boarded and inspected." He threw her a snide grin. "And no, I didn't mention any cargo. We're supposed to be a pleasure yacht, remember?"

"Ouch, I deserved that. Care to sock me again?" There was more than play behind her mock masochism, but it was overwhelmed by the rising tide of wealth on the counter. "How much do you think they're worth?"

"Your guess is as good as mine. I haven't the faintest—a couple hundred thousand, a million? I doubt I've ever seen any but one- or two-carat diamonds. These look twice that size." Somehow, vocalizing the figures made them seem less impressive. Josh's talk of fifty million tied up in the white powder made everything else sound puny in comparison. What was happening to his sense of value?

An instant later, Dyna suggested keeping it a secret from the others for now, and he readily agreed. Only on second thought was he troubled that he'd acquiesced in another deception. Was it the habit of those involved in big stakes and easy money, or just his own peculiar weakness? He began putting the diamond trays back in their hiding place.

"I have to pee, and I'm thirsty," Dyna sighed, knocking her knees together. Excitement always hit her on one end or the other, and big excitement hit both ends simultaneously. She slipped her jeans and panties down to work on one problem while Benjie turned away to run her a glass of water from the basin spigot.

She had a flash of doubt about her lifelong sense of charmed luck, quite apart from the recurring windfalls of the past week. She'd discarded the notion that Weeto might snitch on her, but while in the past it wouldn't have stuck in her mind, now it troubled her; she sensed a loss of control.

"Am I embarrassing you?" she teased.

"No, I know it has two uses." He grinned and tapped a kiss on her forehead as he handed her the water.

"Aren't you going to check the other hiding place?" she reminded him.

"First things first. If I don't get us plotted on course, we may not live to enjoy our profits. We could end on a reef like the galleons of old. Or like this fine lady almost did a month ago—four hundred fathoms under."

"You don't sound all that excited about the diamonds."

Benjie shrugged. "What's one more fortune piled on top of another? I'm already staggered by all the numbers being thrown around. A month ago we had no boat, lousy jobs and an uncertain future. Suddenly we've got a millionaire's yacht, a half-million dollars in pot, fifty thousand in emeralds and God only knows how much in that hoard of diamonds. I feel like a bloody rock musician who finally hits it big with a gold record. I can't believe it's for real yet."

"You sound like Josh when you say 'bloody,'" she snickered.

"Company rubs off," he reasoned. "Anyway this comes first. I'll get excited if and when we get it all cashed in. Why don't you check on what other surprises might be hidden in the lazaret?"

As he was demonstrating how to trip the lock mechanism, she sensed a failing excitement. Something had worn thin. Were there other treasures she'd been neglecting? She kissed the back of his neck where blond fuzz made tiny golden curls on his tanned skin, finer than the finest artisan's filigree in the Gold Museum. "I love this part of your anatomy, luv. I'd fuck you right now, but I know you wanna get the chart work done. You're so bloody dedicated to duty."

"To staying alive!" Benjie corrected, then smiled at her. "And Josh is bloody well rubbing off on you, too!"

"Jealous?"

"Should I be?"

"Not a whit! Meet me on the fantail at ten—if the coast is clear and weather permits. A new trick to show you." She warbled lascivious laughter and kissed the back of his neck again before squeezing out of the door.

Part of her felt like a hypocrite. Not that her feelings were any less genuine than before, but because her action with Weeto had cast shadows on them, they were suspect. Her practical side resisted the notion of confession, seeing no virtue in volunteering slips that only hurt. Who had a right to expect it? Or getting it, who truly benefited? Who says it takes two scars to heal a wound?

A few minutes later she was back, pushing the door in against Benjie, stopping only to offer a deflated comment. "It opened, but there's nothing inside—zero, zilch. My wand must have lost its magic."

"Disappointed?" he asked taking her hand. "You're expecting a new fortune every time you turn around?"

"A fortune an hour gilds the ugliest flower. Who could deny wanting it? *Un milagro,* as our crazy taxi driver would say. Why not! We've been getting them nearly that regularly for almost a month. Are we dreaming or is it for real?"

"I'll let you know when we cash it all in."

"When it least matters," she said slowly, pulling her hand away. "Isn't the fun always more in the anticipation than the realization?" Her tone was so weighted, so curiously uncharacteristic, he glanced up to look at her. But she was already gone.

He bent over the chart, walking the dividers along the course line to compute the distance to the Cat Cays, south of Bimini. Her presence still permeated the closed cubicle, making his body swell with a sweet ache for the pleasure she brought him. Definably physical, yet indefinably vastly more. The thought of being deprived of it, of losing her, overshadowed his optimism. He fought the sinking impulse. But the realities behind it continued to pull on him, dragging him down from below, like a buoy weighted to ride low in the water instead of floating free on the surface. The shadowy ghost of his father was still lurking nearby.

Chapter Twenty-Three

From their 5:00 P.M. position to the rendezvous island, Benjie calculated they could make it before dark the next day if they maintained their present speed. Ordinarily the Gulf Stream added a mile or so to their progress, but the storm's effect would cut into that. Severe northers sometimes slowed it to a standstill; close along the bank it could reverse it at times. Even with the storm passing, it would take a day or two for the stream to return to normal.

Conditions, though vastly improved over the night before, were still rough and choppy. Benjie noted conditions and the suit of sails he had flying, reefed main and jib, exactly right for the night. The big lady was responding with no excessive heel or helm and her bow was riding high and proud as she slashed through the waves. Running along the lee of the bank where waves didn't have the momentum to build into slammers, they were riding smoother than he had any right to expect.

Back on two-hour watches, Weeto was at the wheel when the wind changed as Benjie anticipated—five degrees to starboard of the compass course and the sails stayed full. There was no point in compensating for the earlier hours, however, and chancing going up on the bank. They could close with it in the morning. In the red glow of the binnacle light, they exchanged satisfied smiles.

"Pretty good boat, eh?" Weeto asked as if the vessel itself had induced the wind change.

"A beauty," Benjie agreed. "She's got good balance, she's stiff and rides smooth and goes nicely to windward. Wish I could feel she was really mine."

"Still can't feel it?" Weeto laughed. "Think that you're only borrowin' it then. Hell, everything's borrowed. We got to give it all up someday."

"That's true." He was curious where Weeto's line would take them. "Crazy world, you know? A month ago we were haulin' ass to get outta here. I thought I could never come back. That's a bad feeling, to think you can't go home again. Like you been robbed of what belongs to you.

"Everything's borrowed, you've got to give it all up someday," Benjie parroted, offering him a joint. He took without hesitation and lit up.

"Sure, when I'm dead. Meantime, it belongs to me, like that five-year-old monkey's mine till he grows up. I don' mean to work or abuse or treat like a toy. Jus' to help him grow up and learn about life. It's knowin' you don' die out completely, a piece of you still lives on in your kid."

Benjie absently ran a hand over the stubble on his jaw. "What about people who choose not to have kids? Isn't it enough to know the race survives? Personal immortality isn't important, only the survival of the species."

Weeto chose his words carefully. "My son is a link in the chain of my existence. I'll stay in his mind until he dies."

"An adopted child can serve the same purpose."

"For me, it's not the same. I din help to create him."

"He's a really fine boy," Benjie said. "Aren't you afraid all those Texas millions might spoil him?"

"You din tell the others about that, did you?" Weeto asked, glancing sideways at him. "Not even Dynamite?"

"It's still our secret."

"Because, you know," said Weeto, visibly relieved, "I'm afraid somebody's playin' a big joke on me. Sure I'd like some money to do what I want, to set Chico up right—but millions!

That's crazy! Nobody should have that kind of money." Taking another drag on the joint, he handed it to Benjie. "I tell you one thing, though. You won't see me kissin' that ol' man's hand to get his money. If he don' like my Spic accent, I'll tell him where he can shove his dough!"

Benjie admired, perhaps even envied, Weeto's commitment to principles. He knew he was racing to deliver heroin to a bunch of underworld thugs because he feared what they might do to him if he didn't. Would they really pursue him, or was that just another excuse? If they dumped the load, pot and all, and sailed off to Europe with changed papers and names again, how far would the Mob go to find them? They resorted to violence and killing when it was profitable or convenient. He doubted they'd search the entire world just to punish people who were neither threats to them or their future profits.

The diamonds, even shared with Weeto, looked like enough to make them all comfortable. The profit from the drugs was a swilling, a piggish excess. So why was he delaying a showdown with Josh on the horse and hurrying to the rendezvous unless, in truth, he was just another on that long list of greedy bastards? Weeto could tell an old man to shove his millions, but what could he say about himself?

"I'm sorry I got on your back about this stuff," said Weeto, taking the joint back from him. "It's one thing you're doin' something illegal, and you know the price you gonna pay if they catch you. But I meant it was evil stuff and you were doin' a bad thing. I don't think so now..."

"It's not an unmitigated good," Benjie hedged. "But maybe it's no worse than other ways we abuse ourselves."

"Yeah, but those hard junkies involve little kids," Weeto spoke up. "They use teenagers and children sometimes to make their drops. Pretty soon the kids get hooked too. Who can stand for that?"

The indisputable fact behind mass public fears, cornerstone of popular demand for Draconian measures. Who could argue with the need to protect children from alcohol and tobacco as well as the pharmacopoeia of pills and powders in the marketplace? But people always get the cart and the horse reversed. Pushers use kids for deliveries to avoid the severe punishments. So did the bootleggers of Prohibition days.

"Bad laws breed more crime and mounting punishment," he added. "I could tell you some really crazy examples from the past and present ..."

Weeto was astonished to hear that coffee-drinkers and tobacco-users were once punished by death in Central Europe. Chocolate was once forbidden to all but royalty. In some Muslim countries today, hashish is legal and widely used, while use of alcohol is severely punished. Absurd reactions are everywhere, giving the impression of madmen let loose among the lawmakers. And with a stranglehold now on the most profitable trade the world has ever known, underworld interests would fight tooth and nail to influence the masses, the media, and governments to keep it mythicized and illegal. We'd pay hell to get the laws changed now.

"Jeez, I din know," said Weeto, shaking his head. "You mean they gonna get it anyway, so why not control it like liquor and tobacco and get some taxes out of it instead of all those big profits goin' to Mob bosses?"

"And enticing the young with promises of big profits," Benjie added, "which is only filling our jails. Something like that. There'd be no need to use kids anymore and it would defuse or at least minimize the problem."

Accepting the joint from Weeto, he took a last small puff before tossing it over the side, pleased he had such a supply he could afford to discard it before it scorched his lips.

Because of the morning's mix-up, the old order of rotation at the helm had changed. When Weeto went off at ten and Benjie took over, Josh came on as relief watch. Conditions were almost good enough to dispense with lookouts, but his talk with Weeto had cleared his thinking and he was determined to have it out with Josh. But when he came up bearing mugs of coffee for the two of them and in good spirits, Benjie knew it wouldn't be easy.

"She's the end, that momma of yours. Know what she told me? If we get intercepted, she's gonna stuff the emeralds up her you-know-what! Both apertures, in her case. She got the idea from Papillon and the prisoners on Devil's Island. Said she figures she's got double their carrying capacity!"

"I think they're onto that ruse," Benjie said. "Don't they have X-ray machines that can tell if you're carrying anything in your body cavities?"

"Better believe it. They can tell what you had for your last meal. Nothing's private or sacred anymore, not even a woman's womb. Bad as they treated guys on Devil's Island, they didn't make them spread their cheeks and fart just to prove they didn't have contraband up their assholes."

As usual he sounded like he was talking from experience, but didn't he always on any given subject? Just as quickly he became an expert on diamonds when Benjie revealed the latest discovery. When Benjie described the size and number of the stones, Josh went bananas.

"If they're for real and of any quality, we could be talking millions!"

"There you go again," Benjie uttered irritably. "You're always talking millions. Let's be conservative. Say they're two- and three-carat stones and of only average quality. Say they could wholesale for three to five hundred each. That's three hundred thousand to half a million, more than I ever hoped to hold in my hand at any one time in my life."

Josh had caught on, his face long and drawn. "You wanna trade the diamonds off for the H is what you're getting at."

Benjie bulled ahead. "We never contracted for the H. It was never in our plans."

"You know we can't deliver the pot without the other," Josh reminded him.

"We dump it all, we don't deliver anything. We skip the rendezvous and keep going, up to Savannah or Charleston. We fence our other goodies and wait for the right weather to take off for Europe and cruise the Mediterranean." Saying it aloud made it sound so simple. Josh looked pained to the point of being sick.

"Oh, man, no! Not a cop-out! After all we went though putting it together? The dealing and dickering, transfer at sea, the storm, the fire—and now you wanna dump it? Oh shit, man, that freaks me out!"

Squirming and twisting on the seat, he folded and unfolded his arms, squeezing his hands while little moaning sounds rumbled in his throat.

"Beyond a certain point, money becomes meaningless," Benjie stated. "Or ought to."

"Fifty million," Josh muttered, a dazed look on his face. Suddenly he bolted from the seat and flung himself against the cabin, slamming a fist onto the cabin top. Benjie had never seen such a display of frustration.

"It's not the pot so much, is it? It's dumping the H that bothers you!"

Josh took no notice at first. Keeping his back turned, still pounding his fist, he continued his crazed wailing. "A sixty-million, maybe a seventy-million-dollar cargo! Maybe the biggest haul ever, first of its kind! Man, doesn't that do something for you?"

"Yeah. It scares the hell outta me!"

"Sixty, seventy, maybe even eighty million—"

"Street figures. You said so yourself," Benjie challenged, his voice rising. "After it's cut and diluted a dozen times. You're hypnotized by the big numbers!"

"Fucking well right I am!" Josh spat venomously. "The biggest haul ever! A record run, the slammer of the century! A day away from scoring the most lucrative coup in history and you wanna feed it to the fishes!"

"It's not a game, Josh—"

"Everything's a game!" he shouted, his face livid with rage. "Unless you choose to be a sheep and let the wolves make all the rules!"

Turning, he shot out his fist and struck the compass with such force the whole binnacle shook. "I'm owed one, by God!" he raved as he turned to the bulkhead and began rapping his fist on the cabin top again. "The shits owe it, they owe me this one!"

Josh pivoted abruptly and dropped next to him on the seat. He clamped a hand on Benjie's knee, squeezing tightly. "Look, good buddy, here's the story. Short and sweet."

It came instead bitterly, painfully. "I was in the slammer for a year and one month. My year in Afghanistan! In my mind, friend, strictly in my mind! To hold onto my sanity. I got busted down in dear old Texas, coming across from Juarez to El Paso. Two very hip guys I befriended turned out to be narks. They rapped me for possession and selling. I admit I intended selling some later to friends, but I never sold these guys a thing—I gave. I gave because I liked them. But because they lied, I got busted. They took away a year and a month of my life for three lousy loaves of Oaxaca Red!"

Benjie was stunned. The idol of his youth, master of the switch and double-switch, magician, schemer, leader, had been victimized by the manipulations of others. No matter how unfairly the punishment fit the crime, it was the risk of flouting laws and getting caught—a price they'd all have to pay if they ran into the Coast Guard.

"You see why the bastards owe me this one?" he asked bitterly, his eyes ablaze with anger and hurt. "The cruddy shits already took my time, so now let me have my crime!"

Josh related stories of young Americans caught in Mexican dragnets, aimed largely at satisfying U.S. demands for action. Many were innocent, but rotted anyway in Mexican jails for the minimum eighteen-month period before their cases even came to trial, always at great legal cost and mental anguish to themselves and their families. Even the guilty, subject to inmate extortion and physical abuse, were paying disproportionately for their crimes. It was the reason he had cleared out of Mexico.

"The shit was *demasiado*! Too easy to end up a statistic in the drug war. And it's Uncle Sam behind the screws down there. He'd rather punish you with prison, anybody's prison, than allow you to flout his list of no-no's."

Josh stared down at his hands, then slowly raised his eyes to Benjie. "I swear, Benjie, smack is one thing I wouldn't ordinarily deal in. But who am I to say the guy who needs it shouldn't have it? How can I deny any adult the right to choices that don't infringe on the rights of others?" He stood up, waving his arms. "Agreed, heroin's bad shit, but so is the law that gives the underworld control of the price and distribution. They put me in the slammer because I like to smoke a little pot and provide it to my friends. Now I can repay them with the biggest load of horse ever brought in and do the poor junkies a favor as well. Such a quantity will drive down the price, even restore some quality to the product. They might not even have to shoot, and they won't have to pay so much for their bags."

An elated chuckle seemed to lift him right up to the dizzy heights where he normally operated. "Hey, buzz your head on that awhile. We're not only playing doctor to those poor junkie wretches in New York, we're driving down the price. And there's a social factor—we'll be bringing down the crime rate at the same time!"

"You're foaming, Josh," Benjie laughed, but not without some respect. There was undeniable validity to some elements of the argument, though judged against the standards of other civilized nations like the British, Dutch, Swedes and others who treated addictions as medical problems rather than crimes, it left gaping holes.

Josh hyped his rationalizations until Benjie's shift was up. As if the subject of dumping never came up, he avoided it as carefully as a cautious skipper giving wide berth to a treacherous reef.

Nothing was settled as far as Benjie was concerned, but at the moment he didn't have the heart to press Josh anymore on the subject. It wouldn't be his sole decision in any case, he reminded himself. In a showdown he knew he'd have Weeto with him, but where would Dynamite fall in? He decided to sleep on it until morning.

Before Dyna came up to take over the relief post, he again cautioned Josh to keep the matter of the heroin between themselves. Josh agreed, but if Benjie had noticed the sudden fire in his eyes, he might have guessed that he had just reminded him where his ammunition was stored.

Chapter Twenty-Four

B y the time Benjie learned Josh had "inadvertently" leaked the problem of the heroin to Dynamite, it was too late. A helicopter swooped down on them in the midmorning hours when they were halfway between Dog Rocks and Orange Cay. Looking up at the sound of its beating rotors as it beelined for them from the northwest, those topside feared the worst. The Coast Guard.

Benjie was in the engine compartment, pumping the bilges, when they called him. Rushing on deck, his pulse eased as he realized from the chopper's size and color it was somebody's private toy. It circled and dipped low behind them, apparently intent on verifying the name on the transom, then came alongside at near eye level. It was pretty obvious it was the Miami connection checking on the progress of their merchandise.

"How about that? Big league stuff, huh?" Josh shouted over the noise, waving at the men in the bubble. "Nobody said anything about choppers coming to meet us."

"They act like they're expecting us anyway," Dyna said.

"Maybe jus' friendly cops," Weeto joked. "They don' look like Mafia guys to me."

The two men in the helicopter who smiled and waved back to them had the fresh appearance of crew-cut college boys out on a

Sunday lark. The passenger pointed straight down their course line, then clasped his hands over his head in a victory gesture. The chopper wagged in salute, then veered off in the direction of Miami.

"Well, they know where we are," Josh announced loudly. All his ranting the night before had been unnecessary, the decision had been made for them. "No point in pretending we vanished in a storm."

Dyna raised a hand to shield her eyes and peered into the distance. "Did you understand from his signals that a boat's waiting for us up ahead? Our arrival time isn't until dusk or later. Are they planning to unload us at night?"

"They're crazy if they plan to send powerboats across the Gulf Stream today," Weeto declared. "Unless they got heavy fishing trawlers."

Benjie wondered. Even in the lee of the bank the seas were running four to six feet. Out in the middle of the stream they'd be twice that high and more. Even heavy long-keeled boats would have trouble maneuvering in such conditions. Shallow-draft power-boats would be planing half the time, props out of the water, subject to being broadsided or buried in the troughs.

"I bet it's rough as a cob out there," said Weeto, echoing his thoughts. "I wouldn't want to cross today even in this boat."

"Unless it's already parked at the key and waiting for us," Josh offered, scratching his beard pensively.

"For a few tons of grass?" Weeto scoffed. "I'm surprised they went to all the trouble of the spotter."

Benjie saw Dyna's wink and knowing grin at Josh, and knew she was privy to the secret. He spit over the side to rid himself of the bad taste in his mouth.

Later, when they were alone on the stern having lunch together, he confronted her.

"Stop trying to put me on a pedestal," Dyna exploded, as if eager for the confrontation. "You expect too much of me, of everybody, including yourself. We're none of us angels, not even you! Somebody dangles a fortune under my nose and, damn right, I'll grab for it! I'm not ashamed to admit it!"

"But heroin, Dyna!"

"Don't lecture me, Benjie. I'm not shoving it down anybody's throat or sticking needles into their arms. I didn't create the problem and nothing I do or don't do is going to solve it."

"You're rationalizing."

"Damn right I am! And one definition of that word is 'conforming to reason.' Not a bad start for any human head. I'm not a moralizer or lawgiver. You know me—keep your goddamn laws off my body! The same with having kids. No busybody's going to tell me I have to have a baby because I ran out of pills or your rubber broke. Bad enough for the mother, but think how much worse for the kid. Babies should come wanted, otherwise you're just cluttering the world with more problems!"

She took a savage bite of her sandwich and continued, angrily spitting out the words as she chewed. "If I'm nutty enough to want to shoot up on drugs and waste myself, or if I get suicidal and put a gun to my head, don't put me in a straitjacket and lock me up for life. Reason with me, help me if you can, but then leave me be. It's my body, my life, my choice! Maybe it's the only way left for the human race to rid itself of its misfits and miscreants!"

He supposed he should be shocked by her words and the attitude behind it, taboo in a society so rich it seldom had to face ultimate choices. But he wasn't. Nature clearly demonstrated not only the expendability of individual organisms, but the necessity of their periodic culling for the maintenance of a healthy species. Why should mankind be any different?

Color flooded into Dynamite's cheeks and highlighted her prominent cheekbones, glowing bronze even in the overcast day. The green eyes flashed in their pools of pure white, luminous as gems, illuminated by a mind which alternately amused and dazzled him like a kaleidoscope. Her blond and creamy softness concealed the toughness and strength within.

"You agree with Josh then," he said, his anger dissipated.

A slice of bacon fell from her sandwich to the deck. She snatched it up and stuffed it into her mouth.

"If you had your way, I wouldn't even be in on your little secret," she rebuked, tossing her hair back indignantly. "Why are you always treating me like a stupid-ass kid?"

He wanted to say it was to protect her, but even in his head it rang hollow. Maybe he hoarded decisions the same way some people hoarded wealth. Still, his decisions belonged to him alone— he owned them.

"Why did Josh?" he countered hotly. "Can't you see he was using you to manipulate me? Why'd he drop that on you after he promised me he wouldn't?"

Dyna blushed slightly. "It just slipped out, it wasn't on purpose—"

"Things don't just slip out with him, you know that."

"What's it matter?" she concluded, her impatience squirming to shed the superfluous. "The helicopter made the decision for us. Isn't that enough? Why must we go on agonizing over something we have no control of any longer?"

Dynamite's agitation rose from sources other than Benjie's accusation or the moralizing over the heroin cache. What bothered most was the memory of the other night's rejection. Its unflattering implications were only a twinge in her vanity; worse was her sense of having damaged what she was beginning to see as the most meaningful part of her life: Benjie.

At two in the afternoon, when they were still a few hours from the Cats, a second helicopter appeared on the horizon. Coming from due north, it followed the edge of the bank. The same small size as the other, but this one was painted yellow. The color, brilliant against the gray skies even from a distance, saved them unnecessary concern—the Coast Guard's were white with orange stripes. It went through the same circling and hovering maneuvers, studying the stern for identification. Coming alongside, the pilot waved before turning back across the stream for Florida. "Hey, you are getting some welcome," Weeto shouted to Benjie in astonishment.

"Didn't I tell you." Josh elbowed Benjie. "Nothing moving. They're anxious to get business going again."

"Helicopter!" Chico squealed, taking a rifle sight along his fishing pole and "shooting" at the fleeing target.

Too bad he missed, Benjie thought. The first chopper had been perplexing, but this one had him worried. Weren't the two in radio communication? Why send a second when the first had already spotted and identified them?

Half an hour later, Weeto spotted a sportfishing boat coming across the stream on a crossheading with the *Gorda*. For twenty minutes they watched as it closed on its intercept course. Benjie checked it out through the binoculars, but his knowledge of power-boats was limited and he asked Weeto to take a look.

"Looks something like a Hatteras Fisherman," he reported, squinting through the glasses. "Maybe forty to fifty feet long. Good sturdy boat for sportfishing."

Benjie whispered to Josh, "Did they specify the kind of vessel that would be meeting us?"

"No. I supposed they'd have no way of knowing. But they'll identify themselves with a white flag and black crossbars. Which reminds me—" He was already on the move to hoist the recognition signal.

"I can't see no flag with black crosses," said Weeto, bracing his elbows on the cabin top for a steadier look. "He's taking some beating though. Look at him wallow in the troughs!"

Benjie looked and saw all but the top of the flying bridge hidden by the wave building in front of it. On its course from Florida to the Bahamas it had the stream broadside, uncomfortable even in calm conditions. At the tail end of a norther, it was churned into a maelstrom. Without the benefit of steadying sails, the powerboat skipper had to maneuver crab-fashion, accommodating the craft to the climbing waves by turning sharply to quarter them. Scooting straight on the flat stretches, he had to watch for the next building wave and time his quartering. If a wave lifted it high and sharp enough, the props would be spinning in air, momentarily out of control and the vessel left to the mercy of the next comber. Even here in the calmer lee of the bank, the vessel at times rolled horribly.

"He's a damn fool or desperate to come across on a day like this," said Weeto, handing Benjie the glasses.

Four men were visible on the deck, but the craft was rolling so violently he couldn't bring them into any clear focus. On the stern he picked out the U.S. ensign and from her short radar mast two triangular pennants whipped in the wind. The white flag with black crossbars was nowhere to be seen. Had they forgotten to hoist it, or felt no need to since the choppers made positive identification beforehand?

One thing was certain, however. She was heading straight for the *Gorda*, she wasn't just crossing her path. And that was odd. Why not head for the designated anchorage and wait there? Surely they didn't intend transferring cargo out in open waters? Then Benjie noticed she wasn't equipped with cargo booms. In a pinch they could rig the *Gorda*'s main boom with block and tackle and jury-rig a hoisting system, but it would be a slow and awkward operation. He expected the contact ship, like the *Miraflores*, would come rigged with working cargo booms for a swift unloading. This was purely a sportfishing boat and, from the looks of her, brand spanking new. He asked Weeto about her speed.

"Fifteen to twenty on a flat sea. Today she's lucky to make half that, even in spurts. She's gotta watch those troughs. She'll get swamped if she digs in too deep."

Minutes later he was glad he gleaned that patch of powerboat information. As the craft rolled toward them, an uneasy feeling made him glance at the set of the sails and verify from the telltales the direction of the wind. East by northeast.

Just before reaching the crossing point, the vessel turned and came to meet them. It circled to come alongside the *Gorda* on her port side, a courtesy passing of the sail-driven vessel so as not to steal her wind. But Benjie suspected it was to gain protection by getting on her lee side. He switched on the engine, in case the sails had to be dropped in a hurry.

Now only one man was visible, the one at the wheel on the bridge; the other three had disappeared below. But as it nosed to midships of the *Gorda*, they suddenly rushed on deck with leveled submachine guns. The loudspeaker system crackled static, then the helmsman's voice boomed over the loudspeakers.

"*Dragon!* We know your identity, *Dragon!* We are seizing you in the name of the rightful owners. Do as we say and no one will get hurt. Repeat, no one will get hurt if you follow orders!"

Benjie made his decision instantly, somehow instinctively prepared for the worst. Scooping Chico off the coaming and shoving him to the floorboards, he shouted for the others to duck. He jerked the wheel out of Dyna's hand and twisted it to port, his foot lashing out in the same instant to kick the speed control lever to maximum. Pushing Dyna down, he crouched behind the wheel.

The *Gorda* reared like a spurred horse from the double shot of engine power and the extra pump of wind brought by the broadened reach, slicing smartly to port in a wide arc. Being long-keeled she couldn't turn on a dime, otherwise she might have chopped the bow of the other craft. She could only deal it a glancing blow on the leading edge of the pulpit, sufficient to stop it dead in its tracks and throw the men with the guns to the deck.

The *Gorda* slipped past. Shots rang out, the bullets whizzing overhead. Warning shots. They were doubtless under orders to take the vessel intact and it was easy to guess why. Orders must have been so strict that in their first panic they feared even shooting holes in the sails. From their clumsy deck actions they were obviously landlubbers who hadn't found their sea legs yet.

Still in his crouched position, Benjie checked the set of the sails and his heading on the compass. It was as good as he could hope for. He had a soldier wind on a broad reach, on a course of due west. He couldn't hope to outrun or outmaneuver the other vessel unless he could draw her far enough out in the stream where the seas would halve her speed and force her into intricate maneuvers to keep from being pooped or capsized. But that would take time and extra canvas; he needed the reefed main unfurled. Shouting orders, he handed Dyna the wheel while he jumped on deck and raced to the cabin top to slip the reef points in the mainsail.

They had only the momentary advantage the surprise move gave them, ten boat lengths or so. When the other craft finally surged forward in pursuit, it began gaining on them in bursts of speed between breaking waves.

"Oh man, we'll never shake those guys!" Josh wailed from the stern, while his bony fingers frantically worked slipping the knots. "Not in a fast boat like that! I'm all for a parley and making a deal!"

"The only deal you gonna make with those guys," Weeto scoffed, "is a bullet in the head."

"We're gonna lead 'em out to the rough stuff where they can't use their speed," Benjie shouted. "Hurry up with your reef points!"

Finished with his, he raced to the mainmast and readied the halyard for hoisting. He shouted instructions to Dyna.

"Do it fast when you head up! Don't slow down!"

"Aaiiy, it's catching us!" their five-year-old lookout screamed from the coaming.

Dyna glanced over her shoulder. The powerboat was to port and still some six or eight boat lengths behind. A deliberate jibe, if she could bring the boat across the wind smoothly and fast enough, would not only surprise and confuse them, it would put the *Gorda* downwind and in a position to use the current for propulsion when she wore around to change tack again.

"I'm gonna jibe first," she shouted to Benjie, "and don't say no! We'll scare the shit outta those bastards! Duck your heads and hang on, everybody!"

Accidental jibes in strong winds can be a wrenching, even damaging experience for boats. Sails are taken from behind by the wind and with explosive force slammed from one side to the other. Lines sizzle and smoke through sheaves. Blocks and cleats dance and groan, threatening to rip or tear loose from the strain of having to contain the suddenly bottled wind. Sheared rigging and blown sails were also a part of the calculated risk.

Benjie watched as she waited for the boat to reach maximum speed. Then, in a single swift stroke, she put the wheel over hard. The bow swung cleanly to port in a stretch of flat water. The wind momentarily lost hold of the sails, then they cracked like gunshots. With a thud they were dumped into the opposite heel and, shuddering from the sudden gush of pressure, the boat took off like a spooked horse. Benjie was at the coaming and shifted the jib sheet while Dyna continued her turn to the left. By the time the wind was broadside and at its best, she had the other craft dead on the bow and was hurtling toward it at full speed.

A deft maneuver, beautifully executed. Benjie stood beguiled a moment like a proud teacher seeing a prize pupil perform to perfection. The move accomplished exactly what Dyna had predicted. It panicked the other skipper.

Though their craft was nearly the length of the *Gorda* and with a higher freeboard and bridge, those on her must have felt dwarfed by a bowsprit battering-ram with giant sails that stretched some eighty feet above water. It must have seemed a floating skyscraper was about to spear them.

The skipper reacted on impulse, turning simultaneously with the sweeping turn of the *Gorda*. He turned northwest, which put him upwind and downstream. The *Gorda* was free to cross the wind again, getting the lines shifted to the other side while the current kept her momentum going.

As she carried over into the eye of the wind and the sails began luffing, Benjie brought the mainsail snug to the top of the track, took a turn on the cleat and quickly winched down the gooseneck. It took only seconds and Dyna kept the turn going. By the time the sails were stretched taut and the halyards cleated, they were off the wind's edge and the sails were full. Benjie shouted to Dyna from the mast where he stood coiling the excess line, "Good girl! Beautiful seamanship!"

Even Josh had picked up enough sea experience to appreciate the skill of her handling. There was hardly any loss of momentum as the boat came hard on her new tack, the wind over her starboard side again, pointing northwest in a pounding pursuit of the enemy craft.

"Good crew!" Dyna yelled back, pointing to Chico. *"Viva la tripulación!"*

"Viva la tripulación!" he shouted back, tap-dancing on the floorboard grates. *"Andele, mas rápido!"*

Three times in a row was too much to expect. He saw, however, she was aiming straight at the stern of the other boat with deadly concentration, as if intending to ram the bowsprit right up their exhaust pipe. With the extra canvas up and full engine throttle they were doing nine, possibly ten knots. They were in fact overtaking the other, whose name he saw painted in gold letters on the transom: *Catch U*.

For the third time the enemy goofed. In his flustered state, seeing himself being charged and overtaken from the rear, the powerboat skipper swung left into the current. It might have meant he knew something about handling powerboats in rough seas, but it clearly demonstrated his ignorance of the strengths of sailing ships. It was no trick, with powerful twin engines, to turn and easily sidestep a charging long-keeled sailboat. His mistake was leaving the strongest quadrant of space, northwest to southwest, for the wind ship to maneuver in at maximum advantage.

His oversight allowed her to swing after him in full strength, aiming at him broadside now. They closed enough to see the surprised faces of the men on deck, who started to raise their guns, then bolted and ran to the other side, seeking the protection of the cabin. Benjie yelled for everyone to stay low in the cockpit. He was certain now they would fire.

A huge wave temporarily stopped the *Catch U* dead in her tracks. For a fleeting moment, Benjie thought they might catch her and ram her stern. But, in the final seconds before impact, the skipper found a stretch of flat water he could dig his props into and spurted out from under the bowsprit that was about to skewer his port quarters.

"Now head up, northwest!" Benjie shouted as they shot past the exhausts of the *Catch U*.

Dyna veered off and away, grabbing a good lead before the *Catch U* realized she was no longer being chased and turned to become pursuer again. Shots rang out but nothing hit. They were only meant to intimidate.

"He's still got too much advantage with those big gas engines," Weeto cautioned Benjie. "And I don' know if you got time enough to get him out into the rough stuff—"

"*Mire! Otro bote!*" Chico yelled, pointing in a direction they'd all been ignoring.

In the tense excitement of maneuvering and sail hoisting, no one noticed the vessel bearing down on them from the northeast. A trawler type with a fair-sized mast and boom aft of the bridge, she looked to have the kind of draft that would give her a good hold in the water and allow her to work in rough seas. Making a cursory check in the binoculars, Benjie could only make out the man on the bridge. He passed the glasses to Weeto.

"Not a Grand Banks but something like that," Weeto reported. "About the same size as the other guy, but she'll be slower. She's diesel. My guess is she can do twelve to fifteen maximum. Hey—" he paused, adjusting the focus, "I think she's the one you were lookin' for. She's flyin' the flag with the black cross."

Benjie took the glasses. Halfway up a support shroud, stretched taut in the strong wind, was the matching identification flag. Their contact ship. *Sporty II* was blazoned in red across the front of the bridge.

"Then who the hell is the other boat?" Josh blurted out. "And who do the choppers belong to?"

"They're not from the group I worked with," Weeto declared in answer to Benjie's stare. "I thought maybe, when they let us know we were the *Dragon*. But I never saw any of those guys before. And they sure din own no helicopters. I don' understand what's goin' on here."

"They're not coming for us, they're headed for the other boat. Look!" Dyna yelled, pointing.

The *Sporty II* had veered left and pointed to stern of them, in a heading to intercept the *Catch U*. The other, momentarily abandoning its chase of the *Gorda*, had turned to meet this new challenger. Within minutes, as the vessels neared each other, shots rang out.

"Stay on course and keep the engine revved to maximum," Benjie shouted to his helmsman.

"They got repeater rifles for distance," Weeto reported, back on lookout with the glasses.

"Which boat?" Benjie wanted to know.

"Both. Those submachine guns are only good at close range." Men stretched flat on the decks of both boats could be seen squeezing off shots. Four hands were visible on the trawler; only three were firing rifles on the *Catch U*. The trawler appeared stabler in the water but lacked the speed and agility of its adversary. Still, she looked to have the advantage with her sturdier construction and deeper draft. She plowed ahead directly for the other. Shots were heard thunking home; fiberglass exploding in puffs of dust where bullets penetrated the hull.

When the two closed to within a few boat lengths, still pointing bow to bow, the trawler suddenly turned off to the right. Whether it was the helmsman's intention or a rogue wave was impossible to tell, but the fateful move was almost instantly fatal. Submachine gun fire raked the stern of the trawler in a chattering fusillade and almost at once an orange and black explosion puffed out of the cockpit in a whoosh.

A dozen boat lengths away on the *Gorda*, they felt the concussive force and heat of it. Eardrums rang, vibrating painfully. Their skin and hair tingled as if licked by tongues of furnace fire.

A second explosion, larger than the first, followed an instant later, repeating the assault on their bodies. Their quadrant of sight was almost entirely engulfed by the pyrotechnics aboard the trawler as it blew apart like a giant firecracker. Bodies were catapulted into the air with pieces of metal and fiberglass, etched against the reddish ball that bloomed above the greasy black smoke. The air reverberated with shock waves. The cataclysm left the spectators on the *Gorda* stunned and mesmerized.

Seconds later, the boat had vanished. Where a solid object had been only moments earlier, now only flaming splinters and twisted pieces of debris rained down from the soiled sky, splattering into the water. For a timeless moment the crew of the *Gorda* stared in silence, dazed and unmoving. Even Chico was speechless.

No sounds or movements came from the inert bodies floating in the water, all visibly mangled, some without limbs.

The explosions stunned the crew of the *Catch U* with the same mesmerizing effect. Only the machine gunner was erect in the cockpit, the others still flat in their deck positions, heads cocked in the direction where the craft had vanished from the horizon. Some bits of burning debris showered down on the deck behind them, and for a few seconds they seemed unaware of it. Then, at a shout from the helmsman, they ran to extinguish the fires, kicking some of the still burning debris overboard.

"Jeeesssus, what happened?" Josh gasped.

"They musta been gas engines," Weeto speculated. "I swear they had diesels."

"Maybe jerry jugs of gas for the outboard," Benjie guessed.

"When they went, it ignited the propane."

"Sounded like dynamite to me," Dyna said.

Benjie grinned broadly. "You would know."

"What puzzles me," Dyna wondered aloud, squinting up at the sky, "is why they haven't called in their helicopters? Whichever side they belong to."

"Can you doubt they haven't by now?" Benjie's ominous look grazed Josh, whose face had gone suddenly pale.

"Maybe they're afraid of alerting the Coast Guard by talking on the VHF," Weeto suggested.

"Why not CB's if they're afraid of the VHF?" Josh asked.

Weeto shook his head. "The Coast Guard monitors the CB band too, now. They sure as hell don't want the Coast Guard joining their party."

"Christ, they must have heard those explosions all the way to Miami." Josh banged a fist on the cabin top, tension etched in his face. "If that doesn't bring the Coast Guard down on us, nothing will."

Chapter Twenty-Five

Their contact vessel destroyed and its dead crew left for shark bait, and with every reason to think their pursuers had the same thing in mind for them, even the Coast Guard began to seem preferable to being caught by the thugs chasing them. Still, the prospect of years behind bars made Benjie shudder and cling to some hope for another way out. Something less extreme than spending the prime of his life in prison, or being dropped in the deep with bullets in his head.

Josh's revelation the night before shocked him into thoughts of what it would be like to have his wings clipped for a year. Imagine for ten years—twenty! Imagine what any kind of sentence would do to his mother, or the good name of his father! He turned and made his announcement.

"Time to start unloading."

Playing tyrant didn't bother him this time. Wasn't that the skipper's role, especially in an emergency? If they could rid themselves of the contraband cargo before the Coast Guard happened onto the scene, they had a chance of bluffing their way through the rest of it. Or minimizing the risk, at the very least. Josh groaned aloud when he heard the decision, but even he'd come to realize it had to be done.

"You're destroying my brainchild before it had a chance to be born," he protested. "I hope you feel like a dirty rotten abortionist!"

Dynamite surprised him most of all, until he suddenly realized how consistent she actually was. Don't let worry of possible dire ends deter risk-taking, but if worst arrives, don't let it hypnotically have its way—act! The game had switched, it had a new batch of rules. Now she was anxious, even enthusiastic, about dumping the cargo.

"The sooner the better," she agreed, endorsing his decision. She raised a fist and glanced back at the vessel gradually closing on them. "Man the torpedoes! Let's give those damn killers something else to dodge!"

Weeto began working from the saloon while Benjie and Josh started in the aft cabin, pitching their cargo over the stern rail. Their wake was soon littered with floating bales. They saw the *Catch U* approach the nearest one, slowing to make an inspection.

"Maybe that's all the fuckers wanted in the first place," Josh grunted, in the desolate undertone of a child seeing his candy snatched away.

"Not on your life!" Benjie scoffed. "They're after the diamonds and God knows what else might be hidden on this lady!"

Josh's face brightened. "You think there's more?" The depression at losing his contraband fortune momentarily gave way to the prospect of possible other treasures cached aboard.

"Nothing would surprise me anymore," Benjie grunted as he heaved another bale over the rail. "They sure as hell have got something more important than pot on their list. Look!"

The *Catch U* had gaffed one of the black packages and hauled it into the cockpit. After tearing through the plastic and burlap wrappings, they dumped it back into the water and resumed the chase. They ignored the other bales.

"Open it up, you fucking dummies!" Josh yelled back at them, then turned to Benjie. "The bastards probably don't know about the surprise packages inside."

"Or don't care."

"Don't care?" Josh stiffened, an incredulous look on his face. "What, my good man, could possibly be more valuable than a hundred-and-some kees of smack?" His eyes suddenly glinted with some secret thought.

"Let's float a few bags of the white powder and see if they nibble," he suggested.

Benjie doubted they'd even float. But when he cut through the wrappings with his rigger's knife and tossed one overboard, it bobbed in the water like a cork. Machine sealed in double linings of clear heavy plastic, it had enough air pockets between the liners or in the powder itself to make it buoyant as kapok. He cut open five bales and threw the glistening centerpieces into the water. Floating alongside the black plastic of the bales, they stood out like proverbial sore thumbs.

They watched as the *Catch U* slowed again to examine this latest jettisoned enticement. The first was scooped aboard with a long-handled fishnet. A minute later, they veered over to the next nearest bag, continuing until they had retrieved all five.

"They want us to do all the work for them," Benjie joked, feeling his spirits rise a little. If they were so willing to transport the heroin, might it mean the Coast Guard's arrival wasn't the certainty he imagined? Or did they have powerful connections which made that scene less worrisome for them?

Josh watched them intently, astonished. "The dumb shits haven't made the connection yet!"

Benjie shook his head. It was obvious their objective was neither pot nor heroin, but something else on board. He couldn't believe anymore it was the diamonds alone. Something even more valuable was involved. The trawler, part of Don José's operation, had been after the pot and heroin. The *Catch U* gang, who knew about the *Dragon*, were clearly determined to seize the boat intact—even with the cargo jettisoned.

"It could be something which has value only to them," Benjie wondered aloud. "A set of keys to safe-deposit boxes or secret Swiss bank accounts. Maybe only some blackmail evidence, or a list of competitors, or politicians they've got in their pockets—"

Josh's eyes widened. "When you're hot, you're hot! Did you have to steal the Godfather's boat and—"

Dyna's warning shout cut him short. Looking up, Benjie saw the *Catch U* was again coming up fast, no more than a quarter mile behind. The bobbing bales curved in an arc behind them for several miles, but *Catch U* was racing nicely along upcurrent of them, without having to dodge or slacken speed.

"I'm gonna zigzag," Dynamite yelled to him. "West-southwest for five minutes, then west-northwest for five. We'll litter a broad path so they'll have to thread their way through."

"Just what I had in mind," Benjie called back, thankful to have her at the helm.

The strategy almost backfired on the first pass. The tack to port allowed the other craft to close at an angle, bringing them near enough for shots to ring out. One went through the main sail, leaving a small scorched hole which could give them trouble if it started to tear.

On the swing right, following a new line of bales at a ninety-degree angle to the old line, the *Catch U* skipper was forced to make a decision. He could run upcurrent along the barrier of the bales to the elbow or chance threading through the lines. The first was safer but wasted time. The latter could close the gap quicker, but he'd run the risk of ramming a bale or having one dumped on him by a careless wave. Already they were far enough out to feel the effects of the stream, which they could now see as well as feel. Waves, mounting ever steeper, residues of the storm, were beginning to roll with an authority that demanded the attention of shallow-draft vessels.

The powerboat skipper, playing it safe the first round, stayed upcurrent and bypassed the bales, but lost much of the gap he had gained earlier. He regained some again on the second feint to the left, but it was becoming obvious the *Gorda* wasn't going to be so easily overtaken. Jettisoning cargo had shed weight and given her a lift. She was almost at the point of matching speeds with the high-powered lightweight, and her deep draught and long keel gave her stability and control in the water the other could never match.

On the *Gorda*'s next sweep to the right, the frustrated skipper was compelled to risk threading the needle. Finding an opening and some flat water, he shot cleanly through the first line and roared towards them on a diagonal cut, gobbling up a big chunk of the gap. He closed enough for another round of shots to go off—still aimed high, at worst to put holes in the sails. Obviously, they weren't dissuaded from their original intent of taking the vessel intact.

Before they could breach the second line, Dyna tacked left again, then in two minutes back to the right. The water between became a maze of bobbing obstacles, with *Catch U* caught in the middle and all but surrounded. She was forced to slow down and weave her way through. With any speed on, colliding with one could cause serious damage. Forced into erratic maneuvers, she dodged and dipped her way along like a drunken sailor on shore leave caught in rush-hour traffic. She lost much of the ground gained earlier.

The aft cabin cleared, Josh and Benjie went to help Weeto bail out what was left in the forward cabins. The three-man team soon had the remaining cargo going over the side at a steady clip, emptying the vessel quickly. All the while Dyna kept up her game of feints and dodges, slowing the *Catch U* and keeping it confused and out of range.

Finally, they were down to the last bale and Josh pleaded to save it. His sour face was the profile of a rich man suddenly bankrupted, being asked to surrender even his pipe and tobacco.

"Aw man, you mean we don't even get to keep one for our own personal pleasure?"

"One's as bad as a hundred so far as the Coast Guard is concerned," Benjie lectured.

"We don't know if the Mounties are on the way. We're only guessing they might be."

Benjie yielded. It was agreed they'd fill two brown bags, toss the rest and the wrapping overboard, and be ready to deep six the petty reserve at the first sighting of any Coast Guard cutters or choppers. While Josh and Weeto stayed below to sweep up and rid the interior of any traces of the marijuana, Benjie went topside.

"Helm's alee!" Dynamite sang out as his head popped out of the hatch. Chico mimicked her with a repeat salvo.

She was coming about, the bow already swinging, heading into the wind to reverse direction and head southeast back into the field of bobbing bales in a charge at the enemy. Before he could react or protest, the sails were already luffing and Dyna, throwing the wheel hard over, had momentarily abandoned it for the chore of switching the sheets. He immediately sprang to help, seeing they'd already passed the eye point and that she was determined to carry through with or without his assistance. She said it all with a saucy wink as she handed him the winch lever and bounded back to her wheel post.

It had taken just over two hours to dump the cargo. They were now out in the middle of the stream in waning light. Past five o'clock, the sun was only a baleful hint behind the gauzy gray curtain of horizon.

"We lost our protection when we ran out of garbage!" Dyna shouted to Benjie. "The wind's lessening, and they've been closing the gap. Our only chance is to run 'em over and sink the bastards!"

The cold intensity of her words would have alarmed him in any other setting. Was it fear or exhilaration that drove her into such a frenzy? She was crouched behind the wheel, her trademark golden hair whipped in waves by the wind funneling off the mainsail. The bronzed cheekbones, jaw jutting determination—a fine fierce carving for a man-o'-war figurehead in an earlier era. Athena in her helmet and war face. His pulse raced with pride.

Blasting straight for the other vessel, now no more than a dozen boat lengths away, she held to an unswerving course. As the gap narrowed, Benjie wondered why the other skipper made no move to sidestep. Were they caught by surprise again, too used to being the hound to believe the rabbit could turn on them? If they thought the bales would prove to be the same obstacles for the sailboat as for themselves, they were wrong. The heavy wood hull of the *Gorda* would sweep them aside like so much straw. Dyna proved the point just then, as she entered the strewn field and went slicing between two closely spaced bales rather than alter course. Parting them like swing gates, the hull brushed them aside like harmless flotsam.

The surprise on the other boat was evident. First it headed left. Then facing a rising swell, it faltered and reversed to the right. Dyna shot Benjie a grin, winked and continued on course. Shaving the side of another bale, she cleared the spot the other craft had just vacated, upstream of the hemp patch. Then she swung into a port tack. Shouting orders for the sheet changes, she brought the *Gorda* charging back through the wind, using the momentum of the current to increase speed. In so doing she had driven the *Catch U* back into the obstacle course.

Panic added to confusion aboard the *Catch U*. Two towering waves hit in quick succession, the first lifting her high in the air, her screws spinning vainly for a hold in the water which had suddenly vanished. She was dropped in the trough and nearly broached. For a second she disappeared between walls of water.

Then another big one lifted the *Gorda* high enough that Benjie could see the powerboat struggling to get its bow back on to keep from being swamped by the next assault. But a black plastic gift ribboned in hemp rope was being lofted on the crest's curl. As it broke, the bale, like a garish Christmas gift, slammed on the foredeck and rammed the windshield, shattering the glass.

The big wave hurtled the *Gorda* like a surfboard on its rush of energy, simultaneously dooming the struggling *Catch U*. Thirty tons thundered down on it like a collapsing skyscraper. The *Gorda*'s bow smashed into the flying bridge. The slicing momentum of the iron keel cut the lightweight craft in two, cleaving it diagonally from port bow to starboard quarters. The great weight of the sailboat plowed down and through it, driving it completely under.

Its air pockets and flotation material popped it back to the surface after the *Gorda* passed over, but it came up mortally wounded, ripped like a can bludgeoned by a giant meat cleaver. Before there was a chance to think about survivors and retaliation, an explosion blasted out of the smashed stern. Debris and flame shot in the air. A column of smoke billowed up.

Gorda was upwind of the explosion or they might have caught some of its fallout. One of the ruptured gas tanks, spilling its contents over the water, erupted in a whoosh, the gas spreading like a lake of fire. One of the marijuana bales caught fire, then a second and a third. Greasy smoke engulfed the scene with mushrooms of Halloween black and orange, ghoulish columns shouldering the sky's expanding inferno. The air crackled with the sound of hungry flames.

It was too eerie, too stark, too diabolical. It all happened too quickly, too miraculously to be understood as anything but a nightmare. On the *Gorda* they stood transfixed, looking back on the scene like stone statues. No sign of life showed anywhere. Black plumes rose solemnly from what was left of the smashed wreck of the hull. Even upwind, the acrid smell of burning fiberglass reached them. Josh was first to break the spell.

"Jeeesssus, Dynamite! Remind me to stay clear of your path!"

Chico laughed with the others without quite knowing why. He would remember this moment as the solemn instant he recognized his own mortality and saw for the first time the finality of death and dying.

Benjie kissed Dynamite on the cheek. "I don't know how, but you did it," he said, still dazed.

"*La cara del santo hace milagros.* I had my lucky charm along." She squeezed Benjie's hand, as if she needed it for balance and reassurance, whispering, "Take the wheel, I'm godawful thirsty and I gotta pee."

"I might have figured." He winked at her, then suddenly remembered what his father had once told him about the human condition. He had not fully grasped its meaning until that moment. Boredom is the eternal affliction. The spirited animal, human or otherwise, will go to great lengths, sacrificing peace and harmony, even security and life itself, to avoid it.

They'd just killed four men and he could honestly say he felt not a shred of remorse. Before that day he had never in his life seen anyone killed. It came as a surprise that he shared none of the anguish of the dying, only the victor's sense of triumph. Like the small boy looking dazedly up at him, he too had made a leap into new understanding. The human heart, though infinitely more dangerous than he ever suspected, was infinitely more worthy for the endlessness of its questing.

"'We have met the enemy and he is ours.' Wasn't it an American admiral who said that?" Weeto asked, reassured by Dynamite's wink that the episode between them had been forgotten and their friendship preserved.

"'We have met the enemy and he is us!' So says Pogo," Josh crowed his version.

He had never faced anyone out to kill him before, not in an open confrontation with guns drawn. The exalted feeling of being the survivor swept aside much of his chagrin over loss of his scheme and cargo, which he could see floating away in the stream like so much debris. The Coast Guard hadn't come after them. They still had a stash of grass for their own pleasure. They still had the diamonds and emeralds, and what Benjie didn't know, the two kilos of coke in the sugar jar. There was also whatever else was secreted aboard that was so valuable the Mob had sent helicopters, a boat and armed men to seize it. Remembering that he had to search for it, he turned to go below.

Just then, Dyna exploded out of the hatch.

"Water's coming in!" she shouted. "Already up to the floor-boards!"

Chapter Twenty-Six

The leaking came as no surprise. From such a jarring collision they were bound to have damage. Open seams at the very least. Likely cracked ribs. Possibly some stove-in planks. Benjie already noted a new, alien sound in the propeller or engine. Broken blades, a bent shaft? Revving the motor low he heard the burring noise of something loose or out of alignment. He turned the wheel over to Weeto and dashed below to start the bilge pump. Dyna had already started it and was tearing up the loose floorboards to open the bilges.

One look and Benjie called up for Josh to take over the helm so Weeto could check for leaks in the aft cabin while he and Dyna checked the forward compartments. He found a gaping hole in a waterline plank and used bedding from one of the bunks to plug it. A second opening was lower and aft of the other. He stuffed it with wadded pillowcases. Dynamite reported she found one on the same side in the head. On a tack heeling to port when the collision occurred, he expected the port side would take the brunt of the punishment. Dyna crammed the gap with Kotex from under the counter.

Checking the open bilge, Benjie saw the pump wasn't getting ahead of the water, which was nearly to the floorboards in the main cabin and six inches deep in the lower section of the forward area. He whispered to Dyna, "If we've got holes along the waterline, it means we've got them lower down too. We'll have to bail to get down to where we can find and plug them."

She glanced down at the water swirling around her ankles. "No Mayday calls?"

His look was merely reinforcement of what they both knew. They didn't dare. Beginning with the boat itself, they trailed such a wake of evidence any official help would only bring more trouble. They were on their own. Sink or swim. Their eyes met, sealing the agreement.

Benjie heard the increasing clatter of a laboring engine or propeller assembly. He sprinted up to the cockpit and threw the gearshift in neutral. The noise gradually halted as the prop stopped spinning. He sighed with relief. The problem was in the screw or shaft; he could live with that. At least the motor, needed to run the bilge pump, still functioned.

"It's damn lucky we got rid of the grass," Dyna called out as he came back down. "We'd be up to our asses by now if we hadn't."

Benjie rummaged in a seat locker where he remembered seeing buckets stored. "With no way to get at the equipment, " he completed her thought.

"The bucket brigade," she laughed when he handed her one of the plastic pails.

They improvised a mix of methods in bailing the water. Dyna dumped hers in the galley sink where it flowed out the drain. Benjie worked two pails in tandem with Weeto, who took them from the top of the hatch, dumped them over the side and handed them back. Chico, refusing to be shunted aside, was allowed to work with a smaller pail which he also dumped in the galley sink. Working with a serious concentration new to him, he rebuffed Dyna's efforts to provoke some playfulness. Even when she dipped into Spanish to please him, he shrugged indifferently. She couldn't tell if he truly understood the nature of the danger they had just passed through, or whether he was old enough to understand death and the threat of their present plight. Sinking was a distinct possibility.

Half an hour of bailing brought the water down a few inches, below the floorboards. While the others continued bailing, Benjie took a hammer and nails, a can of roofing tar and pieces of scrap canvas, to reinforce plugs and goop seams and cracks. It was the best he could lay hands on; he had no store of modern glues and epoxy resins which would stop a leak even under water. Another reminder of the price one paid for being in a hurry and failing to check and provision properly.

When he came to the hole in the head and found it stuffed with Kotex, he laughed but couldn't resist marveling at the ingenuity behind it. Anything in a pinch, even a Rembrandt if it's the nearest thing at hand. It all begins with a will to survive and ends when desire runs out.

When he glanced outside again it was night and pitch black. No starlight or moonglow showed anywhere between the heavy cloud cover. Running without lights, in case the Coast Guard or a search helicopter came by, the tarry darkness was ominous yet comforting. He reflected that one good thing had come with the flooding of the floorboards. Any residue of marijuana had been washed into the bilges. With luck they'd get it all pumped out, leaving no trace when they were boarded and inspected by Customs and port authorities.

The thought made him stop. Did he really have it in mind to sail into a Florida port and bluff it out with officials? He was getting as bold as some others he could name. He wanted to get Weeto and Chico safely ashore, sensing a special duty owed for the perils they'd been put through. The Bahamas were safer, but Florida was closer by half or more. In any case, he wasn't at all sure they could keep the vessel afloat long enough to make it back across to the Bahamas. The decision was being made for him, and for once he didn't rail against it.

Called back to bailing because of rising water, he relieved Dynamite by putting her back on the wheel and bringing Josh down to help bail. Shining his flashlight on the open bilge, he saw the water was nearly up to the floorboards again. It hit him that they were wasting time and effort dumping it over the side.

"Throw it in the cockpit, it'll go down the drains!"

"I think I see shore lights, guys!" Dyna shouted a few minutes later.

Looking out one of the forward ports, Benjie saw the faint glow, some part of the eighty-mile stretch between Miami and the Palm Beaches known as the Gold Coast. He guessed they were north of Miami Beach, maybe Dania or Hollywood, possibly Lauderdale itself.

The slogan for the crossing was "Head for Miami and you'll end in Lauderdale." The forty miles of northward push was courtesy of the Gulf Stream. Unwittingly, *Dragon*—her cover blown, Benjie reverted to her true name—was heading for the barn, back to where it all began. When had that been—not much more than a month ago? Was it possible thirty days had the power to undo twenty-two years of a life's course line?

The lure of land lifted spirits and spurred their efforts, as Benjie saw when he shone his light on the open bilge again. But he knew that their slow pace in a waterlogged boat with punctured sails and malfunctioning propeller, with fifteen to twenty miles to go, represented some heavy hours of steady bailing before they reached shore.

"Vamanos, mas rápido!" Chico barked, mimicking one of his Poppi's earlier commands. The others picked up on it and soon they had a chain gang chanting in unison. *"Vamanos, mas rápido!"*

Josh elbowed Benjie and snickered. "Just like old times down among the bean pickers in dear old Texas!"

The fact he could joke about it said something about his relieved state of mind. Satisfied they were making progress, Benjie checked the bilges again with the flashlight and tools. He found his covering for the big hole in the port bow had partly washed loose. Restuffing it, he nailed new edges and daubed it with tar, then tacked another piece of canvas over it and daubed again. He smashed off a piece of the bunk railing with his hammer and nailed it on top. Water still seeped in.

He reinforced other cracks and holes the same way. He discovered a couple of new ones which he canvassed and tarred, then nailed over them strips of wood which he had ripped from drawers and paneling.

Surmising there were worse openings farther down, under the water where his roofing cement wouldn't adhere even if he found them, he saw his patching efforts as stopgaps at best. He couldn't save the wounded lady, only extend her death throes long enough to get them to shore. When he returned to the bucket brigade he saw Dyna had relieved Weeto and given him a turn at the wheel.

"No way to stop the leaks, huh?" she asked when Benjie flashed the light and they saw the water on the rise again. He admired her stoicism. Not a trace of panic, just a question establishing fact.

"Too many below the water where I can't get at them. And we can't get it out fast enough to get down to them."

"Is the boat going to sink?" Chico asked, dipping his pail in the water.

"Not with you around to help," Dyna sang in reply.

Determination shone in the boy's dark eyes. "Don't worry, I can swim."

Before Dyna could speak again, they were interrupted by the sound of an approaching chopper. Benjie bolted topside like a guard dog. Behind them in the east he saw the blinking lights, skimming close to the water as if searching for something on the surface. He watched as its flight took it south and finally out of sight and earshot.

He had barely resumed bailing when the inimitable whap and whir drifted back into range, lights blinking back in their direction. Its higher pitched sound convinced him it wasn't one of the big Coast Guard choppers but likely one of the smaller ones which greeted them earlier in the day. Were they looking for their missing boat and buddies or searching for the *Dragon*?

Benjie called out to the others. "Don't show a light of any kind, anybody! Nada! Don't even strike a match!"

Nearer but still miles astern, the chopper's course took it north this time, and now he saw the beam of a powerful searchlight knifing down from it. Raking a zigzag path like a theatrical spotlight piercing a darkened stage, the big eye gobbled chunks of darkness as it traced the route the *Dragon* would have taken on a crossing to Florida. Any doubts Benjie might have harbored about its mission were eliminated by the searchlight. Only the *Dragon* had reason to run in darkness with its running lights doused.

A few more of the same measured passes and the chopper would intersect the *Dragon's* path, no matter what evasive action he took. As its sweep took it twenty to thirty miles in a matter of minutes, there was little hope of avoiding being spotted by the spotlight beam.

"Josh, give me a hand!" he shouted down the hatch. He jumped onto the cabin top and began unlashing the rubber dinghy from its cradle under the boom. Together they launched it over the side. By the time he lifted the outboard motor from its taffrail mount and handed it down to Josh in the dinghy, they all knew what was happening. No one protested or questioned it.

While Benjie gathered emergency supplies and equipment, Josh scrambled back aboard and ducked below for more rations. Guessing his intentions, Benjie shouted after him but he had already disappeared from sight.

Dyna emerged from the hatch, and he handed her the set of oars as she seated herself in the dinghy. Then he passed down the other items of survival equipment. Weeto, in the stern with Chico between his knees, pushed the button to start the outboard. Benjie stopped him. "No motor, we'll only use the paddles for now."

Benjie shut off the ship's engine when Josh popped out of the hatch. With the bilge pump stopped, the vessel would begin rapidly filling with water.

Josh was clutching his two bags of grass and the big camera case Benjie had only seen once. As he was handing down his leather purse and treasure bags to Dyna, the camera case slipped from his arm and plopped in the water. Josh cursed and promptly dove in after it.

There was no danger of his being raked by the vessel. With no one at the controls *Dragon*, even without a bloated belly, would have reacted like any well-balanced boat. Nosing into the wind, she had come to a virtual standstill, her sails luffing and filling, then spilling again before she could gather any momentum. When Josh's head finally broke the surface, bellowing another curse, he clambered for the safety of the dinghy.

"What was so important in that case?" Weeto asked as he helped boost him aboard.

"A camera, what else?" Josh replied, squishing water like a sponge as he settled himself in the bow next to Dyna. Helping him into his life vest, she smiled in the darkness and decided he had used up his fair share of luck.

Chico's fishing pole was lying on a cockpit cushion. Benjie grabbed it and tied the hook end to a stanchion, then unlocked the reel. Passing it down to Chico, he instructed him to let the line run out when they got underway, like an umbilical cord to lead them back to the mother ship if she somehow survived the next hour. Slipping into his life vest, he handed Dyna a jug of water, squirmed down and untied the painter.

Shoving them off, he picked up the other oar, synchronized his stroke with Weeto's and began paddling for the shore lights. He knew that lights could be deceiving. From his dead reckoning he guessed they were at least five, possibly as much as ten miles from shore and the stream nudged close along that part of the Florida coastline. They were still out in the rough stuff where the strong current had been known to carry disabled craft north to the Carolinas and beyond. His hopes rested in the outboard.

The helicopter came by on another, closer pass, its spotlight a frantic eye probing the surface like an enraged Cyclops. Still far enough away to miss them, it continued south and disappeared into the night. But on the next pass it found its prey and began circling. A burst of machine gun fire rose above the whir of rotary blades. In the glare of the searchlight's beam, they saw the puffs where the sails were being stitched by bullets.

The lights circled and studied the ship once more, the chopper hovering lower and circling closer. Then bullets sprayed the hull. They must have guessed by then, from its lowness in the water and its lumbering, that the *Dragon* was sinking. Machine gun fire raked the other side. Then, angling closer, a half dozen magnesium flares were lobbed into the cockpit and onto the decks.

Intense molten flames raced over the rocking vessel. The decks caught like a gasoline spill. Fire erupted everywhere at once.

In an instant the sails caught a lick of flame from the cabin top and morphed into yellow tongues licking the shrouded sky. From half a mile away, the anxious faces in the raft reflected the glow of the blazing inferno.

Benjie cut the fishing line with his rigger's knife. When he looked up the chopper had veered off and was heading southwest, presumably for Miami. In the illuminated sky he made out its color—white, like the first one seen in the morning. Whatever was so valuable aboard, one thing was certain. They wanted it sunk or destroyed rather than falling into other hands.

"Whatever the bastards wanted is on its way to the bottom," Josh muttered. "That would've included us if we'd been aboard."

A wave swept the dinghy and nearly capsized them, a not so gentle reminder they were still in dangerous waters. Dyna grabbed the pail and started bailing. Benjie started the outboard.

"I forgot all about the goddamn diamonds and emeralds," Josh shouted over the outboard noise into Dyna's ear. "All I could think of was saving my grass and coke."

"Don't worry," she shouted back, pleased the laws of compensation sometimes operated even in Josh's world. "I didn't get my priorities mixed up."

"You got them? All of them?" He nearly whooped in his elation before he asked, "Where?"

"Remember, what you don't know can't hurt you!" she laughed. She patted her big leather shoulder bag, which looked uncommonly stuffed.

"Easy come, easy go, eh?" Weeto nudged Benjie. "Can you believe she ended up where she was scheduled to go, only a month later?"

Benjie nodded and grinned. "Everything's only borrowed…you've got to give it all back someday."

It pained him to see such a splendid vessel suffer such a fate. He'd be hard pressed to find her likes again at any price. Strange he should be thinking of a replacement, he thought. But a part of him was beginning to read Dynamite as easily as the telltales on the shrouds. Without having to ask, he knew she had the diamonds and emeralds—or some of them anyway.

If they proved to be less valuable than hoped, they'd still cover the cost of deep-sea diving lessons and a charter boat. He already knew scuba, the hard-hat stuff couldn't be that much harder to master. Renting a dive boat for a few months, they could go down and see what other valuables might still be aboard the *Dragon*. The diamond cache was below the waterline where it wouldn't burn. There could be other hidden things similarly placed, and the laws of salvage at sea were generous. After that, with luck, on to another boat and back to the good life of free wind, unfettered space and the lure of distant landfalls.

Suddenly he caught himself questioning his old carefree dream, wondering if it was as unshackled as he always insisted. If he thought Josh obsessed with wild schemes and dangerous enterprise, what was his own obsession with the sea and small boats but an insatiable desire to test his own nerve and endurance?

The passages were often rough and dangerous, the reward little more than satisfaction in surviving the plights one invited by going to sea in the first place. When gold and spices were the quest—or simply undiscovered lands beckoning—there was a point to voyaging. But what could he say of aimless journeying over charted waters, to mapped and settled lands, except that it was just another form of tourism?

The cargo took on importance—it came clear as the bell on the foundering vessel, dinging last warnings as she was going under—because it gave a point to the return voyage. However contraband, it lifted the passage above aimlessness. As the high purpose of transporting Weeto and Chico had on the passage down, and as the secrets of the sinking vessel were already doing to his future.

To his surprise, his father's face came to him—the worn, kindly face he hadn't been able to picture in his mind's eye since that fateful day of violence. Studying it carefully, afraid it would vanish forever before he grasped its message, he felt a sudden calm pass through him. His father's brutal and senseless death said nothing about the man or his nature. But his lifework spoke eloquently of him and the potential of humankind: the quest for the good, true and beautiful. The purposeful life.

Slowly, with a serene acceptance, he let the face fade back into its dark niche, certain he'd be able to summon it forth at will without fear of its familiar pain.

The fiery torch in the water had attracted shoreside attention and several fast boats could be seen racing out to investigate. Benjie steered away from them. He had the flare gun in his pocket if they capsized or needed help. But until such time, he preferred finding his own way to shore, landing on a deserted stretch of beach somewhere.

Unexpectedly, he felt remarkably good. Higher than a kite, as his father used to say. Better still—as Dynamite always told him and the day proved so convincingly—born with a lucky star.

Epilogue

A t the time of this story, Colombians were just beginning to infiltrate the U.S. drug trade. Cocaine was only a trickle then. Heroin came via the French Connection in Marseilles; Mexico was our marijuana supplier. Not until 1977, when the Mexican government began using the herbicide Paraquat to destroy its crop, did an opening occur. With established infrastructure from their trafficking in cigarettes, liquor, and appliances, Colombian *contrabandistas* were naturals to take over. With the French Connection forced to detour its heroin shipments via South America, Colombians soon took over and added a local product, cocaine, to the traffic.

Into the 1980s cocaine was still a powder people snuffed, and it had a relatively benign reputation. Not until it was made into a paste and smoked (*basuco* or freebase), or reconstituted as crack, was its deadly and addictive power made manifest. By then a decade of social tolerance—even advertised chic—had spread its usage. Not just thugs but military ex-pilots hired out for the trade, which soon transformed petty dealers like Pablo Escobar of Medellín into drug lords with the power to bargain like sovereign states.

This says nothing about the role our government unwittingly played in promoting the drug trade. Stories abound of CIA covert actions in the Cold War against communism in which trafficking was allowed or fostered to underwrite clandestine actions, as far back as 1951 against the Chinese communists, to support anti-Castro Cubans in the 1960s, Golden Triangle tribes in the Vietnam conflict, or the Contras in Nicaragua in the 1980s. Aside from official winks at illegal activity, worse damage doubtless came from cops and undercover agents seduced by the lure of riches. As early as 1968, a Federal Bureau of Narcotics internal investigation revealed "at a minimum a full fifth of the agents were corrupt, actively colluding with major heroin traffickers and making major heroin sales themselves. It may well have been more, but investigations were not pursued on agents who decided to resign or retire" (Jill Jonnes, Hepcats, Narcs, and Pipe Dreams, p. 268).